Sherlockian Musings:
Thoughts on the
Sherlock Holmes Stories

By

Sheldon Goldfarb

I suppose there is no harm in
in this book - it could
substitute as half of an
argument or discussion -
point - counter - point about
Holmes - but it really is just
a gathering of notes and fragments -
it's not very satisfying.

Paperback ISBN 978-1-78705-481-3
ePub ISBN 978-1-78705-482-0
PDF ISBN 978-1-78705-483-7

Published by MX Publishing
335 Princess Park Manor, Royal Drive,
London, N11 3GX
www.mxpublishing.co.uk

Cover design by Brian Belanger

In Memory of

Peter Wood,
my first Priory Schoolmaster

Contents

Foreword

In 2003 while researching a murder mystery I was writing set in the Victorian era, I happened to meet the late Peter Wood, "Priory Schoolmaster" of the Sherlockian group in Vancouver, the Stormy Petrels. I soon became a member of the group and especially enjoyed their monthly discussions of stories from the Sherlock Holmes canon, presided over by Peter.

After Peter died, the schoolmastering was at first taken over by another Petrel (Orilea Martell), but eventually fell to me. I brought a slightly different perspective to the job, something deriving more from Academe than Baker Street. Peter then and the other Petrels now tend to be more traditional Sherlockians, interested in the "real world" of Holmes and Watson, in explanations going beyond the text of the stories, and in evaluating the stories. I was trained at graduate school to ignore everything except the text and to analyze rather than judge. However, the Petrels were very generous in listening to this different approach, which I embodied in "Musings" on each story as we did them.

Peter and Orilea produced background notes and study questions, and when I took over I began to do likewise, but I soon developed my own musing style, leaving annotations aside and instead plunging into everything the stories made me think of, drawing on other literary critics and my own interest (a Holmesian-style interest?) in figuring things out.

My first musings (on "The Stockbroker's Clerk," the story the Petrels were doing when I became Schoolmaster) in part followed my predecessors' style by including background notes before I turned to my musings, but by the fourth set I had abandoned background and dwelt solely in the realm of the Muse (though I have learned that "musings" and "the Muse" have different derivations and are not connected).

In any case, I hope the Musings will both entertain and provide fodder for discussion of the stories. That is what Mark Alberstat of the Spence Munros (the Sherlockian group in Halifax, Nova Scotia) thought they might do when he commissioned a special set on "The Red-Headed League," a story I had not yet Mused about, and I hope this collection can assist Sherlockians seeking ideas about the stories and academics looking for approaches to teaching them.

Mark suggested that I collect the Musings and offer them to MX Publishing for book publication, so here they are.

My thanks to Mark and to Steve Emecz of MX Publishing and of course to all the Stormy Petrels of Vancouver, who have listened to my musings over the years, including Gary Spence, my biggest fan; Brian Collins, who says the Musings make him too lazy to read the actual stories; and of course Fran Martin, the Petrels' long-serving president and keeper of my predecessors' notes.

Last but not least, thanks to my girl-friend, Roberta Haas, who was the first to say these Musings would make a good book. I hope she is right.

Sorry, Roberta

A Study in Scarlet

So here's how it all begins: Or maybe not. And I don't mean in the Baring-Gould sense that since there are earlier cases, the Holmes canon actually began earlier. No, I'm talking about publication and how *A Study in Scarlet* was the first Holmes story to be written and published, to be followed of course by 59 others. And how tempting to refer to those other 59 when discussing the first. The origin story which led to all the others, which you perhaps can only understand by referring to all the others. But …

There's a problem here: When Arthur Conan Doyle wrote this story (novel or novella, really), it does not seem that he was planning a series, still less to write 59 sequels. He had to be dragged, kicking and screaming (or bribed by huge payments), to write some of them. And after finishing *Scarlet* in 1886, he didn't immediately write another detective story; instead he wrote a historical adventure called *Micah Clarke* and then embarked on another, *The White Company*. His great aim, when not trying to be a doctor, was to write serious historical novels; he would later complain that Sherlock Holmes distracted him from that more serious work. It was not for a few years after *Study in Scarlet* that he decided to write some more Sherlock Holmes stories, so let's try and look at the *Study* as a work in itself.

And how does it begin? Not with Sherlock Holmes at all (except as the title of Chapter One), but with that other character, without whom there would really have been no series, and who may even have been thought of first: Dr. John H. Watson. The sources are unclear, but perhaps Ormond Sacker (Doyle's original name for Watson, and thank God he abandoned it) was going to be a sort of combined doctor-detective and the hero of the whole thing. And why would Dr. Doyle have thought of making his hero a doctor? The question perhaps answers itself, though one should also remember Dr. Joseph Bell, Doyle's deducing professor in Edinburgh. In any case, we begin with ...

Watson: And what a Watson. A wornout, wounded, aimless Watson. An idler drawn to that great "cesspool," London, where he is squandering his government pension and feeling sorry for himself. The ideal situation for a life transformation, a typical beginning for an adventure story in which someone will be swept up into exciting situations and made to become a hero. Will Watson be the hero? Perhaps like a Marlow going to discover Mr. Kurtz? And his Kurtz will be Mr. Sherlock Holmes, a mystery man he is warned about by young Stamford – and by the way, all the characters are young here, are they not? Holmes is some sort of student, Watson only graduated a few years before: these are very young men, not the middle-aged codgers we may think of from later in the canon. But let's not think about the canon. Let's just think about *Scarlet*.

Thinking about Scarlet: And thinking about it from the point of view of the character who is positioned as the hero, not Holmes, but Watson. Reminiscent a bit of the situation of Violet Hunter (oh, there I go, thinking about the canon again), who ends up in a strange establishment and has to figure out what is going on. Here Watson tries to figure out what is going on with his new companion, who seems quite mysterious. What is his profession, first of all? And why does he swing between moods of enthusiasm and periods of languor? Drugs, I hear you say – but no, no, no, you're thinking of later stories. We are reading *Study* as if there are no other stories, and our hero, Watson, is sure there can be no drugs involved. Perhaps he is wrong; perhaps he is naive; and don't we know from the very next story ... But we don't know that, not yet; let us stick to our text.

Let's forget about the drugs and think about the profession: Watson is strangely "delicate" (his word) about asking directly. Is this Victorian reticence or a sign of how passive he is at the start? I note that the very text of the novel begins in a passive way: he is "removed" from his brigade and later, after being struck by the famous Jezail bullet, is removed again (to hospital), then is struck again (by enteric fever): the very grammar is passive. Later his adventures begin when someone else taps him on the shoulder (not the one he got the bullet in, I hope), so he is not at first very assertive. Instead, he makes his famous list of Sherlock Holmes's attributes and tries to deduce something from them: but he is not the master of deduction and gives up in despair. Poor Watson.

Humorous Watson: He does have a sense of humour, though, and when confessing his bad habits (laziness and an aversion to rows) adds, "I have another set of vices when I'm well, but those are the principal ones at present." What are those other vices? Well, later in the canon we might note his eye for the ladies, but we must stick to this story, and we don't really see Watson when he's well here, so we don't know.

Does Watson get better? Yes, I think he does, and it begins perhaps when he is roused to action by reading Holmes's article, "The Book of Life": a rather high-falutin title with perhaps Biblical overtones that suggests grand things when it's really only about detective work, and is detective work all there is to life? Not a question Watson raises, but he does question whether this science of detection is valid, and he does so by wielding as his weapon an eggspoon. Another humorous moment, but effective because in calling the article "ineffable twaddle," he provokes Sherlock Holmes into defending it, owning it as his, and explaining his profession as the world's only consulting detective.

Does Watson find a profession? Yes again, he does. Not as a detective; he only accidentally provokes the discovery of what Holmes does for a living. But by the end of this novel Watson does seem dedicated to something. If the hero's journey traditionally is a journey of self-discovery, then Watson does discover in the course of this tale what it is he wants to do. Not doctoring; he seems uninterested in that, really, though later in the canon ... (but never mind later in the canon). In this story, after being rather skeptical of Holmes to start with, Watson becomes quite a quick convert and celebrator of him, a sort of hero-worshipper, which makes sense since he is quick to quote Thomas Carlyle, the author of *Heroes and Hero-Worship*.

So Watson's role is to be what? A devotee? Perhaps, but something much more concrete than that. In a world in which the true hero, Sherlock Holmes, is not getting his due, Watson will take on the role of chronicler. Imagine that, a doctor who becomes a writer: who ever heard of such a thing? But it does seem to invigorate Watson: he will tell the world the truth.

But what about Jefferson Hope? Who? What does Watson say about him? Well, not very much, because mostly we get his story about fighting the Mormons in Utah from the strange middle section of the novel told not by Watson but by an anonymous, omniscient narrator. As several critics note, Holmes and Watson, thanks to the odd construction of the novel, don't even know this Mormon story. They are on one plane, solving a murder in London, while Jefferson Hope is on quite another, trying to save the Ferriers and then plotting their revenge. How do these things even connect?

Doesn't the Mormon story disrupt the mystery? So say some, though the critic Joseph McLaughlin says that presumes that what is going on here is a mystery story. Conan Doyle, the writer of historical adventures, may have thought the main point was the Mormons in 1847 and 1860, not the detectives in 1881. Or maybe not. In any case, on either side of the Mormon tale we have a tale of detection, but the Mormon tale itself is more an adventure, a historical romance, romance in both meanings, with a love story between Hope and Lucy and an adventure in the mode of *The Count of Monte Cristo*, in which an evil organization has to be brought down by a brave individual, or maybe individuals plural because John Ferrier is another who opposes the Mormons alongside young Hope, and if they don't succeed in bringing down the Mormons altogether, at least Hope is able to avenge the Mormons' murder of John Ferrier and the virtual murder and forced marriage of his stepdaughter Lucy.

Stepdaughter? Yes, I suppose we should call her that. John Ferrier is fierce in claiming her, though it seems she is not his own flesh and blood. And why should the story be set up this way as a story of adoption? Are we echoing Watson's adoption of a new career? Or Conan Doyle's?

Echoes: Does Jefferson Hope echo Sherlock Holmes? They're both solitary trackers, unofficial, not part of any organization, certainly not part of an authoritarian organization like the Mormons, and not even part of a more bumbling organization like London's Metropolitan Police, personified by Inspectors Gregson and Lestrade. Though actually are they so bumbling? Lestrade discovers RACHE, though he thinks it means Rachel, and Sherlock Holmes laughs at him: he is always laughing at them, but to be fair, they laugh at him too, and for that matter so does Watson at times: yes, Watson the worshipper.

Laughing: Should we be laughing at Sherlock Holmes and at all of these London detectives? Maybe Jefferson Hope is a more solid type to celebrate. But he's a murderer. Well, there is that, so he is the villain of the outer story even while being the hero of the inner one. In his murders doesn't he do good? Isn't it good to get the simian Enoch Drebber out of the way? Well, perhaps, but murder? Here we have the clash of the Wild West and modern London, of the adventure novel with its rougher code of morality and the detective novel based on codes of law.

Clash or mixture? Perhaps, anticipating later stories (and I know we mustn't do that), this is one of those Holmes stories in which two different approaches to life need to be combined. We have Holmes on one side, for whom blood belongs in a test tube; and on the other we have Jefferson Hope, for whom blood belongs in the heart (or perhaps the nose): Hope is full of feeling, full-blooded feeling that makes his face red and his nose bleed. Holmes is the man of logic and reason. And yet even here he is also a man of the arts who knows his art jargon and his violin; still, he is not a man of passion. Does Watson strike a balance somehow? Or is that left to the readers who know not only the London murders but the tale of Utah?

Choosing: Watson chooses Sherlock Holmes over Jefferson Hope; he becomes Holmes's chronicler, not Hope's. Is the message that in modern times we cannot follow the path of Hope but must stick to logic and reason? Of course, the paths are not entirely different: they are both hunters, trackers, bloodhounds, almost literally, just one will go beyond the law – and wait, won't Holmes in later stories go beyond the law and become his own judge and jury just like Jefferson Hope here? Except not his own executioner; he won't go that far. So maybe the two parts from this story will combine later on. But for now Jefferson Hope has to die – peacefully perhaps, satisfied, but still he has to die. He must answer the second summons to Baker Street and have his career of vengeance stopped. Of course, he's already completed it, and we are invited to feel grateful to him for it to a certain extent, but it has to stop.

Politics: The newspapers write up the events from their particular political standpoints. One blames foreign socialists and revolutionaries; another blames the Continental despotisms that create such revolutionaries. We don't actually have a Continental despotism on display here, but we do have the Mormons, who stand in for the Catholic Inquisition and other tyrannies. And on the other hand, we have their enemy, the Jefferson Hopes fighting for freedom who resort to violence like some modern-day anarchists. What we need perhaps is some middle path between them? A Holmesian detective who won't go in for violence but who won't become an agent of tyranny either. Perhaps.

Religion: We don't like the Mormon religion as displayed here. It's not even Christian, says John Ferrier. Is there any other religion in the story? Is Holmes's *Book of Life* a sort of religious text? It sounds as if it should be. How about anything supernatural? Well, the constable is afraid that the ghost of the typhoid victim may be about, and Jefferson Hope is certain he sees the ghosts of John Ferrier and Lucy leading him on. There are those numbers that appear inside John Ferrier's house: what sort of strange necromancy is that? And Holmes declares the importance of having faith in reason or a chain of reasoning even if the facts seem against it. And there is Nature, wild and frightening in the American West, with its great desert, or just broad as described by Holmes. And the great chain of being alluded to by Holmes, a traditional philosophical concept.

Demons: Besides ghosts, there is a demon: John Ferrier is described as being the genius or demon of the desert. He is part of that Old West? Later Jefferson Hope crawls like a serpent: is that demonic too? But maybe demon is meant here in a good way.

Numbers: Back to those numbers appearing in the house. Very Gothic, as the critic Nils Clausson says: this is not a Western; it's Gothic horror, he says. And there are other numbers: nine to seven and seven to five, the sign and countersign of the Avenging Angels (oh, more religious terminology). And then there is the number four: Four Mormon elders, four houses in Lauriston Gardens, Gregson's four men with a stretcher to carry out Enoch Drebber, the four million inhabitants of London (Sherlock Holmes's estimate), the group of four who tackle Jefferson Hope (Holmes, Lestrade, Gregson, and Watson), and the three key dates in the story: March 4, when the murder investigation begins; May 4, when John Ferrier and Lucy are rescued by the Mormons; and August 4, when John Ferrier is murdered by the Mormons. All pointing to *The Sign of Four* perhaps, but that's the next story.

Providence: Back to more direct references to religion, there's Jefferson Hope's belief in a Providence that would ensure the guilty Stangerson would choose the poisoned pill rather than the harmless one (is he right?). And there's the "higher Judge" who summons Hope via death: what will He decide? Watson seems to believe that there is such a judge, so seems to side with Hope's belief in Providence. Otherwise is it mere chance that is ruling our world? The critic Sarah Heinz sees Victorian England as fearing violence and chance: perhaps Sherlock Holmes is meant as a bulwark against both. But the police force could say the same. Or even the Mormon Church – unless it is the source of violence. Does the *Study* ask us to trust in God? Or are there more earthly supports? But Holmes, Lestrade, and Gregson seem almost more interested in one-upping each other than providing protection, and they are all wrong at various points, even Holmes, who is fooled by an old woman who is not an old woman, but who is really – well, who? We never learn. Some mysteries remain. Will God preserve us? The God who created the whole world – or did He? Little Lucy is dubious. He created the country in Illinois and Missouri, she says, but whoever created the Great Alkali Desert did not do as good a job: "They forgot the water and the trees."

Alkali, alkaloid: One seems to mean salt, as in the salt desert; one is a poison Holmes would happily test on a friend – or a poor little terrier. Also the poison Hope makes Drebber take, right after showing him Lucy's wedding ring: at least that was his plan, that Drebber's dying eyes should see it. But in the moment, what does he shake in front of Drebber's face? Not the ring that signifies the horrifying forced marriage, the crime of the past, but the key to the door that has locked Drebber in, locked him in the room from which he can only escape by death. The symbolism has changed, and we seem now in a story about how we cannot escape retribution for our sins: we are locked in a room with our judge and executioner, the instrument of Providence.

Drunken Drebber reading his Boccaccio, harassing young women, looking like a baboon. Perhaps he deserved to die? Is Jefferson Hope justified? But Sherlock Holmes captures him, perhaps protecting England from the transportation of foreign grudges to its unspoiled shores. The idea is not to take sides in these grudges, but to make sure violence is not done in the name of them. And most of all to celebrate this protective activity, as Dr. Watson will do by publishing his account. And that perhaps is what *A Study in Scarlet* is about.

The Sign of the Four

What's up there in the attic?   Here's a story about something up at the top of a house, something that looks like one of the major characters except that it's become all twisted and distorted. It seems that whenever the character commits a sin, the picture upstairs becomes distorted, and while he never ages, the picture gets older and ...   No, wait, that's *The Picture of Dorian Gray*, not *The Sign of the Four*, but *The Sign of the Four* is similar in presenting a Thaddeus Sholto out in the real world and a twin brother whose face has become distorted, though not by sin but by an Andaman Islander's poisoned dart.

Did they consult?   Conan Doyle and Oscar Wilde, that is. How unlikely, you say, and there's no evidence of that, except for the strange fact that the two of them were both commissioned by the managing editor of *Lippincott's Magazine* at the same dinner party. Yes, if you can imagine it, Conan Doyle and Oscar Wilde sharing a dinner and hearing from the editor how he'd like a short novel from each of them. Did the editor say, Maybe you could each try something with a strange-looking double in an attic? Who knows? Anyway, both stories were published in *Lippincott's* in 1890.

Not exactly the same, of course: Dorian Gray is a beautiful young man, and only his picture is hideous. Bartholomew Sholto looking like a disembodied head at the top of Pondicherry Lodge is hideous enough, but Thaddeus Sholto is no beauty: rather, he's a twitching, terrified, blubbering mess, with a great bald dome of head looking like a mountain-top amid a fringe of hair that reminds Watson of fir trees.

Watson! Yes, Watson is there, of course, in this second Sherlock Holmes story, and doing all the narrating this time, not leaving half to Jefferson Hope, though actually he does leave a large chunk to Jonathan Small and then complains that Small is too frivolous in his story-telling. Professional jealousy?

But back to the Sholtos: There's twisted, hideous Bartholomew in his chemistry lab, the sort of place you might find Sherlock Holmes and conjuring up notions of scientific rationality, as several commentators note. Is Holmes like Bartholomew Sholto? Or is he more like Jonathan Small the tracker? Or the complete outsider, Tonga? Critics have suggested all these comparisons for the man who we first see in this story injecting himself with cocaine – not perhaps the most rational thing to do, and prompting (eventual) objections from Watson that he's ruining his constitution: symbolizing the English constitution ruined by foreign substances? (That's a suggestion from the critic Joseph McLaughlin. The critics have a field day with this story, especially with all the references to Empire.)

But Thaddeus Sholto: His head makes me think of a barren Arctic landscape, and there's much that is barren in this story, or bleak and muddy and like a desert. Thaddeus, though, has an oasis of art in "the howling desert of South London" and so in the midst of fog and coarseness, there is a room full of Oriental, Eastern luxury, not to mention French paintings. (Some see the influence of Oscar Wilde there too.) And yet Thaddeus himself does not seem a happy man. He is continually twitching and worrying about his health, even getting Watson to check his heart. "Have you your stethoscope?" And oddly it seems Watson does. And there's nothing really wrong with Thaddeus's heart, though if there were, one could see that as symbolic of heartlessness – except it's Thaddeus's brother and father who seem the heartless ones, too greedy to share the Agra treasure with Mary Morstan, whereas Thaddeus insists on sending her pearls and making sure she gets her fair share.

But he's so twitchy: Some would call him the good Sholto, even if a bit thoughtless in so casually mentioning the death of Mary Morstan's father. Now, there was a man with a bad heart: Captain Morstan. Was he heartless too? But the real villain was Major Sholto, stealing the treasure that belonged to Jonathan Small. Or did it belong to him? Who did it really belong to? Maybe better not to know: it just brought a curse to all who handled it. Or so says Jonathan Small. Of course, he's a villain too, though he has his defenders (loyal to his fellow murderers, you know, the Sikhs, and friendly to Tonga, even if he does make racist remarks about "black devils," and then he bashes someone over the head with his own wooden leg: shades of Long John Silver: hmm, I'm not so thrilled with Jonathan Small actually).

But Thaddeus: It's so hard to stay focused on him, but there is something very interesting about him. Also something rather off-putting, with his airs about art and finding policemen and other things unaesthetic or distasteful. Just a little too affected and pretentious for my tastes, but he does try to do right by Miss Morstan, and he suffers so, though maybe the suffering, the herky-jerkiness, the perpetual covering of his yellowing teeth, his self-indulgence with the hookah – it's all perhaps a bit much. I suspected him at first of having nefarious plans: is there really a twin brother in the attic? Maybe it's all Thaddeus. And even Watson, when he glimpses Bartholomew through the keyhole, has to check to see if Thaddeus is still beside him.

It's all this Eastern stuff: Is Thaddeus some sort of warning to us? Is this what happens when you try to assimilate all the things of the East, the Oriental vases, the hookah, and so on? The Sholtos are British; maybe they shouldn't pretend to be from India, though of course Major Sholto was stationed there and brought home money, "curiosities," and native servants. But maybe that's just the problem, maybe the moral is the one stated in the opening line of another famous work from just before 1890: "East is East, and West is West ..." But Thaddeus Sholto tries to mix them, and perhaps Doyle is warning about the results.

The problem of Empire: Here we get into a subject that activates the critics, the evils of the British Empire. And what is the message of Doyle's novel concerning that? It does not seem pro-Empire, though it's true that the description of the non-white people of foreign lands does not seem very complimentary. But then the British are not portrayed in a very complimentary way either. Major Sholto is a greedy liar, Jonathan Small's villainy I have already alluded to, and the motivations of the British colonizers are perhaps best summed up by the Sikh murderer who tells Jonathan Small, the British guard at the fort in Agra: "We only ask you to do that which your countrymen come to this land for. We ask you to be rich."

And how does one get rich in India? By exploiting the natives? By running an indigo plantation as is done by Abel White (a perhaps allegorical name, though he doesn't seem so able in the end)? Or simply by stealing the Agra treasure. Even Watson gets into the act in a very symbolic way in the end: he takes a poker to smash the Buddha-shaped lock on the box where the treasure was. Is this what Europeans are doing: smashing native culture (Buddhism) to grab the loot?

But there is no treasure: Yes, that's the irony. Smashing and looting leaves you with nothing. And perhaps this has nothing to do with Empire-building: as one critic (Nils Clausson) says, the Empire was more about those indigo plantations, not loot, especially not loot that got hidden away in an attic and never used. For Clausson, this is primarily a moral fable, echoing stories as old as Chaucer, stories about how greed for money leads to disaster. And it may be that, but still the whole thing has roots in India; it has the air of Empire about it; it takes place at the time of the Great Mutiny, the uprising of Indians against British rule. If not about Empire, what is it about?

Well, many things: Sherlock Holmes and his drugs perhaps, Watson's marriage, Sherlock Holmes's views on work, or need for work, the growth of London with its monster tentacles (perhaps a bit of Empire-building at home). But certainly also about Empire, the depiction of which seems to amount to saying it's dangerous out there, and those who are growing our Empire are motivated too much by greed, and the danger may lash out and hurt us (i.e., the British) there in India and even here at home: we may get convicts and cannibals coming to our shores. Better to send them and their treasure back into the primordial ooze. This is an anti-Empire story written from the point of view of those who think the British are being contaminated by their overseas possessions.

But what about Sherlock Holmes? It is a Sherlock Holmes story, isn't it? Or is it? Just as *Study in Scarlet* almost seemed more about Watson finding a purpose in his life (to write up accounts of his new friend's exploits), so this second entry in the series seems about how Watson will find yet another purpose in his life: marriage, domesticity, settling down. Which, as he announces at the end, will mean an end to his adventures with the great detective. It's almost as if Conan

Doyle is shutting down the series before it even begins. And why is that?

Perhaps Sherlock Holmes is just too irritating: Never mind his drug-taking, how about invading Watson's privacy by announcing that his brother was a drunken failure? Or how about dismissing Watson's first story as not very well done at all: mixing too much romance with the pure Euclidean geometry of Holmes's deductions. Watson begins to get tired of his friend's egotism, his need to be at the centre, and is there also a suggestion that Holmes doesn't really know as much as he thinks? He first dismisses the map as of no relevance, he thinks the pearls are compensation for Captain Morstan's disappearance, not for any treasure, and his hound-dog gets confused on the creosote trail. Poor Toby. But it's true Toby gets set right, and Holmes does in the end track down the murderers, though he underestimates the speed of their boat and so cuts it very close, as Athelney Jones is quick to point out.

But adventures: Yes, it is a glorious adventure, capped by the high-speed boat chase, like something out of a Hollywood movie. But can you really go adventuring forever? Isn't the standard journey of the hero one that takes him into exotic climes, lets him show his stuff, teaches him something, and then sends him home? And by home I don't mean 221B Baker Street. Or maybe I do. Maybe that's why the ending of this novella, though meant to wrap up the series, doesn't really work. What we get at the end is almost like something out of Jane Austen: the characters overcome obstacles (in this case the horrible Agra treasure that Watson fears is putting Mary out of his reach) and come together in marriage. It's the traditional marriage plot, more typical one might think of a heroine's story, an Emma or an Elizabeth. Some see Mary Morstan as the wisest character in the story (and perhaps she is for her lack of interest in money), some even see the love story as convincing, but most I think find it insipid.

The contest for Watson: It's Holmes and Mary battling it out over the poor doctor. Not that Holmes seems to care; he'll just reach for another shot of cocaine. And perhaps that makes him even more alluring. Or perhaps Watson ends up feeling that responsibility for Holmes's constitution that I alluded to earlier. And then Holmes has perhaps become even more interesting than in *A Study in Scarlet*. Not only is he taking drugs, but he's philosophizing about men in the aggregate and whether even the toughs down on the docks have a spark of immortality in them. He can even talk about pink flamingos. And he does after all solve the case, so perhaps there is something about him that Watson wouldn't want to lose.

And so a mere year after sending Watson packing, Doyle revived the partnership in "A Scandal of Bohemia" and created a series of adventures for those who are always children at heart, perhaps a bit childish even, and who aren't quite ready to settle down in tranquil English domesticity but who want to go and figure out exactly what happened to a naval treaty or a stolen racehorse. Or if not go and do these things themselves, then at least read about them in a never-ending series. And thus the remaining fifty-eight stories.

A Scandal in Bohemia

Never to return: That's what we learn of Irene Adler. She's left England, never to return. She has this one brilliant turn in "A Scandal in Bohemia," and then is gone – poof! – never to be seen again. (Except in countless pastiches, adaptations, and the fantasies of Sherlockians.) I shouldn't make that a mere parenthesis, though: it raises a big question: Why the fascination with this opera singer from New Jersey?

New Jersey? Yes, I know, how can that be right? Here she is, the one woman who can outsmart Sherlock Holmes, and she comes from New Jersey. One's class snobbery rises – and perhaps that is the point. The whole series is about not judging by class or caste or status. There can be brilliance come from New Jersey: why not?

But back to the significance of Irene Adler: For Sherlock Holmes, of course, she is always *the* woman. Why? Because she was smarter? Like Mycroft? No, that doesn't take us anywhere. Or perhaps it does. It humbles Sherlock, perhaps humanizes him. And how daring of Doyle to do this in only the third appearance of his detective, and the first in the *Strand Magazine*. This would be the first introduction of many readers to the man who is supposedly the master, the incisive reasoning machine who is invariably successful – and he fails! He is bested by a woman, who sees through his disguises, or at least one of them, who fools him with her own disguise, and even drags him into her own wedding and tosses him a coin for his trouble. This is what made fans out of the readers in 1891?

Well, perhaps Doyle knew what he was about: It reminds me of the opening of *Butch Cassidy and the Sundance Kid*, when the heroes are unable to shake a posse. They are failing despite all their tricks, but this somehow impresses us: we just know that usually they get clean away. Just as usually Sherlock Holmes outsmarts all he meets. But this time …

This time he meets a woman: Yes, and what's a woman doing in the canon? I mean, there are lots of stories in which Holmes comes to the aid of women, but here is one who impresses him. Some Sherlockians imagine she does more than that, and see a repressed romance here, but is that what's going on? Is there in fact any place for romance in the canon? Well, among the clients, of course, but can our heroes give way to it? Oh, come on, I hear you say, Watson is always falling for the latest pretty face; he even marries one in the story just before this one, and is still married and perfectly happy, he says, as this one begins – and yet he can't help venturing back to Baker Street and even ends up sleeping over there.

Watson and Holmes: There's the real couple in the canon. I don't mean romantically (though some Sherlockians speculate about that too). I mean more like Boswell and Johnson. Holmes even calls Watson his Boswell here, and says he'd be lost without him. Why? Does every man need a biographer, a sidekick, a butt? Perhaps, perhaps, a Sancho Panza for every Don Quixote, a Robin for our Batman. But then how does Irene Adler fit in?

Well, she doesn't: And she could be very disruptive, as could Watson's wife if she had any reality. The true reality in the stories is Holmes and Watson as a team. It's a very male bonding thing, a boys club, no girls allowed. So again, what is Irene Adler doing in this keystone story?

Maybe to show the limits: With Holmes and Watson we are in a world of *Boy's Own* adventures, or if you prefer, the single-minded knights pursuing the Holy Grail, or Curly the cowboy in the movie *City Slickers*. It's a man's world, even if part of it is spent investigating the crimes involving women. But there is a world beyond, a world of romance, marriage, domesticity. As the critic Michael Atkinson points out, Holmes dresses up as a groom and ends up at Irene Adler's wedding – as a groom! Is he marrying her? Well, of course not, she's marrying Godfrey Norton, and yet how odd …

And he keeps her picture: Rather than a snake ring (which admittedly doesn't sound nice), Holmes prefers a photo of *the* woman. What will he do with it? Some speculate that he will keep it under his pillow (does Holmes have a pillow?). Some say it is merely for his files. I think it is probably meant to be a keepsake to be admired, not necessarily in a romantic way, and yet there is something of the pining knight in all this, the courtly lover. And like a courtly lover, he is drawn to an unattainable woman: she is married to another, and by now she may even be dead (Watson calls her "the late Irene Adler," though there is dispute over what that means).

So that other world is delineated but kept apart. There she is, *the* woman, and she will always be *the* woman, precisely because she is hurried off the stage to become a mere memory or memento. Holmes had his moment with her, penetrating into her inner sanctum even, finding the one thing she would show no one, but then she is off, she is gone, he is deflated, defeated, and it is over, but not in a sad way, more in the way Curly in that movie describes the young woman he once glimpsed while riding the range. He saw her only once, but she is the love of his life – and having established that, he can get back to being a cowboy, just as Holmes can get back to what he's meant for: solving crimes.

And developing a relationship with Watson: His Boswell, whom he needs. But why does he need him? To tell his stories? Perhaps. He also gets him, in this story, to throw a smoke bomb through a window. It seems rather unnecessary. He hires a whole street full of accomplices: why couldn't one of them throw the bomb? Why drag in Watson, good old flat-footed innocent Watson, who here declares his willingness to break the law and be arrested, all because it's in a good cause. What cause? Serving the King of Bohemia? That turns out not to be such a good cause at all. Conspiring against Irene Adler? That makes him ashamed. No, the good cause is the partnership with Sherlock Holmes; that's what this story is setting up. Watson will do anything for Holmes, and so will we.

And who is this Holmes, anyway? Watson says he has a Bohemian soul. Who, Holmes? In some ways he seems the furthest thing from an artsy, passionate Bohemian. And yet he is unconventional and does drugs, so maybe, but … It is interesting that there is a scandal in Bohemia, or there almost is, until it is averted, and here we have Holmes the Bohemian. What does it mean? Is the Bohemian scandal really about the relationship between the King and Irene, or is it more to do with the relationship between Irene and Holmes? The scandal of a woman intruding into Holmes's "Bohemian" world? But she doesn't intrude very long.

Lingering Questions: Why does the King say the matter will be of no importance after two years? Will the photograph not matter once he is securely married? Yet in the meantime it could threaten the peace of Europe. And what is the significance of grouping Irene Adler with a rabbi and the naval officer who wrote a tome on deep-sea fishes? Adler, by the way, means eagle in German, and therefore, well, who knows?

But the main thing is that this story sets up a Master who impresses all, and who wins the loyalty of his biographer, and yet someone who, despite Watson's description, is not an infallible machine. Throughout the canon we will frequently see touches which qualify or modify our sense of Holmes as some sort of automaton – and that's all to the good, for who can identify with an automaton? And yet he will still have the whiff of superiority about him; we will marvel at his triumphs, and we will identify above all with his relationship to Watson, the ordinary human being who is just like us. And the woman? She is just a photograph.

The Red-Headed League

The Front of the Picture and the Back: They are very different, aren't they? On one side is the bustling artery to the City, filled with fine shops and stately businesses. On the other, the shabby genteel Saxe-Coburg Square, with its poky pawnbroking establishment. The good and the bad? The fine and the declining? The rich and the ... Well, you get the idea, but what exactly is the point? To show the variousness of London? To draw a contrast between the financial heights and the struggling shopkeeper? (The bank with its gold bullion is on the fine side.) Is there some class symbolism here? One commentator at least, in the Twayne literary series no less, thinks so ...

Theory, Theory, who's got a theory? That would be Rosemary Jann, in her book on the *Adventures*, who sees an alliance between aristocrats and the lower orders going on here. In contrast, in another study in the Twayne series, Jacqueline Jaffe turns more to Jung and Joseph Campbell than to Marx, and sees the hero's journey, the struggles in the dark, the quest that leads the hero (heroes?) underground to grapple with powerful forces ...

Maybe. And of course there's also the notorious Samuel Rosenberg, who sees homosexuality in the story, with Holmes thwarting a homosexual assault to defend order and propriety. (This assault consists of John Clay's attempted attack on the bank from below.)

John Clay: The Moriarty-like villain, one of the smartest men in London, says Holmes, who later compliments him on his clever red-headed scheme. A young (well, not that young, says Jabez Wilson) criminal genius. Almost womanish in his appearance: no hair on his face and a womanish hand. There are no women in this story, just John Clay as a pseudo-woman, perhaps lending credence to the Rosenberg hypothesis? But maybe we should look more to the pseudo part of this. Clay is not really a woman; he is not an amiable clerk named Vincent Spaulding; and his accomplice is not really named Duncan Ross or William Morris (the latter alias, by the way, was the name of a noted Victorian socialist and craftsman, perhaps lending credence more to the Jann thesis about social class).

Things are not what they seem: As I was saying, John Clay is not really a woman, or young, or an innocent. You have to beware of surfaces and schemes. And especially of Red-Headed Leagues. A Red-Headed League, what a notion. And a street full of red-headed men, all applying for an imaginary job copying articles out of the *Encyclopaedia Britannica*. What is going on here?

Of course, yes: It's all a ruse to lure Jabez Wilson from his pawnbrokerage so that Clay can dig in the clay, down deep, where he pretends to do photography. Holmes and Watson travel to the location by Underground (the only time they go Underground in the whole canon). It must mean something, plunging into the depths, looking at the backside of the picture.

But why such an elaborate ruse? Why summon hundreds (thousands?) of red-headed men when you want just one, and one particular one. And when you have him, why do you almost turn him away, shaking your head when he says he has no children, for the point of the Red-Headed League, founded by that fabulous American, Ezekiah Hopkins, is supposedly to propagate red-headed men (as if genetics really worked that way). Haven't we got a little carried away, believing our own ruse?

And then to pull on his hair! Causing pain, seeking for a wig. We wouldn't want to have a pseudo-redhead, would we? But wait, why do we care? The redhead thing is just a hoax, a ruse. We seem to have here a case of believing one's own propaganda, or just getting carried away playing a role … But it also makes one wonder about the significance of redheads for John Clay or Conan Doyle, or someone. There are all sorts of prejudices and stereotypes about redheads, but the story indulges in none of them. So why this obsession? What does redheadedness signify in this story?

Or maybe that is to miss the point. As yet another commentator (Martin Priestman) notes, the important thing about Jabez Wilson is not his hair but his shop: the shop borders the bank. This is a story about stealing gold, not about an alliance of redheads.

Or is it? Of course, the plot is about stealing gold, but the theme? And the title? What is surface and what is reality? Is it the fine shops and stately businesses? Or is it the shabby shop? Was England still a nation of shopkeepers, or something else?

Maybe both? This is a story of duality after all. Watson goes on about Holmes's dual nature, the languorous aesthete and the severe rationalist. Or is he such a rationalist? Near the beginning Holmes threatens to destroy Watson's reason (over the issue of whether truth is stranger than fiction, and this in a work of fiction, I note). And he will destroy Watson's reason by means of facts. Facts versus reason? On the other hand, don't all these things work together in a sort of creative synthesis? Isn't Holmes following a standard method of creativity: gather the facts, meditate upon them (smoking three pipes if necessary), then take a break, listen to Sarasate, then eureka, you've solved it.

But how? Holmes is almost godlike here. Or as Watson puts it, he knows what has happened and what is going to happen. Holmes versus the devil (Clay, that man of the earth). And then Holmes explains – a dangerous thing to do: when he explained to Jabez Wilson how he knew Wilson was a Freemason who had visited China etc., Wilson dismisses it as nothing. (Only after the explanation, I note: beforehand he is astonished. But then the magician explains the trick. You should never do that.)

Admiration: Watson, though (at least this time), expresses admiration for the Holmesian chain of reasoning and calls Holmes a benefactor of mankind. Holmes turns suddenly modest, disclaiming anything but having been of slight use. But it's not really modesty, is it? Some see Holmes as seeking acclaim, but what he yearns for here is the game, stimulation, something worthy of his talents. How sad for a man of talents to not be able to use them, or have nothing to use them on. The Red-Headed League gave him a chance to shine, but he doesn't care so much about shining as about figuring things out and saving himself from boredom. That is perhaps what the League is really about: a first-class problem for a first-class mind to solve. Something mundane to winkle out from underneath the bizarre. It is reassuring in the end: life presents its oddities, its baffling mysteries, but there is our God, Sherlock Holmes, to figure things out for us and assure us that life can go on without further disruption (at least until the next case).

A Case of Identity

Depend upon it, there is nothing so unnatural as the commonplace: So says Sherlock Holmes, and it sounds profound. But what does it mean? That ordinary things are actually extraordinary? And thus the extraordinary are ordinary? That the most unusual things happen all the time in everyday life, more unusual than what the most extravagant artists could dream up? But as more than one commentator has noted, it is ironic (hilarious?) that Holmes makes this argument by dreaming up a completely fictional, even science-fictional scenario of flying over London, gently removing the roofs, and peeping inside. (A little voyeurism, by the way? I guess that's what detectives do, though: spy on other people.)

So which is it, fiction or reality? Which is more extraordinary, unnatural? If reality is unnatural, then is Nature unnatural? It is very confusing. And of course made even more confusing by being a claim made in a work of fiction (my apologies to those who think these are non-fiction accounts). Could any story-teller invent something as bizarre as the husband throwing his false teeth at his wife? So says Holmes. But who after all invented that bizarre scenario except the story-teller Arthur Conan Doyle – or is there a real case of that? If not, what on earth is the significance of the teeth-throwing? One commentator says it points to the comedy in this story. Perhaps, and ...?

False teeth, false teeth: Replacement teeth for the real thing. Just as Hosmer Angel is a replacement for a real lover? Poor Mary Sutherland is stuck with this make-believe delusion which Holmes refuses to disabuse her of, thus allowing her evil stepfather to succeed in his plan to control his stepdaughter's money and, say some, maintain the evil patriarchal system of oppressing females. It does give one pause: Holmes justifies it with a sweeping generalization about women (you better not take away their delusions, he says, supposedly quoting a Persian poet). What is going on here?

Martin Wagner has an idea: This critic does an interesting analysis of Holmes's opening analysis of the "interesting" Mary Sutherland. By the way, the well-respected Sherlockian Sonia Fetherston notes that this story sets up the whole canon, being one of the first to give us all the standard elements of Holmes and Watson, from their cosy fireside chat to the pipes and tobacco to the analysis of a client that never fails to astound. But let's look at that analysis, or follow Martin Wagner's dissection of it. He focuses especially on Holmes's conclusion that Miss Sutherland is a typist (or typewritist, to use Holmes's word) because of the marks on her plush sleeves. But, says Wagner, she wouldn't wear her plush sleeves for typing. This makes no sense at all.

And typing's not difficult even if you can't see: Mary Sutherland says that, noting that an experienced typist knows where the letters are. This in response to Holmes's suggestion that her short-sightedness must make it hard to do her work. This seems not really an error on Holmes's part, and Wagner doesn't push the point; it's more that Miss Sutherland has made an accommodation to deal with the problem. But let's look at that accommodation: she can type because she knows where the letters are? The letters on her keyboard, presumably, but every good typist looks away from the keyboard because their focus has to be on what they're transcribing: some handwritten manuscript usually. How does she see that with her short-sightedness? Well, with her pince-nez, but still …

37

Is anyone telling us the truth? We have Holmes in essence jumping to an impossible conclusion because there should be no signs of typing on the plush sleeves. We have Mary Sutherland confusing the matter by referring to letters she already knows rather than the ones she has to discover. And yet the reader is willing to suspend disbelief and accept all this. Why? I think it's Watson's fault. Here is Watson celebrating his great companion, talking of his "incisive reasoning" and saying he had so many reasons (how we repeat that word) to believe in Holmes's "subtle powers of reasoning." Reason, reasoning, rationality – that's what Holmes is all about, no? And yet, suggests Martin Wagner, it's not true, it's a fiction. The truth is a fiction, as one might put it in a moment of Holmesian (or anti-Holmesian) profundity. Figure that out.

And what about the incest? Well, yes, I know, they don't actually commit incest, this stepfather and his stepdaughter, but there's an icky quality to the story, or perhaps just a sense of a father figure keeping his daughter from rival males. Sort of an Oedipus complex inside out and upside down (I fear all this flying over the roofs of London has disoriented me). Later in the canon, and even in the earlier tale of Bohemia, we have Holmes himself (and sometimes Watson) seeming to step in between a young woman and her proper suitors, even if the suitors are fiancés. Nothing like that here, though Chris Redmond detects a whiff of it. Miss Mary Sutherland, a rather large woman with a vacuous face and a preposterous hat, doesn't seem our heroes' type. There is no Holmesian interruption of the course of true love; instead, it's the stepfather who intervenes, disguised as an Angel.

Hosmer Angel: And he's no angel, of course, except perhaps in the fact that he doesn't exist (apologies to those who believe that angels do exist, and fairies too). He doesn't exist, and yet Miss Mary Sutherland believes in him, a belief that Sherlock Holmes is loath to challenge: she would bite his head off, he suggests. She has a simple yet noble faith in her supposed fiancé; she swears loyalty to him on a Bible. This is religion of a sort, and not the only religion in the story. We do talk of these stories as a canon after all, with Holmes as a sort of God, and Watson, I will venture to add, as his prophet.

And why do we need this God and Prophet? Why, to deal with all the unnatural occurrences of everyday life. To bring order to the universe. That's what Holmes can do for us: he'll take the most mysterious of circumstances and make them clear. Whether he lets the villains go free or not, that is not the point. He explains things, that's what's important. Now we understand what Hosmer Angel is; we have settled the mystery; and we can go back to our own everyday activities, comforted in the thought that there is a reason for everything (even if it's a fiction to say so).

Lingering Questions: Why is the mother angry? We don't see her, but we learn that she was in on the plot and was – but wait, was she in on the plot? We have only Holmes's conjecture for that. Was she taken in too? But how could she not recognize her own husband? On the other hand, how could Mary Sutherland not recognize her own stepfather? I know she was short-sighted and he was wearing a disguise, but really ... Of course, we must suspend our disbelief. And what we do know is that the mother was all for the match and, as Mary puts it, was even "fonder of him [Hosmer Angel] than I was" – well, of course she would be fonder of her own husband, if she recognized him as her husband; would she be fonder of her daughter's suitor even if she didn't know it was really Mr. Windibank? Is she eager to have her daughter marry? Why? To free her of Mr. Windibank? But if she knew all along, then she was helping to bind her daughter to Mr. Windibank. But if that's so, why be angry when Hosmer Angel vanishes? Or was that an act? Or was it just a spark of maternal affection springing up for her poor, deceived daughter – even if she was willing to go along with the deception at the beginning. Do we have mother-daughter rivalry here? Or mother-stepfather conspiracy? Or mother-daughter alliance? Or some mixture of all three? Oh, the strange ways of families.

And one more question: Why is Holmes sure Mr. Windibank will end on the gallows? Is this actually just some Holmesian social snobbery at work, looking down on the jumped-up wine salesman who thinks he's better than a plumber, or anger at a heartless cad? But why should deceiving a stepdaughter lead to capital offences? Will he murder someone in his greed? Ah, well, who knows? Perhaps Holmes is just jealous of someone who so successfully uses a disguise, rivalling Holmes himself, reminding him of his defeat by Irene Adler, who also was good at disguise. So it's a story of rivalry perhaps: Holmes versus Windibank, Windibank versus suitors, mother versus daughter. A story of rivalry and faith.

The Boscombe Valley Mystery

The only mystery in the canon: Well, of course it isn't; they're all mysteries, aren't they? Or mostly. But this is the only one called a Mystery. There's one Case (as we've just seen), but then mostly Adventures. According to Jacqueline Jaffe, *Adventures* is a good title, summoning up the archetype of the hero's journey: is that what's going on in the stories? I rather think they are more mysteries. On the other hand, this one begins like a classic adventure tale: there's our hero having a humdrum breakfast with his wife when he is summoned by a telegram.

Oh, wait: That's Watson, not Holmes. Is he the hero? Not really; he's just the Boswell – but then again our Boswell is important. Still, in the later stories more often there is no summoning like this: Watson is already with Holmes at Baker Street. And then a client drops in with a mystery to solve. And yet we call them Adventures.

Have fun with your friend, John: So says Mrs. Watson in this tale, or words to that effect. She is almost the mother sending her little boy off to play, and this in a story with few mothers. Both Mrs. McCarthy and Mrs. Turner are not on the scene. The main female presence is Alice Turner, daughter of the murderer, bank robber, etc. etc., who led a wild life in Australia, making much money in an ill-gotten way and then retiring to the Old Country, where his little daughter somehow civilizes him. Or maybe it was England that civilized him. He seems perfectly respectable now; it's only his past that's appalling.

And that past comes back to bite him: In the person of Charles McCarthy, another ex-Australian, who knows all about Turner's criminal exploits (adventures?) – indeed he was the victim of one of them – and yet it's this victim who's described as a devil with wicked eyes. Of course, the person doing the describing is Mr. Turner, so perhaps the description is biased? But no one seems to dispute it in the story, and if there is a villain, it is not the mass-murderer, but the one who witnessed his mass murder. How odd.

And why is that? Well, as we will see elsewhere in the canon, one of the worst crimes is blackmail, and one of the main concerns is reputation. Some see this story as depicting the way Victorian England exploited its colonies, making money in unspeakable ways, ways which are literally not to be spoken of. If you start speaking about them, or threatening to speak about them, if you use that threat to extort money, land, and a wife for your son, then you are the biggest villain around, whatever peccadilloes (like a few murders) your blackmail victim may have committed in Australia long ago.

The past is a hidden country, as someone might have said: we keep our skeletons there. And as a doubling of this crime-in-the-past motif, there is the bigamy that the younger McCarthy (James, the son who loves Alice) got mixed up in. Or at least his secret marriage, which prevents him from marrying Alice. She thinks he hesitates because he is not ready for marriage – but really he is already married. At least he thinks he is, but it turns out the low barmaid he married was married already, so we have bigamy twice over, and he is free, and can marry Alice after all – which is not at all what her father wants.

So who wins here? Sherlock Holmes, playing judge and jury, lets off Mr. Turner, who however is dying. Turner killed McCarthy to keep him from forcing a marriage of James and Alice – but James and Alice do marry. Only, they somehow never learn of their fathers' criminal ways, and Alice apparently is not told of the barmaid. Really that barmaid affair is just some sowing of wild oats, isn't it? With a euphemistic cover as a marriage – for the benefit of the tender sensitivities of the readers of the *Strand Magazine* (where this story first appeared), at least according to Rosemary Jann. And maybe so. And doesn't that suggest that Alice was right after all? James was sowing his wild oats, what a young man gets up to before he's ready to settle down and marry. It is as Alice says: James wasn't ready, though not quite in the way she meant. And his premarital adventures (that word again) are something to be hidden, concealed in the same way as her father's murders. The past is a hidden country, as I've said. We did things then that don't bear looking into, but now we can go forward into a respectable future.

Even if her father killed his father? Apparently. They are not to know. The murder of Charles McCarthy will remain publicly unsolved, though we know who did it. And that murder, by the way, is not in the distant past; it is here and now, and yet Holmes will let it go: because blackmail is worse than murder apparently, and because vigilante justice is acceptable. At least one critic (Les Klinger) shakes his head over this, but the point is surely to defend the currently respectable. It is a bit odd, though, that Holmes jumps to protect a member of the landed gentry; he's often at odds with them, as in "The Reigate Squires" and "Silver Blaze."

But above all the important thing is to defend respectability and reputation – why, we'll even defend the reputation of the King of Bohemia, though not that of Isadora Klein or of Baron Gruner. But perhaps things are different in those later stories.

Moonshine versus Fog: Lestrade is here, oddly acting as a sort of private consultant to Alice Turner (is that even legal?), and he has no time for Holmes's theories. Moonshine, he calls them, prompting the response that moonshine is better than fog. Brighter. You can see by moonshine whereas you get lost in the fog. The regular police, like Lestrade, are often in a fog; it takes Sherlock Holmes to set them right.

And how? By becoming a dog on the scent, embarking on a frenzy of detection at the crime scene, like some Romantic artist caught up in the throes of creation. Is this how Conan Doyle felt writing these stories? There's animal lust here, anticipating the later animal stories like "The Creeping Man." Those who think of Sherlock Holmes as a mere detecting machine must not forget this side of him. He is transformed from quiet thinker to Coleridgean poet with flashing eyes, from Dr. Jekyll to Mr. Hyde – but a good Mr. Hyde, using his animal powers for a good cause, much in the nature of the archetypal hero on his journey. So Holmes is the hero after all, and this really is an Adventure?

Poor Watson: And if Holmes is the hero, what is Watson? The recorder, the sidekick – and the butt. What do we make of Holmes calling Watson slovenly in his shaving? He called him away, made him get ready in a hurry, and then complains because he doesn't look right. Well, to be fair, he's not complaining, just making an example of Watson to prove his superior deductive abilities. I can show you what a great detective I am by explaining why it is you shave so badly. Hmm. Putting one up to put the other down: is that really necessary? Or is it all part of making us Watsons feel unworthy in the presence of the Master? Holmes has a reputation to maintain too, after all, and so what if he does so at the expense of yours?

The son's just deserts: Why does James feel he deserves to be arrested and blamed for his father's death? Because he quarrelled with him? Because he's frustrating his father's desire for a marriage between James and Alice? Or frustrating his own desire? Because he married that barmaid? For whatever reason, he does get punished in this story, having to endure a trial even though Sherlock Holmes knows he is innocent. Why? Because he is the son of a blackmailer? So much worse to be even the son of a blackmailer than a murderer, it seems. But he does get to marry Alice in the end, and we are left with Sherlock Holmes musing about the tricks of fate, by which, however, he seems to mean the suffering inflicted on old Turner the murderer rather than on James. And Holmes says, "There, but for the grace of God, goes Sherlock Holmes." As if Holmes has some crimes on his conscience too? Does he have a past that does not bear looking into? Ah, who can tell? But the main thing is: he sympathizes with the murderer. How strange.

The Five Orange Pips
Clumsy Lumbering:
Holmes's Failure in "The Five Orange Pips"[*]

The Petrels did "The Five Orange Pips" in December, and it turned out to be a story that provoked an unusual amount of passion. Some members were passionate about its flaws and overall awfulness, though some of us were more sympathetic and noted that Conan Doyle included it in his top 12.

Someone suggested that Doyle did this simply to give an example of something different, and the story certainly is different. It ends, for instance, not with Holmes triumphantly seizing a criminal or even deciding to let a criminal go, but with the miscreants perishing at sea before they can be captured. So it's not that they escape; they do get punished, but not because of anything Holmes or the constabulary do. It's more just the workings of the universe.

The universe works in mysterious ways in this story, or at least in eerie, ominous ways. The wind cries and sobs "like a child in the chimney," reminding Watson of "the presence of those great elemental forces which shriek at mankind through the bars of his civilization, like untamed beasts in a cage." And this is a story of great elemental forces that seem to be beyond the powers of Sherlock Holmes.

Holmes's powers, in fact, seem decidedly feeble here. There's no parlour trick at the beginning by which he deduces what Watson is thinking. He does do something of the sort with the client who is blown in by the storm, deducing that he has come from the southwest, but the client seems singularly unimpressed: unlike clients in other stories, he does not seem struck dumb with amazement, but treats the deduction with indifference, and when Holmes explains how he made it, as if

---

[*]   Before I started my Musings, I wrote this essay for the Petrels'
magazine, the *Petrel Flyer*. It was published there in February 2013.

begging for some applause, the client simply changes the subject.

It is notable as well that Holmes's first conjecture in the story, that the ringing of the bell is more likely to signify the arrival of a "crony of the landlady's" than that of a client, is quite wrong: it *is* a client, John Openshaw, who will go to his death in this story even though Holmes could surely have done something to prevent it: that is part of what annoyed the Petrels.

It is also notable that when Openshaw says he has heard that Holmes is never beaten, Holmes replies, "I have been beaten four times – three times by men, and once by a woman." The woman, of course, would be Irene Adler in "A Scandal in Bohemia," but who are these men? Why is Holmes the great solver of mysteries suddenly portraying himself as quite beatable and not so great?

He is not alone in this self-deprecation, however. Openshaw describes himself, after receiving the latest threat from the KKK, as feeling "like one of those poor rabbits when the snake is writhing towards it." Holmes tells him to buck up and act, but Holmes himself does not seem to act appropriately, instead sending poor Openshaw back home to his death.

Holmes says that the first consideration is to remove the pressing danger threatening Openshaw; as the Petrels noted, the best way to do that would have been to have Openshaw stay overnight and then be accompanied by Holmes and Watson the next morning in daylight when, as it turns out, the storm of the opening pages has passed. But no, Holmes sends Openshaw out into the screaming wind, with the rain still coming down: the "mad elements" are at work, Watson says, and in those mad elements Openshaw meets his doom.

The second consideration, Holmes says, is to clear up the mystery of the KKK, the orange pips, and the demand for papers to be placed on a sundial. But this never happens either. Why does the KKK want these papers? Why are they killing people? These questions do not get answered, because Holmes never catches the criminals, and so we miss the usual denouement in which all is explained.

Instead, we oddly get a recapitulation of the limits of Holmes's knowledge, something Watson first compiled in *A Study in Scarlet*. The difference here is that there is talk of a lumber-room in addition to a "brain-attic." In the *Study*, Holmes says that the "skilful workman is very careful indeed as to what he takes into his brain-attic," adding that such a skilful person "will have nothing but the tools which may help him in doing his work."

Something similar is said in "The Five Orange Pips"; Holmes even says that he is repeating himself: "I say now, as I said then, that a man should keep his little brain-attic stocked with all the furniture that he is likely to use." But this time he adds that "the rest he can put away in the lumber-room ..."

Why the lumber room? This is just a metaphorical lumber room for Holmes, but there is a real lumber room in the story, the one where Openshaw's uncle keeps the papers so much wanted by the KKK, the papers that seem to be the key to the mystery. Someone has made a mistake here: either Openshaw's uncle erred by sending important papers to the lumber room, or perhaps Sherlock Holmes is in error to think of a lumber room as the place for things that are not important. Or perhaps he has put something in the lumber room of his metaphor that should have stayed in his brain-attic, for instance the common sense not to send Openshaw out again on a stormy night.

Holmes is devastated by Openshaw's death and vows revenge. He indeed thinks he has succeeded in that revenge, saying he has the perpetrators "in the hollow of my hand." But he is wrong again. "There is ever a flaw, however, in the best laid of human plans," Watson notes, and the criminals escape Holmes – only to go to their deaths, it is true, but still ... We are left with a sense of the insignificance of human beings and their plans in the face of the elements, which in this case seem to have wrecked the ship the murderers were on, causing them to drown.

And what should we make of all this? When Doyle created Holmes, he made him seem almost supernaturally effective in the fight against crime, and yet in the third Holmes story he has him beaten by a woman, and here in the seventh he has him completely stymied. It is almost as if he has pulled back from the notion of the detective's all-conquering powers in the face of even greater powers, those of Nature and the mysterious Universe. This is more in the order of a Gothic horror story, with helpless victims trampled by evil forces, than a detective story in which the detective puts everything to rights.

It is as if Doyle was having a momentary failure of nerve, a reaction in his own "brain-attic" against how he had built Holmes up as someone well nigh invincible. But it seems to have been only a momentary failure, and Holmes would soon go on to solve the mystery of the speckled band and be able to determine the significance of the dog that did nothing in the night. A failed Holmes would not have remained so much in the popular imagination, no doubt, but it is interesting to see his moments of failure.

The Man with the Twisted Lip

Like birds to a lighthouse: Well, that's nice. People in grief flock to see Watson's wife. But I began to think about this simile. Do birds flock to lighthouses? Indeed, they do, attracted by the light, and they hit the buildings and die. Hmm. Is there something dangerous about Watson's wife? Or at least boring? The story opens with Watson yawning in her presence. It's a tender domestic scene in the Watsons' sitting room, Watson in his armchair, his wife at her needlework, and yet where is the exciting repartee we get when Watson is with Holmes, or for that matter when Hugh Boone is plying his trade as a beggar?

Hugh Boone is good at being a beggar: There's the witty repartee and the professionally done make-up, making him quite a character on the streets of the City, known to Sherlock Holmes even before his involvement in this case. And what a strange case it is: the disappearance of the respectable Neville St. Clair, thought to have been murdered by Hugh Boone, only for it to turn out that Neville St. Clair [SPOILER ALERT] *is* Hugh Boone. There is no murder, no disappearance – well, I guess a disappearance, a disappearance that takes place every day, as Neville St. Clair transforms himself into a hideous-looking beggar in an opium den (but usually transforms himself back every night, except not this time, because his wife intervenes, and the police, and Sherlock Holmes, and he is stuck in his secret identity: a Superman who can't find a phone booth to change back into Clark Kent; instead he ends up in a jail cell in the guise of his alter ego).

So what are we to make of that? I am all in the dark, says Watson at the beginning, and so is Sherlock Holmes, who gets the wrong end of things altogether and keeps trying to figure out how a murder took place, dismissing any difficulties with the murder theory in the best manner of the slow-footed policemen he usually mocks. Only when he settles onto an Eastern divan, meditating and puffing smoke like a Zen Buddhist (or like someone in an opium den) does the real answer come to him. Is this a plea for intuition over logic? He does praise woman's intuition over logic in this story, when Mrs. St. Clair says she just *knows* her husband is alive; she would feel it if he were dead. And of course she has a letter from him to encourage this knowledge, though Holmes at first tries to explain that away – because he has that murder theory to hold onto: very un-Holmesian. But then he smokes a little opium – sorry, tobacco – and he can see straight.

Can opium make you see straight? No, no, that was tobacco. We do see opium smokers, of course. The story opens in an opium den – well, scene two at least after the opening in which Watson's yawning is interrupted by the arrival of Mrs. Whitney, whose husband Isa has gone off on a two-day bender to the Bar of Gold in Upper Swandam Lane. Mrs. Whitney, by the way, is dressed all in black, including a black veil: why? Is she in mourning? Her husband is an opium addict, and is in essence dead? Is that what this means? Is their marriage essentially dead? Because after all opium does not make you see straight; it makes you confused even about what day it is, and it means Isa Whitney cannot function properly: what would he be functioning at, by the way? What is his profession? His brother was the head of a theological college, and he read De Quincey at college (most men read Classics or Divinity, but there you go), but what does he do now? Nothing?

That opium den: Watson goes to the Bar of Gold to rescue Isa Whitney and bring him back to domesticity, and it is there that he runs into Holmes disguised as an addict, who is there looking for the vanished Neville St. Clair, last seen at an upper storey window. Why is all this taking place at an opium den? Why does Neville St. Clair make an opium den his dressing room? What has opium to do with it?

Evil opium: From the Far East, brought in by nefarious foreigners, like the "sallow Malay" and the "rascally Lascar" (a native of India) and, oddly, a Dane: something rotten there, perhaps. Anyway, in the late nineteenth century there was quite a panic about opium and the evils of the East, which some commentators see Doyle channelling, and perhaps he is. But there is always this doubleness in Doyle: the foreign can be dangerous, can in this case destroy you and your ability to pursue a livelihood, but it can be liberating too. Is opium liberating? Maybe, though we don't quite see that here, unless the fact that Neville St. Clair uses an opium den as his base of operations indicates something liberating about it.

Liberating from what? Well, Neville St. Clair gets liberated from the arduous work of journalism and makes five times as much just sitting around. Holmes, too, just sits around, on his self-built Eastern divan: is that a better way to go than pursuing logic or journalism? Is begging better than a real job in the City? Is being a detective better? Or a writer of detective stories? (Some, like Stephen Knight, see Neville St. Clair as a self-portrait of Arthur Conan Doyle slumming among the potboilers instead of being a serious author or eye doctor.)

And Neville St. Clair works with the rascally Lascar, so in a way he's involved in the opium trade, making money through it, at least by association, and thus much like the British government and its involvement in the opium trade. Is this an indictment of British imperialism? Or praise of it?

Liberating from what, Part Two: Opium liberates Isa Whitney from his wife. The opium adventure also liberates Watson from his wife. Tell her you've thrown in your lot with me, says Sherlock Holmes in getting Watson to go off on the Hugh Boone expedition. So is it opium versus domesticity? Detective work versus domesticity? Which side are we supposed to be on?

But at the end Neville St. Clair is sternly told that there can be no more Hugh Boone. Of course, being Hugh Boone in itself was no threat to domesticity. It was only being caught in the midst of transformation that kept Hugh/Neville from his wife. You should have trusted your wife, Holmes tells Hugh/Neville, patting him on his arm. And then what would have happened? What will happen now? If Neville St. Clair renounces Hugh Boone, will he go back to a "normal" job? Should he? Will he be happier with his wife? Or will he yawn at her like Watson?

Is this a story about settling down? You can't be a beggar (or a detective) forever? Why not? True, you can't be an opium addict forever: in fact, being an opium addict is a bad thing already: Isa Whitney is a mess. But is Neville St. Clair a mess? Is Watson? It's a conflict between respectability and adventure, and in fact aren't a lot of the Holmes stories about that? At least they're about respectability or reputation and the threats to it. Here you are, a respectable landowner or whatever, and someone shows up who blackmails you because you were a criminal in Australia; you can't have that.

In this case there's no Australia, just an opium den and playing a beggar, but again there's a threat from a secret that may destroy a respectable appearance. And Neville St. Clair does want to keep up appearances; he doesn't want shame visited on his children; he wants them to be able to build something proper with those building blocks he buys for them.

Well, then, he can't keep on playing the beggar: That's what the story says at the end, clearly. And yet what fun it was to do that. You can't keep playing detective: is the story also saying that? There is a push all along in the canon to get Watson married and away from Sherlock Holmes. There's even a push to kill Holmes off altogether. Enough of these childish adventures: you have to grow up, settle down, be an adult.

And yet who ends up really dead? Not Holmes, or not permanently, but Mrs. Watson. And whose bedroom do we see Watson in, even in this story: not the one he presumably shares with his wife but one he shares with Sherlock Holmes.

There are several couples in this story, but which one is the most likely to last? There's Kate and Isa Whitney, but Kate is already in mourning for her marriage because opium has killed it. The path of opium seems a mistake. There's Watson and his wife, but that seems boring or deadly or both. There's the St. Clair marriage, and that one does seem to involve real connection: Mrs. St. Clair can tell if her husband is still alive, and when she gets the note from him she dresses up in a seductive chiffon gown in eager anticipation of his arrival. But will that marriage survive if Neville can no longer go off on his Hugh Boone adventures?

And then there is Holmes and Watson: that's the real couple in these stories, and they go on forever, continuing to satisfy our child-like interest in play, though partly we know this is just a game and we have to settle down – but not just yet.

The Blue Carbuncle

We were compelled to eat it: The bird that is, the goose, the Christmas goose. So says Holmes, talking to Henry Baker. Not that Holmes ate it exactly; it was the commissionaire, Peterson, though Holmes and Watson will eat a bird soon, a woodcock, though not without checking its crop first for carbuncles. (No, that's just a joke, one of many in this light-hearted Christmas treat.)

But is it so light-hearted? A gem in a goose, ha ha, an inept jewel thief, yes, and the festive season and all that, a time for compassion and forgiveness, letting the jewel thief go, but I'm not so sure. I keep thinking of poor Henry Baker. He does get a goose in the end, that's true, and also his hat back – but what a hat … A battered old felt thing that has seen better days, as has poor Henry himself. Some critics say the jewel theft is rather pushed off to the side in this story, and one of the things it is really about is Henry's hat.

That hat: It must be the most famous hat in the canon,[*] the excuse for Holmes to launch into a series of deductions about the life and lifestyle of Henry Baker, sight unseen, much to the astonishment of Watson (and to the dismay of some Sherlockians, who quibble about the Master's conclusions). And what does Holmes tell us about poor Henry? That he used to be well-to-do but has fallen on evil days. He used to be far-sighted but now has been driven to drink. And most astonishingly of all he has lost the love of his wife.

Poor Henry: And what is more, how does Henry Baker even enter this story? By being set upon by a gang of roughs and getting the hat knocked off his head, after which he raises his

---

[*] Well, next to the deerstalker, which isn't really in the canon.

stick to defend himself but accidentally breaks the shop window behind him, prompting him to flee when a commissionaire arrives on the scene. Oh, poor Henry, fearing the roughs, fearing the law, down on his luck, losing his goose (and his hat).

But he does get his goose back: Or not his goose but another. And his hat. Not the gem hidden in the goose, of which he knew nothing, but that's really not his affair. But does he get back the love of his wife? He is bringing her the goose as a peace offering: did it work? And will his fortunes be repaired? Will he get some more shillings and free himself of drink? This we do not know. Sherlock Holmes can identify him and lay out his problems, but those really aren't the sort of problems a consulting detective can fix.

So what good is he? Well, he restores the blue carbuncle to its rightful owner, but do we even care about that? The rightful owner is some countess we never see. She never hired him; she was not the client. Nor was Horner, the unjustly accused, whom we also do not see. If there is any client here, it's the commissionaire who brought the problem to Holmes, and Holmes does solve it, it's true, making everything clear: he finds Henry Baker, restores him his hat, and also discovers how it is that an expensive jewel made its way into the crop of a Christmas goose.

Assuaging our anxieties: That's what Stephen Knight says Holmes does in the stories, by restoring order and letting us know what has happened, dispelling any fog and mystery. But another critic, Nils Clausson, wonders how assuaged we can be in this case, knowing that Holmes is out there letting criminals go free. I myself, as a reader rather than a property owner in 1889, am more likely to be in the assuaged camp, except I am troubled – not by the fact that a jewel thief may be on the loose thanks to Holmes's arrogating to himself the powers of commutation and soul-saving, but by the fact that nothing has been done to help poor Henry Baker.

The limits of detection: Perhaps this story lays those out. Problems, disorder, puzzles: Sherlock Holmes can put those right. Declining fortunes, fading affections – not so much. And what sort of universe does that give us? A strange one, as the critic Joseph Kestner says, where passerbys' breath resembles pistol shots and the stars shine coldly upon us. The more I think about it, the less assuaged I am. Solving puzzles is all very well, but where is happiness in this universe? Is Henry Baker happy? For no reason that we know of, he has come down in the world. How about James Ryder, our jewel thief? Holmes lets him go, as he lets Henry go, and yet ... James Ryder was supposed to get a goose for Christmas. His sister has promised him one. He takes it, or at least takes another one, but he ends up leaving it with his criminal accomplice in order to go after the goose with the golden (or at least carbuncular) egg. But he doesn't get that one either. He ends up without a goose at all.

And what does that signify? One pair of commentators (Enda Duffy and Maurizia Boscagli) suggest that this story tells us that geese are more important than gems. Perhaps, in the sense that geese here stand for Christmas cheer, for conviviality, family gathering and celebration. James Ryder doesn't get any of that; he has to flee. And why? Because he gave way to a criminal impulse. Perhaps there is a lesson here: don't give in to such impulses, or you may risk jail and, even worse in the early canon, a loss of reputation: Oh, I have given away my character, says Ryder (by which he means his reputation). And don't tell my father or my mother: as if that is more serious than actually going to jail.

Reassurance? Some see reassurance, redemption even, in that James Ryder is give a second chance. Holmes himself seems to think this. And yet the last we see of him he is clattering down the stairs, fearing that he has been branded as a thief. It makes me think of Cain sent out of Eden with a mark upon him (and Ryder does keep talking about God and the Bible). So the lesson is a stern Old Testament one of, Do no evil, or you will suffer. This would hardly assuage those young men from the City reading this story in the *Strand Magazine*. Nor would the mysterious fall from grace of Henry Baker: that would be even more disturbing. At least one can learn from Ryder's tale that you shouldn't steal carbuncles. But what can you learn from Baker's? Don't indulge in drink? Don't wander the streets at 4 am?

Is it Henry's fault? One critic (Rosemary Jann) does say the story seems to be blaming him for wandering around drunk in the middle of the night. But the commissionaire was out at the same time, and not in an official capacity but after some Christmas Eve "jollification." Was he drinking too? But he profits from it. Why, though, was he up so late away from his wife? Is that a happy marriage? Are there any happy, festive Christmas-celebrating couples in this story?

Couples: There's the unhappy Bakers.   There's the commissionaire and his wife: they may be happy, and they do get a Christmas goose. Ryder is outcast from society, the Countess we know nothing about, John Horner is still in custody and we know nothing of his family life. And all this in a city of four million inhabitants constantly jostling each other – and worse. What about those roughs? What kind of world is this where roughs can attack you for no reason at all?

And yet: Under this cold starry sky we do have one couple that sits down happily to a roast bird in this Christmas season:

Holmes and Watson, of course, having figured out all the puzzles and made themselves feel better by being charitable towards James Ryder, and now being able to sit down to a woodcock prepared by Mrs. Hudson. (And where is Mrs. Watson in all this? Well, never mind her.)

So that's all right, then? But I'm still uneasy about Henry Baker. There is decline here, something that will feature repeatedly later in the canon, but at least in the later stories there are suggestions that fresh blood from afar or below may help out. Here it's merely a shrug and a substitute goose, which is good as far as it goes, but how will we pull someone like Henry out of his decline? Or is that simply not what detecting, however brilliant, can do?

The Speckled Band

Live by the snake, die by the snake: I think that about sums this one up, Conan Doyle's favourite story, and one of the most popular too, but is it just because I remember it that it didn't grip me so much? After all, can there be any question who the villain is? It's more one of those howdunits, like "The Devil's Foot," than a mystery with various suspects.[*]

And how did he do it? With a swamp adder, the deadliest snake in India, if you believe the story. However, if you listen to the commentators, you'll discover that there is no such snake and certainly not a snake that answers to a whistle and drinks milk or, most importantly, can climb ropes. And who needs both a rope and a snake in the story? It's all rather "over-determined," to use a fancy literary term meaning something like: there are too many reasons here, too many symbols, causes, whatever.

Phallic symbols, anybody? So we have a snake and a rope and a hunting-crop, which is a sort of whip, and a dog-lash, which I think means a leash, and which serves as a whipcord, which I think just means a whip. So two whips, a snake, and a rope, not to mention the cane Holmes uses to bash the snake when it comes down the rope after being removed from its cage/safe with the dog-lash by Grimesby Roylott (and what a name for a villain that is, as Samuel Rosenberg says).

But just to complicate things, some of these phallic symbols can function as symbols of femininity too, if you believe some of the critics, especially the snake when it is

---

[*] Actually, as Thomas Leitch notes, most Holmes stories do not focus on who among a group of suspects is the guilty one. On the other hand, most are not "howdunits" either. Leitch says they are mostly "whydunits" or "whathappeneds."

curled up into a headband on the dead Roylott's head, reminding you of Medusa perhaps or the Dionysian Maenads, those ecstatic female devotees of the God of Wine. Hmm. Too many causes and too many results.

But let's stick to the phallic aspects first: Here we have one of the *Roylotts of Stoke Moran* (which is an anagram for "snake story tomfool rot," according to John Hodgson, who thinks Conan Doyle may be having us all on and subverting the whole detective genre in this story). Anyway, here we have Grimesby Roylott, eager for his stepdaughters' fortune and not wanting them to marry out (the same problem the stepfather had in "A Case of Identity"), and so he decides to pretend to be their fiancés. No, no, that's not right, that's what Mr. Windibank does in the other story. Grimesby is much grimmer than that: he plans murder, and since he's been to India (where he's already committed a murder), he uses an Indian instrument (that swamp adder) to do the deed.

But where's the phallic part? Well, the snake, of course, climbing down the rope. Not to mention the whole idea of penetrating a stepdaughter's bedroom (which Holmes and Watson do too, of course, suggesting ... well, who knows?). And then he pierces the other stepdaughter's bedroom with building renovations. I mean, really. Some critics talk of symbolic rape. Is this another veiled incest fantasy? But I thought he was after their money. Perhaps both. Perhaps as some recent critics argue it's all part of a program of patriarchal control or a rearguard action against the new rights women were being granted in such things as the Married Women's Property Act.

And don't forget the snake is from India: Not to mention the cheetah and the baboon (though actually there are no baboons in India) and the Turkish slippers and the fact that

Grimesby lived in India and went thoroughly bad there, if he wasn't bad to begin with. Perhaps the tropics just exacerbated his inherited bad temper, as his stepdaughter says. In any case, this seems to be one of the stories in which Eastern elements are thoroughly bad (unlike some of the other stories where the East is perhaps a source of wisdom). Sherlock Holmes does not indulge in Buddhist meditation here; he is the severely rational one, testing his hypotheses, and setting them up against the Eastern training of his antagonist.

But is he as severely rational as all that? This is one of the more physical stories, as one commentator (Rosemary Jann) points out. Holmes unbends the bent poker, beats the poor adder (which after all is only doing what an adder does), and then of course he becomes just like his antagonist, using a snake to kill (and before that, there was the entry into the bedroom).

Eastern contagion? Some critics see the story as a lament about the effects of Empire on the homeland: all this colonization is bad, not for India, but for England: it brings back snakes and cheetahs and baboons and makes dissolute English aristocrats even worse than they were before they went there. And look what it does to Holmes: he becomes just as bad, unless you think killing with a snake is okay if the person you're killing is someone sending a snake against you (or your client) – and perhaps it is, but still ... Is England being corrupted? It seems already in decline: the Roylott family, an ancient Saxon clan, has lost its fortune, and in the changing conditions of the late nineteenth century its scion has been forced to take up something as middle class as doctoring, and meanwhile the ancient manor house has become a picture of ruin.

Gloomy? Is there any hope? Well, Holmes does prevent the second murder, the evil Eastern-inflected aristocrat is done away with, and Helen Stoner is free to marry – what's his name again? That absent fiancé who had tried to reassure her by saying oh, it's all in your head. No, it's all on Grimesby Roylott's head, though only after Sherlock Holmes sends it there. In a canon full of useless fiancés, this one wins a prize for being worse than useless. If Helen had listened to him, she'd be dead.

Come to think of it, she is dead, at least by the time Watson writes the story. Why is that? Why kill her off? And did she marry the worse than useless Percy? We're not actually told that: we simply see her ushered away to live with an aunt. Maybe that's what women need, to stay away from men. But then she dies. Is England not going to go on, the England of good Englishwomen like the Stoner sisters?

And what about the band? That band of the gypsies with their speckled kerchiefs. But they're not the band; they're a red herring, like the cheetah and the baboon. The speckled band is the snake, looking like a headband when it takes up residence on the head of Grimesby Roylott. One can see how it looks like a band then, but before? Why does Julia Stoner call it a band? It's just a slithering snake at that point, or did it wrap itself around her head too? Or more likely it is just described that way to make us think of the gypsies, another foreign element. Of course, they're perfectly innocent of the crimes, but this is more of that over-determination: foreign Otherness everywhere, scaring us even more than the snake.

The True Villain of the Tale: Not Grimesby Roylott, not the snake, certainly not the gypsies or the fiancés (did you notice that there are actually two in this story? talk about over-determination). No, the true villain is the banking system.

You scoff, but what is it that has ruined the Roylotts? What does Helen say? There's nothing left, she says, but a few acres and a two-hundred-year-old house, "which is itself crushed ..." Crushed, I say, crushed, by what giant Godzilla of a horror? What could crush a house? "Crushed," says Helen, "crushed under a heavy mortgage." Mortgages, they're the villain, along with Eastern training, the whole British Empire, and the wastefulness of the British aristocracy. And if you import aristocratic values and Eastern methods even into an upright middle-class profession like medicine, watch out.

Is there anything positive here? Well, despite the undercurrent or subtext, the tone of the story does seem upbeat, at least at the end. Holmes is quite happy and not feeling guilty at all about using the snake to kill someone – though if he has to say that, maybe he does feel guilty. And true, the atmosphere early on is full of Gothic terror, and yet Holmes feels zest over the investigation and Watson wouldn't miss it for the world. Holmes is the magical master here, intuitive yet logical (even if when you look closely – but don't look closely! – some of it doesn't make any sense). And that moment when he unbends the bent poker with such nonchalant power and laughs at Grimesby Roylott – what larks. Though true, he also becomes full of horror and loathing when the snake appears. But no matter, there is something inspiringly powerful and even happy about the story despite its dark undertones. Evil forces may abound, but we have Holmes and Watson to fight them.

The Engineer's Thumb

All my medical instincts rose up against that laugh: That is Watson's comment on Victor Hatherley's hysteria at the beginning of the story. Watson is alone at the beginning, and he seems different somehow, not the sidekick but the professional in control of the situation. Stop it, he tells Hatherley. Not that that works. But eventually Hatherley calms down and returns to his normal self (except how can he be quite normal now, missing a thumb?). Anyway, he returns to himself, very weary and "pale-looking" or "blushing hotly," depending on your edition.

Wait, how can the editions be so different? Well, the original edition said blushing hotly, but the American editors thought that made no sense, since he has bloodless cheeks a few lines later. Let us stick with the original, though: why would Victor Hatherley be blushing hotly? Is he embarrassed at his hysteria? Watson certainly disapproves of it. Stiff upper lip and all that, I suppose. Pull yourself together, be a man. Of course, he's lost a thumb and some critics have a field day with this, suggesting the thumb represents another appendage, and thus perhaps Victor Hatherley is no longer a man at all, or a castrated, emasculated one. A eunuch perhaps? Do eunuchs blush? Over their loss? Though what a eunuch has lost is perhaps not exactly what Victor Hatherley has lost.

Other approaches: Some critics, sometimes the same ones who talk about emasculation, see an anti-German flavour to the story. This was a time of anti-German sentiment in England. The new Kaiser was making expansionist noises, threatening his neighbours so he could get their fuller's earth: no, that's just Lysander Stark. Colonel Stark, I note: very military. Is this all symbolic of war by Germany against its neighbours? By 1890 this was already a fear, even though Germany was the land of science, poetry, and music, as evidenced by the harmonium and the books of poetry and science that Victor Hatherley finds in the German house.

How can England protect itself? This is an early example of the foreign motif in the canon.   In this case the foreign presence is dangerous; it threatens British manhood, and how can British men stand up if they've been emasculated? Is this a warning? The German colonel does escape, the danger is not really over, even if his hydraulic press has gone up in smoke.   And note that there is an Englishman (Ferguson? Becher? what is his name?) willing to help Colonel Stark. There is danger from within too? Is Ferguson/Becher really English, though?   Hatherley thinks so, but Becher doesn't sound too English, though I find it can be an English as well as a German surname.

Yet other approaches: Stephen Knight has an interesting theory, saying that in this story, and in "The Man with the Twisted Lip," Arthur Conan Doyle is writing about himself. Hatherley, like Doyle, is a young professional without any clients: an engineering consultant who is never consulted, like Doyle the eye doctor without any patients. And then along comes a munificent offer to do something a bit different (inspect a hydraulic press, write Sherlock Holmes stories), and look what happens: dismemberment, crippling. Doyle wanted to be a serious author, not a churner out of potboilers, and he resisted continuing the Holmes stories and eventually would kill Holmes off. Here, in what Hatherley at one point calls a bad dream, Doyle is imagining the horrors of being stuck in the land of potboilers or machines for producing counterfeits: counterfeit literature?

And how gruesome it is: Like a very bad dream. I can barely stand to read the description of what Victor Hatherley's hand looks like after his thumb has been hacked off. "Hacked" is indeed the word, and if Doyle is unhappy about being pulled away from serious literature, is he concerned that he may be turning into a hack? Dreams can be full of puns.

Another pun: I discovered the "hack" pun myself, but Stephen Knight points to another: the word "press" in the story refers to the hydraulic press, but of course for an author the press means something else. Is it the popular press, the *Strand Magazine*, that is crippling Arthur Conan Doyle? Are the villains not so much the Germans as the publishers? Or the whole profession? Victor Hatherley is crippled by something from his own profession, as is Doyle perhaps. In Doyle's case he feels oppressed by his own creation, which makes me think of Frankenstein, and it's interesting that Doyle gives very little to his monster to do in this story, if his monster is Sherlock Holmes. The story starts with Watson alone and consists mostly of Hatherley's tale. Holmes is mostly there to let Hatherley relax on a couch and then tell him afterwards that at least he will have a good tale to tell others: so perhaps he can become an author too? "You have only to put it into words."

Boxing the compass: This I am told means covering all the points of it, as Watson, Hatherley, and the police do when trying to determine which way the horse went to get to Colonel Stark's estate. Holmes tells them they're all wrong, in a way reminiscent of Poe's detective, who when everyone was sure they heard a different language from the murderer said it was no language at all but the shrill sounds of an orangutan. In his only piece of detection in this story, Holmes says the horse went in no direction at all but round and round, or at least six miles out and six back, bringing us back to where we started – which is where?

Poe and others: There is a more obvious allusion to Poe in the near crushing: the hydraulic press coming down is like the pendulum coming down in "The Pit and the Pendulum." And the woman with the lamp puts me in mind of Florence Nightingale, and nursing would come in handy here. But maybe the woman is more an Ariadne to Hatherley's Theseus, since she helps him escape the labyrinth of Colonel Stark's house after he confronts the Monster. There's almost too many allusions here: what can it all mean?

How quiet and sweet and wholesome: That's the garden as seen by Hatherley, admittedly from thirty dangerous feet above, where he is dangling from a window sill and about to have his thumb chopped off after barely escaping being crushed to a pulp by the hydraulic press. If only we could have the quiet garden back, but it seems that is not our fate, or its. At the end the garden is filled with fire engines vainly trying to keep the flames under control. Our garden is on fire? Well, the house in our garden, and the garden will be trampled under in an attempt to put it out.

Perhaps we can just quietly slip away: That's what the station guard fears Victor Hatherley might do, though why should he? Perhaps his hysteria would drive him to it. But he calms down thanks to brandy, bandages, and breakfast and becomes a new man, or so he says. Before that Watson feared he might be some sort of "strange creature" (like the orangutan in Poe's story? or the baboon in "The Speckled Band"? or more truly a thumbless man). And is he a new man? What will he do now? Some imagine that he won't be able to continue in his career, but I don't see evidence of that in the story. Do you need two thumbs to be an engineer?

Of course, he didn't have much of a career to begin with. And he was an orphan, a bachelor, and alone. Still, it's almost as if he has made friends with Holmes and Watson, who can sympathize and then, it's true, send him on his way – but with a strange experience he can relate and so become excellent company. Perhaps he will dine out on this story, perhaps at a dinner party at Watson's, where even Sherlock Holmes has been persuaded to visit on occasion, or so Watson informs us at the beginning. Hard to imagine. But is that the best we can do? Socialize and entertain each other while monsters gather and fires flicker? Perhaps.

The Noble Bachelor

Crime, crime, who's got the crime? What crime is there in this story? It seems that Hatty Doran may have been murdered, or at least abducted (by Flora Millar), but that's not true: she's simply run away during the wedding breakfast: is that a crime? Flora tried to disrupt the breakfast: how about that? Creating a public disorder? There's lots of disorder at this wedding, created by the two women: one causes a commotion and one runs away. And Hatty does technically commit bigamy. But some critics want to blame Lord St. Simon for being a cad or snooty or something, though it's hard to see that he's committed any crime (he is rather the victim, isn't he?) except perhaps against Flora, but what did Flora expect? That he would remain her paramour forever? But perhaps that is his natural role: an aging roué who is only embarking on a marriage (at the "mature" age of 41) because he needs the cash ...

Is it all about the money, then? As we learn in the story, St. Simon's noble family has fallen on hard times: they're selling off their pictures. Is the English aristocracy going bankrupt? It would seem so, and the society papers are complaining that there has been an invasion of American heiresses taking advantage of the situation. Elsewhere in the canon it sometimes seems that importation of fresh blood is exactly what England needs, so why doesn't it work here? What happens in the end is that Hatty abandons her British lord for her first American husband: Americans stay with Americans and don't come to rejuvenate the Brits.

Except some of them do: We learn that in the story itself, and we know from history that the Brits get a Winston Churchill out of the bargain (American mother, British father of noble descent). Is this story saying that is a bad thing? And yet, echoing his creator, Sherlock Holmes hails the British-American alliance at the end, sitting down to supper with the Frank Moultons at a table laid by genii, and imagining some future country which will merge America and Britain under a combined Union Jack and Stars and Stripes.

But maybe marriage is not the way: Maybe the best thing is the friendly supper party attended by two Brits (Holmes and Watson) and the two Americans. And maybe the connection works best without the noble lord who refuses to attend. Like many noble lords in the canon, he comes off badly, at least to an extent: he is superior, and has to be taken down a peg (by Holmes saying that in taking his case he is descending). And yet he has his good points too: he defends both his women, saying Hatty would not do anything dishonourable and Flora wouldn't hurt a fly, even though Flora is hot-headed and Hatty is a volcanic child of Nature.

Maybe the true rejuvenation should come from women? Those two passionate beings here: are they the liveliest pair in the story? Not that we see much of Flora; she is always at second hand through a newspaper report or St. Simon's account. And at the end what happens to her? Is she still languishing in jail? Some critics complain about that, and blame Holmes for forgetting about her. Is that a crime? She surely won't remain in jail, though. Will St. Simon remain impoverished? Will he suffer from public humiliation? But we learn that by the time Watson writes the account, the story has been forgotten, overtaken by other scandals. Just like today.

Does anyone really suffer, and is anyone to blame? Holmes explicitly says at the end that no one is to blame, and the critic Barrie Hayne says there is no serious suffering here, only discomfiture. Is it a comedy, then? Perhaps a bit of a farce? But what is it all about?

The decline of the nobility? St. Simon is greying and stooped over and without heirs. Watson also calls him ungracious, and Holmes mocks him, though in the end he is forgiving, saying, Remember, Watson, he has just lost a wife and a fortune. And though we then are reminded that it is a bleak autumnal evening, Holmes seems upbeat about it all and proposes to play his violin. He has had that supper with the Americans after all and solved the case, which brought a light to his eye. The Americans are perhaps a tad vulgar, judging by the words that come out of their mouths, but they are honest and upright, so perhaps the hope for the future is of some friendly alliance with them: not marriage, but convivial gatherings over woodcocks and pâté.

Dangling his glasses: St. Simon keeps dangling those golden eyeglasses of his, yet never looks through them. Perhaps he should, to see the future? To better understand the Anglo-American alliance? Watson at the beginning is listless from saturating himself in a cloud of newspapers and seems to have nothing to do but nurse his old war wound. At the end there is also nothing to do: the violin is a resort to while away the bleak evening. And yet in between we've had the lively American wife, the disruptive *danseuse*, and the mysterious case. Not to mention the loyal and persistent American husband and the loyalty of his wife. So what does that all add up to? Perhaps the British need to forget the past and their long ancestries and befriend Americans? Perhaps we all need a mystery to keep us occupied and should know our own natures better so as not to embark on marriages when that is not really our way?

Watson is about to get married: Yes, so he says in this story, which is a flashback from earlier stories where he is already a husband. It is only a few weeks before his marriage, and yet he has nothing to do – not until the case comes along. Perhaps another suggestion that Watson lives for cases, not marriage. He and St. Simon (and Holmes) have this in common: leave marriage to the Americans. And don't try to have a middle-class American manage the leap, the "immense … social stride," involved in joining the British aristocracy. Perhaps even the pâté is too much for them. Despite that supper at the end, it's almost as if the American and British worlds are so far apart that the notion of a future American-British union is just an illusion.

The American world: It seems rough, with dangerous Apaches and servants who take liberties. There's mining and claim-jumping (one critic even thinks that's the real crime here: somehow Hatty's father was a claim jumper, though there's not the slightest evidence for it). When Hatty speaks of claim-jumping, she's being metaphorical, of course, referring to St. Simon moving in where Frank has first right. Some critics are disappointed that Hatty uses her freedom and independence mainly to switch from one husband to another, but I think the point is her freedom and independence, her defiance of her father's wishes when he decides Frank is not good enough for her (because he has no money and Hatty's family suddenly does). How easy it is to become snobbish and superior: are the Americans actually no better than St. Simon? But Hatty is, and though she should really have let people know what she was doing, what she did (returning to her first husband) seems the right thing to do. All she needed was the paternal hand of Holmes to encourage her to come clean about it and announce to all Europe and America, as Frank wanted from the first. So the ideal would be American honesty guided by Holmesian (British?) awareness of the proprieties?

And what about that trout? That's American too, courtesy of Thoreau, and means something like: if you see a trout in the milk, it means someone's been watering it down. Circumstantial evidence, like Lestrade thinking that if the clothes are in the Serpentine, the body must be there too. Holmes laughs at this, but it makes perfect sense to me. Why must Lestrade be wrong? Why is he reduced to shrieking when Holmes looks on the other side of the note? The money is there: is money behind it all? Perhaps. Or not in this case: it's true love. And a trout in the milk: a fish out of water? The Americans need to go home to their native habitat, and so should St. Simon and Holmes and Watson. Is that the true meaning of the story? Not a coming together, but sticking to your last? Who can say? But I feel bad for Lestrade. The body should be in the Serpentine, there should be a murder; what kind of detective story is this? But Holmes offers him a drink and a cigar, so that's okay, I guess. Friendship conquers all.   And a man's clothes can be somewhere else, and discarding a wedding outfit merely means the bride is going back to her first wedding, not that she's been drowned in a lake. Still ...

The Beryl Coronet

Here is a madman coming along: And why do his relatives let him out? But can you really stop someone from getting out? Can you stop your niece/adopted daughter from falling for the evil aristocrat? Or your son from falling under the same aristocrat's influence? (I suppose I shouldn't call Sir George Burnwell an aristocrat, since he's only a knight, not like the noble lord, or prince, who gets the story going by depositing a national treasure in a bank: who would do such a thing? There seems to be some confusion of categories, and perhaps this reflects the changing times, times when aristocrats had to resort to businessmen like Mr. Holder for loans, but it shows something of the persistence of an older, more personal world that Mr. Holder at first contemplates a personal loan rather than one from his bank, and then even when he makes the loan from the bank itself, he decides the best thing is to take the beryl coronet home for safekeeping.)

Safekeeping? Well, he does have a safe, or at least a bureau with a lock, but Sherlockians have a field day mocking the idea of keeping a national treasure in your dressing-room bureau which can be opened with "any old key." What could have possessed Holder? But I'd rather ask what could have possessed Conan Doyle. Presumably, a desire to create a story about the effects of bringing an aristocratic treasure into a private household. It's a bit like a fairy tale test, which Mr. Holder begins by failing immediately when he ignores his instructions not to gossip. He tells Mary and Arthur, and perhaps Lucy overhears. Foolish man.

Family circle: It's a story about the pressures on a family circle, though admittedly not a completely typical circle. There's no mother, and the young woman is either a niece or a daughter, or both. Which makes Arthur not only her cousin, but her … Some critics talk of incest, but critics like to talk about such things. Still, what is going on here? Some compare the story to "A Case of Identity," where the father (or stepfather) of the family goes to great, and deceitful, lengths to keep the daughter in the household. Mr. Holder doesn't go so far as pretending to be a suitor – or is he really Sir George in disguise? (No, we'll leave that to the Sherlockians.) And it seems a bit harsh to say, as Martin Priestman does, that he keeps Mary prisoner. True, she doesn't go out, and Mr. Holder doesn't socialize, but could she not go out on her own? Would that not be proper in those days? Mary Sutherland in "Identity" goes out: that's how she meets the fiancé who is no fiancé.

No fiancé: There could be a fiancé in this story, as in so many others, but Mary turns down Arthur's proposals, and is it as a result that we get a young man who is able to act heroically? Usually in the canon, fiancés do nothing, but young Arthur thwarts the crime while at the same time chivalrously protecting the guilty Mary. Innocent fiancées usually don't get protected in the other stories (you're just imagining things, dear), but here a non-fiancée who is guilty of assisting in a robbery finds protection. What does that mean? And not protection provided by Sherlock Holmes, who often protects where fiancés fail, but protection by the would-be fiancé, almost you might say against Sherlock Holmes, who of course is trying to find the guilty culprit, which in this case would be Mary.

Relatives can't keep you down: Even if you're mad, or madly in love, or doing something clearly unhealthy like gambling your money away. Mr. Holder can't keep Arthur from going to that aristocratic club, and when it comes to a crisis, Arthur threatens to leave and make his own way in the world. Of course, what really happens is that he is shipped off to prison, though he will presumably be let go, and then … Well, the story doesn't tell us. Will he go home to live with his papa? Will he track Sir George Burnwell down and capture Mary? But Mary doesn't want to be captured by Arthur, though Sherlock Holmes predicts that she will suffer at the hands of Sir George: would she then be more open to Arthur's proposals? But he's her brother, or at least her cousin. It's time to flee the nest perhaps, but not this way. Maybe by trying to keep this little circle too closely bound, Mr. Holder inadvertently pushes his children to take unsavory ways out: visiting gambling clubs or running off with villainous noblemen (or quasi-noblemen) out of a Victorian melodrama.

Good child and bad: Mr. Holder seems a very poor judge of his two children, a little like King Lear perhaps. The one he thinks is good is bad and vice versa. And the result is personal affliction and near public disgrace, which he tries to avoid by having his own son arrested. Something very wrong in that family circle. What is really going on? You have the disappointing son who loses money at cards and horses, the apparently sweet daughter/niece who lies and steals and tries to blame the maid, and the father who tries to keep too strong a hold on things: perhaps that's why he's called Holder.

Treasure: The true treasure in a family circle would be what? Not a coronet, surely; not money generally. Money is for work time, but Mr. Holder brings it home with him, or brings the coronet home, mixing business and family ties, and business, represented by the coronet, totally disrupts those ties. Is this a plea for keeping work away from home? Don't bring your coronets home with you, gentlemen. Or don't let your family in on your work secrets: don't tell them there's a coronet in the house. If only there'd been a mother in the house instead of an overly indulgent father who wants everything to stay the same: nothing stays the same, and in two days you can go from happiness and prosperity to shame and disgrace.

And prosperity, what is that? A man with a wooden leg? He's named Prosper, but it doesn't sound like prosperity to me. Mr. Holder worries that he's lost his honour, his gems, and his son (and then his daughter too). But wait, how are they his gems? They're a national treasure which he values more than his own son, it seems (or why put his son in jail for them?), but they're not his gems, are they? Well, I suppose they're in his safekeeping, but by trying too hard to keep them safe – and after all he brings them home because he thinks they will be safer there, as if a home is safer than a bank, and maybe it is for some things, though not for keeping money locked away … By trying to keep them safe, he loses both them and his children. Perhaps he is trying too hard. There seems some lesson here about letting birds fly free, or something, not that there are any birds in the story.

Trust: Maybe this is a story about trust. Mr. Holder needs to trust his own bank for keeping the coronet safe. Let business be business. Bankers should be trusted to safeguard treasures, just as detectives should be trusted to solve crimes. Watson has trust, or faith as he puts it: even though he and the banker are sure the son did it, since Sherlock Holmes thinks otherwise, Watson will follow along. But what about trust in people? You can't trust Sir George Burnwell, whose name (as Stephen Knight points out) conjures up images of hellfire. You can't really trust Mary. And Arthur? He squanders money – but in the end he comes through, though he nearly comes to grief trying to be true to both Mary and his father (and the nation, I suppose). Maybe Mr. Holder needs to trust them just to make their own way.

Public disgrace: The canon is full of stories motivated by fears about reputation. In this story Sherlock Holmes himself plays with the notion of reputation: he can suddenly be a poorly dressed vagabond, then return to his "highly respectable self." Mr. Holder fears losing his reputation and puts his son in jail; in other stories those in fear of losing their reputation are driven at times to murder. There's no murder here, only theft and lies and deceit, but is there a suggestion that perhaps too much stock is put in reputation?

Of course, there are other motivations: Mary acts from love or passion. Arthur is motivated in part by his love for Mary, but also from fear of disgrace. He needs money to pay his club debts and can't just leave the club as his father suggests, because that would be dishonourable. (Honour seems like an old-fashioned aristocratic word in this context.) Of course, Sir George has other motives and cares nothing about reputation, only money and lust, but then though honour is an old aristocratic term, in Doyle's time it's the middle class that worries more about it. At least that's the stereotype: you have all these dissolute noblemen not caring whose lives they ruin, while the bankers and shopkeepers worry inordinately about reputation. Is Conan Doyle suggesting they should worry less about it, become more like aristocrats? No, that can't be quite right: the aristocrats are the villains. Still, maybe there's a time to dress up like a vagabond and forget about respectability.

The Copper Beeches

The peaceful beauty of the scene: That would be the scene from the window of the Copper Beeches, but it suddenly ceases to be beautiful when Violet Hunter, who is the one viewing it, sees Carlo the mastiff come into sight, sending a chill into her heart. But that's not the first disruption of apparent beauty: Watson thinks the countryside beautiful until Holmes tells him, No, no, the country is more dangerous than the vilest alley in London, full of hellish cruelty.

Okay, then, so what is beautiful? It is an odd thing in this story that beauty is associated with Violet's hair (and Alice's, but then their hair is identical, so that makes sense) – well, that's not odd, but Carlo the ferocious mastiff is also called a beauty, though that is by his evil master, Jephro Rucastle (Castle of Rue?), so maybe we should not take that too seriously. And Rucastle himself is called a beauty by none other than Sherlock Holmes, but perhaps he is being sarcastic when he says so. And yet … Is beauty simply in the eye of the beholder? Is there any true beauty?

Travellers' beauty: Maybe if you're just passing through, the isolated homesteads can be beautiful, but if you are a tortured child living in one, perhaps not. Not that we see any tortured children in the story; instead we have a child who delights in torturing others: other creatures, that is, and he is a creature himself, according to Violet Hunter, and perhaps not important in this story except as a sign of the cruelty of his father. Or even his mother? That mother is a strange one: a nonentity, Violet calls her, but with a secret sorrow. What secret sorrow? That her stepdaughter is locked up in a room upstairs? Was she not a party to this plan to lock Alice away like a princess in a tower, shorn of her hair so she cannot even let it down to a passing prince?

No, wait, that's Rapunzel: Which some commentators are reminded of (Rapunzel, Rapunzel, let down your golden hair, and so on). Others think more of Bluebeard and locked rooms where you can find the corpses of dead wives and learn that you may be next. Horror stories, Gothic tales. Well, fairy tales, but perhaps that's the same thing. Is this a Gothic horror story? But there's also detection going on. Maybe it is both, an interesting mix of genres, with yet a third one added in, what we might call the thriller. When a detective is under threat, that's more a thriller, isn't it, than a straight detective tale where Sherlock Holmes bustles in, puts things straight, and then goes on to his next case.

So who is under threat? Not Sherlock Holmes and not Watson, he with the gun able to blow the brains out of Carlo the mastiff, and wow, is that Watson's most violent moment in the canon? And done so casually: "Running up, I blew its brains out." There you go; now what were you saying? Our detectives remain firmly in detective land, where they can step in and help others who are under threat, but they are not threatened themselves.

Who, then? Well, Violet Hunter. That's who this story is mostly about. It's her story about being in need of employment, of finding the cupboard bare after several comfortable years with the Spence Munros, and being driven to take a dubious position because she needs the money. It's a bit of a coming of age story: you have to leave the nest, you have to make your way in the world, you can't be turning down positions (or Miss Stoper will upbraid you), but is the world safe? There may be dangers out there.

What sort of dangers? Well, who knows? That's the problem. If we could define them, they would cease to be dangers. Well, so says Sherlock Holmes, though this isn't literally true: Rucastle could easily define the danger of Carlo, but that doesn't save him from it. Still, the point is that there is danger in not knowing, in being in the dark, uncertain, not knowing what might be lurking. And what is lurking for Violet Hunter? Well, the loss of her hair, for one thing.

But hair, who needs it? Many people are improved by cutting it short, says Violet, rationalizing. But is this the price you have to pay for venturing into the world? Your hair? (Which some might call a major part of your identity.) We'll give you lots of money; you can survive now; but we're going to tell you how to do your hair. Also what dress to wear. And we'll make you sit there and there and there at our whim. Is this what being an adult entails? Well, maybe an adult who is employed and has to do what their boss says. Better not to take a job like that perhaps. But then you starve.

So you give up your tresses: Another word for tresses, by the way, or a related one, is Strand, as in *Strand Magazine*, and I wonder if this is another story in which Conan Doyle is chafing against the pressures to keep writing Sherlock Holmes stories (for *Strand Magazine)*. Here I am out in the world wanting to write serious fiction (which doesn't pay), but to get some money I have to keep writing this detective stuff. Oh, well.

But it is all a bit horrifying, though more so for Alice locked away than for Violet. We seem to have doubling here: two nearly identical women with identical tresses, and yet their stories are a bit different. As I was saying, there are different genres mixed in "The Copper Beeches" – and by the way, I have wondered about those beeches: why are they here? What might they signify? There's a coppery colour, sort of red, like a Red-Headed League, and there is eccentricity as in that story, but suddenly I thought, Copper! Slang for police. Is something being policed here? Violet Hunter's desires? Alice's desires?

But back to the different genres: There's a detective story featuring Holmes and Watson, which in a way ends quite early, as Debbie Clark in *About Sixty* points out: there's Holmes pages from the end essentially explaining everything, based on the legwork done by Violet and with details to be filled in by Mrs. Toller, but essentially the detective story ends with Holmes explaining that the plan must have been to put off Alice's fiancé by making him think she is happy without him.

But then we return to the thriller story, going off to rescue Alice, and that story ends with the confrontation with Jephro Rucastle and his unfortunate encounter with his own dog. But then there's a third story, the Gothic horror, to wrap up: the rescue of the princess from the castle, and we find out that this has already been done, by Mr. Fowler the fiancé. The Fowler has got there before the Hunter.

Three stories in one: Yes, and almost not connected. At least Violet's story doesn't connect very closely to Alice's. Alice is the passive victim locked in her room; Violet is the active investigator out-Sherlocking Sherlock, almost (well, no, he has to explain things in the end), but she does act very resourcefully in exploring this strange situation, using a makeshift mirror, penetrating into the forbidden wing, and then bringing in reinforcements. And she ends up with a career while Alice goes away and is married. Watson is disappointed that there is no further connection between Holmes and Violet, but did he really expect … Anyway, Violet apparently marries no one, which depending on your brand of feminism means either she is being punished for being too independent or being celebrated as a New Woman who doesn't need a man. Maybe a bit of both, or maybe Doyle is just delineating various options: If you're a passive Gothic heroine you end up married; if you're a resourceful and brave investigator you become head of a private school. The Entrepreneur and the Bride, a possible title for a pastiche.

And what is the meaning of it all? Which is what Violet keeps asking. That as a child becomes an adult sometimes their parents want to keep them from going out into the world? We saw that already in stories like "A Case of Identity" and "The Speckled Band," not to mention "The Beryl Coronet." But at the same time if you do go out into the world there can be real dangers there. The Gothic story is about the horrors of being locked up. The thriller is about the dangers of being free (which can lead to you not being so free, and can lead you to come up against horrors like the Rucastles and the very eerie experience of seeing what seems to be your own tress of hair locked up in someone else's secret drawer: oh, where are the Spence Munros when you need them?). So the thriller can almost turn into the Gothic horror. But perhaps that is where the detective story fits in, explaining everything so that you know what is going on and can define the dangers. I'm not sure that really means the dangers cease, but at least now you can feel a little bit more in control.

And that is about it for this story, which as Debbie Clark says has everything and more in it: dog, child, eccentricity, detection, Gothic horrors, and above all a very appealing Nancy Drew-like central character in Violet Hunter.

Silver Blaze

Your very excellent field-glass: This is how Sherlock Holmes describes Watson's pair of binoculars, which Holmes wants him to bring along to Dartmoor so that he can – what? Search the ground for vestas (matches)? No, he does that with the naked eye. He often throws himself down on the ground to examine things with his magnifying lens, but that's in other stories. Here he has no lens, just the field-glass, and he doesn't examine the ground with it, but borrows it to – yes, watch the race in which the disguised Silver Blaze romps to victory, satisfying almost everyone (perhaps not John Straker, but he's dead; perhaps not blustering Silas Brown either, but you can't please everybody). All of which is to say that though there is a woman behind it all, and at least one critic goes on about gender dynamics (but that's what he does about all the stories) – despite all this what this story is really about, which is why the field-glass is so necessary to it, what the story is really about is …

Racing. Yes, I know, you're surprised. If not about gender, is it not about the Othering of the gypsies, or the brilliance of detection, or the importance of imagination, or the importance of not theorizing before you have all the facts? (Wait, doesn't not theorizing contradict the use of the imagination? Well, perhaps, and in fact though not theorizing is a watchword of Holmes in other stories, here the emphasis is on careful selection of important facts from amidst irrelevant or misleading details.) In any case, the story may be in part about gender, gypsies, and the imagination, but what it's mainly about is horse racing, which made me muse about the significance of horse racing. Conan Doyle confessed to ignorance about the sport, so what was he aiming at here? What does horse racing signify?

Competition? Perhaps. Manliness? This is a men's club sort of story, and even though the motive for the attempted crime stems from a woman or a man's desire to please a woman with expensive tastes, really the whole focus of the story is on men and their games, in this case the horse-racing game. And why do men play such games? What is it that men want, as Freud might have asked. Mastery? Domination? Triumph? Arthur Conan Doyle liked mastery. After apologizing for his horse racing errors he said that after all he was never nervous about details, and "one must be masterful sometimes." What an odd thing to say, really: you can just be masterful and get things wrong? In this story, though, Sherlock Holmes gets things right. He is quite brilliant in deduction, and thus obtains mastery? Mastery over Colonel Ross, who he toys with. Mastery over Silas Brown, with the suggestive initials (the same as Silver Blaze), who is cowed into doing his bidding. Masterful even with Inspector Gregory in a generous way, congratulating him on his thoroughness but noting his lack of imagination.

Mastery: Of course, some men seek mastery by illicit means: John Straker by wounding his own horse, Silas Brown by stealing his opponent's, and Fitzroy Simpson by seeking to bribe the stable boy (and the maid). They all fall short, and Sherlock Holmes comes out ahead, winning the race. One might summarize it thus:

Race Card:
>   Inspector Gregory's Intelligence
>   Silas Brown's Bluster
>   Col. Ross's Sneering
>   Fitzroy Simpson's Ineptitude
>   John Straker's Greed,
>   and the Favourite: Mr. Sherlock Holmes's Imagination.

And it's Imagination way out in front, and the rest nowhere. But never mind the winner ...

The Game's the Thing: Men like to play and compete and show off, and yes, dominate other men, get the better of them. Some will even resort to underhanded means, but Sherlock Holmes will have none of that: he reveals John Straker's greed (and infidelity), thwarts Silas Brown's attempted theft, pays back Colonel Ross for his cavalier attitude, and shows that an intellectual can get the better of those with mere money or brawn. He even outshines dedicated but limited Inspector Gregory.

But what's it all about? The whole country is convulsed by the disappearance of Silver Blaze. It's a catastrophe, we're told more than once. It is of great importance to so many people. Why? Because racing is so important? Surely not. But competition, that's what men are all about, and a blow to fair competition, a prevention of seeing a favourite run – that is a tragedy. (Oh, and the death of the trainer too, I suppose.) But no, it's the racing, which here symbolizes all competition, I think, and points us to what men want. Money? I suppose. Power? That's closer. Women? Yes, but that's not the main thing. No, I go back to power, mastery, and control. That's what this story is about.

And an overcoat flapping on a bush: Well, that perhaps shows the opposite of mastery, the best-laid plans and all that. Speaking of plans, after all his plans to hobble the favourite, after practising on the sheep, obtaining a special cataract knife, and so on, why does John Straker pick up the red and black cravat of Fitzroy Simpson? What a strange bit of improvisation. The mysterious cravat and the flapping overcoat, symbols of failure: maybe in picking up the cravat of

87

the incompetent Simpson (who can't even bribe a stable boy), Straker was dooming himself to failure. Perhaps.

Other men's bills: One doesn't carry those around, no. And why? Because it's each man for himself, and the devil take the unpaid milliner's bills. Actually, it's the devil that gets into Silas Brown when his first impulse is to return Silver Blaze to King's Pyland. The devil leads men astray and keeps them from helping their fellows. Or is it women with their expensive tastes? But only some women: Mrs. Darbyshire, married to the mythical Mr. Darbyshire, but not Mrs. Straker, who seems simply anguished (of course, this is after her husband's been killed in such a horrific way).

Or is it money that drives things? People think Fitzroy's little packet contains opium, but no, it seems to be money: another drug, one might say. And money, or the need for it, corrupts John Straker, and of course many people are seeking to win money on the race, and yet it seems racing's the thing in itself, and Sherlock Holmes is there to protect the integrity of it, even if he does it by disguising the favourite and no doubt confusing the bettors. He certainly confuses Colonel Ross, who doesn't know whether to complain or to celebrate. Just as we can't have counterfeit money in circulation (see "The Three Garridebs"), we can't have corrupt ways of determining the winners of horse races or the outcome of life in general, or at least of competitive life, capitalism, one might say: one can see Sherlock Holmes as the great regulator in the capitalist economy, making sure everyone plays fair, but not questioning the whole basis of things, the competitive instinct.

Speaking of instincts, the horse's instincts save it from a hobbling. This reminds me of Holmes's praise of feminine instincts in another story. He may be the voice of logic and reason, but he has a soft spot for instinct (and of course imagination). He even pricks his ears up like a horse: is he an animal? Would that be the ideal? Is he at his best following instinct and imagination, less like the serious logical Inspector Gregory and more like, well, like a woman? Sherlock Holmes as a woman: I'm sure there have been pastiches like that.

I follow my own methods: Perhaps Holmes is neither beast nor woman, nor logician nor policeman; he is one of a kind: singular, to use one of his favourite words. He will even contradict himself, and yet he demands our full belief and loyalty, though I must say it is a favourite pastime of Sherlockians to point out his failings: he couldn't possibly have figured out the speed of the train, say some, though others disagree. Why this drive to bring down the hero? Just human nature, I suppose, but even when he's your own hero? But here we are venturing far from the story, and perhaps should just end by smoking a cigar and promising to provide further details at a later date.

The Yellow Face

Racism: Peter Wood, a previous Petrels' Schoolmaster, asked if this story, taken together with the derogatory depiction of the black boxer Steve Dixie in "The Three Gables," indicated that Conan Doyle was a racist. A strange way to put it, because this story is typically contrasted with "The Three Gables" as one that is quite liberal on matters of race. But how then do we square this circle of the liberal Doyle in "The Yellow Face" and the indulger of stereotypes in the later story? Perhaps it is simply a matter of time: in this story and the next ("The Stockbroker's Clerk") a young author subverts conventional racist (or in the Stockbroker story, anti-Semitic) attitudes, whereas at the end of his career a more curmudgeonly author indulged in them.

Perhaps: But perhaps we should look more closely at the portrayals. Can they all be reconciled? "The Three Gables" mocks the black boxer, treats him as a joke and a coward, and disparages his physical characteristics. In "The Yellow Face," the little black girl is treated lovingly and accepted into the Grant Munro family, to the applause of Watson and the silent approval of Holmes.

But what about those physical characteristics? When we first realize that the "creature" behind the yellow mask is not a monster, but a little black girl, she emerges with "all her white teeth flashing in amusement," in contrast to the rest of her "coal black" appearance. She's very non-threatening and even lovable, and yet the flashing white teeth conjures up something stereotypical, I would say.

Or how about Watson's reaction to seeing the picture of John Hebron, Effie's late husband? He is handsome and intelligent-looking (Doyle always thinks you can read character or in this case intelligence in a face): anyway, Watson says Hebron in the little portrait within Effie's locket looks handsome, "but" (the "but" is important) shows clear signs of African descent. Handsome but African. So not so handsome? Or surprisingly handsome for an African? Or does it just mean handsome but now you can see why little Lucy is coal-black?

And Effie's own reaction? Unfortunately, she says, the little girl takes after her husband's people rather than mine. Now, does that simply mean that in a society with racist conventions it would be better to look white? Or does it show Effie's preference for white over black?

Preferences versus actions: Of course, preferences are one thing and active discrimination is another. The whole thrust of "The Yellow Face" is to endorse acceptance of the little coal-black girl. That's why it is hailed as liberal and ahead of its time. And yet, and yet ... "Dark or fair, she is my own dear little girlie," says Effie, which sounds noble, and yet perhaps should be interrogated, as they say. You could replace dark or fair with good or bad, and then which one would be good? Is this a story about accepting someone even though they are black? Which of course is better than rejecting them because they are black, and it says a lot about Grant Munro and Watson and Doyle that they will accept little Lucy. A lot positive, I mean, and yet behind that acceptance is still the notion of difference.

Locket and pipe: But let us move on to two interesting objects in the story, the locket and the pipe. First the locket, which Grant Munro had been led to believe did not open, but it does open and it reveals Effie's secret: the race of her first husband. Grant Munro had begun the story by telling Holmes and Watson that he and his wife had no secrets from each other, that they shared every word and thought, and had not even had an argument in three years. An extended honeymoon, one might call that. But then it turns out that Effie hasn't really shared every thought; she has this whole hidden past that Grant Munro knows nothing about. It is as if after three years Holmes finally revealed he has a cocaine habit. But Watson knows all about that habit, and deals with it as one does when you are one half of a couple that lives together in intimacy. Is the story in part about getting beyond the honeymoon and dealing with the reality of the other person rather than your idealized projection of them?

This is not a pipe: Or at least not just a pipe. Grant Munro's pipe, that is, which he leaves behind, and upon which Holmes bases some character analysis. This is reminiscent of the hat in "The Blue Carbuncle," but in that case what Holmes discovered seemed important. How important is it that Grant Munro is muscular and left-handed? But on closer examination there is something important about the pipe: it has been mended twice, which suggests that Grant Munro is one of those people who prefers to patch up something he values rather than throw it away in favour of something new. Is this symbolic of something? Of his tendency to hold onto things, like his marriage to Effie even if he finds it broken in some way? Even if she's been hiding things from him, even if it turns out she has a coal-black child? Yes, even then he's not going to move on to another marriage; he's going to make this one work.

What did Effie think? Did she think her husband would throw her over when he discovered her black child? Divorce? And what was her plan? She told him to trust her and he would know all some day. When? What would happen to allow that? And in the meantime what was she planning to do? To run off every night to visit her child and still keep her husband in the dark? Effie keeps talking about trust, but she is the one who has no trust: she does not trust her husband to stick by her; she gives him less credit than he deserves, as he puts it. But then he shows what he is made of, and the new family of three walks out of the story together, presumably to become a stronger unit for no longer having a dark secret at its core.

Dark secret: Pun only half intended. That's what's at the core of this story, as it is of so many of the stories. This at first seems like so many of the other stories: a character has some unpleasant bit of history that has suddenly come forward to haunt him (or in this case her). Often this leads to blackmail and then murder. Holmes has seen this many times, and if he is guilty of prejudice in this story, it is not race prejudice but the lazy prejudice of thinking every case is just like another. So he assumes there is something like an American lover come to blackmail Effie, and there is bigamy or infidelity. Even Grant Munro fears there is some sort of infidelity, and though Holmes tells him not to fret until the truth can be known (good advice though hard to follow), he himself tells Watson it's a bad business and constructs an elaborate theory which even Watson dismisses as pure surmise.

Sometimes a cigar is just a cigar. And sometimes a dark secret is only dark because of skin colour. There is nothing criminal in Effie's past. Though if you think of it more, and if we look at this story as an indictment of Victorian mores, maybe (by the standards of the time) Effie has done something wrong in marrying a black man. Such things were frowned on; that's why she is so frantic to cover it up, to hide her first husband and her little girl even from her new husband. Not because of bigamy, infidelity, or any other sin or crime, but because in Victorian times one might be shunned for having done what Effie did.

But is she guilty of something else? We of course see nothing wrong with her marriage, but what about her treatment of her child: leaving her behind for three years or more, and for what? Because she fears losing her husband, over whom she seems quite smitten or something: half crazy with fear of losing him, based on what? Her own misperceptions of his character. It's about time these two came to know each other better. Husbands and wives not sharing fully is a problem Doyle will touch on in "The Second Stain." And of course there is Neville St. Clair's secret in "The Man with the Twisted Lip," but would that have been a good one to hold onto? Ah, marriage.

The Stockbroker's Clerk

Connection/connexion: Watson bought a connection (or connexion, depending on your edition), by which he seems to mean a medical practice, but I can find no other examples of the word used in that meaning. It's not recognized (or even recognised) in the Oxford English Dictionary.

Sheeny: Derogatory term for a Jew. In using it, Hall Pycroft demonstrates not only anti-Semitism, but suggestibility. Pinner is a Jewish surname; Pycroft thus assumes that the man calling himself Pinner is Jewish, and presumably that's why he says he had a "touch of the sheeny about his nose." But Pinner is really the non-Jewish Beddington.

Beddington himself is playing on Jewish stereotypes about money-lending by taking on the Jewish name Pinner when he pretends to be a financial agent.

If only we knew all: The most memorable part of the story for me is when Holmes notes that Watson got the more successful medical practice, which he can tell because the tread is more worn at Watson's new residence. Watson had no idea; he just lucked out. But Holmes knew. If only we could see as perceptively as Holmes, how easy life would be …

Except did Watson really get the best practice? He notes that it used to be a good practice, but it has fallen on hard times because the doctor he bought it from fell ill, scaring off the patients.

So Holmes was right to say, judging by the steps, that the practice *had* been popular, but other factors have been at play since. Even the far-seeing Holmes may not be right, then, and in fact in this story, as in the previous ("The Yellow Face"), we see Holmes stumble. This time he calls himself an idiot for not realizing the importance of the newspaper.

Are we meant to think that even the greatest of us mortals is not infallible and that there are limits to human intelligence?

Greed and gold: "The glint of the gold" in the villain's mouth is what gives the game away, and the glint of gold, metaphorically speaking, i.e., greed, is the main motive both for the Beddington/Pinners and for Hall Pycroft. It leads to disaster for all of them, though: the love of money is ...

Holmes and Watson are pure, though: their motive is not monetary gain, not in solving the crime at least, though Watson is interested in making a living from his medical practice (and yet he is prepared to drop it every time Holmes shows up). But even freedom from greed doesn't guarantee success: Holmes stumbles. Why? Over-confidence? Or just human fallibility as suggested above?

Brothers galore: There are two actual Beddington brothers, and one Beddington brother who pretends to be two Pinner brothers. Why? You might say Holmes and Watson are a brotherly team too. And it's brotherly affection that drives one of the Beddingtons to attempt suicide. "Human nature is a strange mixture," Holmes says: both greed and fraternal feeling can co-exist, apparently: is the result good, though?

Confused identities: Following up on the brothers theme, but from a different angle, we have a lot of impersonation in this story. Is the point to warn that appearances can be deceptive? Pinner is not Pinner; the Hall Pycroft who shows up at Mawson & Williams is not Hall Pycroft.

I note, too, that we have a Harry Pinner and a Hall Pycroft (both HP), and then Holmes and Watson pretend to be Harris and Price (another HP, if you will): does that mean anything? Who is who in this story? Can we tell anything for sure in a world of masquerade?

And why all this doubling? Two Hall Pycrofts, two Pinners, two Beddingtons, two or even three HP's, not to mention Holmes and Watson. Lots of couples, and yet not a woman in sight. You might say there's a lot of asexual reproduction going on: the Beddingtons manufacture a Hall Pycroft and two Pinners, and Hall Pycroft manufactures Harris and Price, but is it a good thing?

The Gloria Scott

Ghosts: "Of all ghosts the ghosts of our old loves are the worst," says Trevor Sr., a wonderfully haunting line (sorry about that), only it turns out not to be true. What haunts Trevor is not an old love; that's not what the "JA" tattoo refers to. He's haunted by his past identity as a transported criminal, and this is the theme of this story, as it is of others in the canon: the threat that the past poses to current respectability. Here is a respectable landowner and JP whose position can be jeopardized in an instant because of something he did years before, when he was in a way a different person.

To me this speaks to a very Victorian anxiety about reputation and propriety. In an era when it was possible to make money and rise in the social structure, there would always be some uneasiness about origins. Prendergast's money enables him to take over a ship. Trevor (aka Armitage) gets money in the Australian gold fields, and turns himself into a member of the landed gentry. And yet, and yet … he remembers what he once was, and fears he may be reduced to that again, losing all his hard-earned social status.

Implausibilities: Les Klinger wonders why Hudson would resort to blackmail over a crime in which he himself was implicated. Baring-Gould can't believe that a convicted felon would take a position as Justice of the Peace. Some people look at issues like this and shake their heads at Doyle; others try to invent alternative stories: Baring-Gould imagines that really Armitage couldn't have been convicted in England; he must have been a colonial.

My approach is different: where a story seems implausible, illogical, or even impossible, I wonder what could have led to Doyle's making it that way. It may indeed be implausible for someone implicated in a crime to blackmail someone else about it, but Doyle needed the blackmail to bring out the threat posed to Trevor's respectability. He cares so much about his theme that he is prepared to run roughshod over the facts (or the plot).

Friends: Watson, it seems, has become a close enough friend to be told of Holmes's first case. And Holmes turns out to have had an earlier friend: who would have thought? It's hard to make friends with Sherlock Holmes, though: you need your dog to bite him on the leg and freeze him in place …

But why is Trevor Junior, a hearty outgoing type, friendless like Holmes? There's an implausibility. How to explain this? Well, let us look to the needs of the story. Here there is virtually no Watson. Holmes narrates; Watson plays no part, except to stretch out his legs by the fire and listen. But these stories need a Watson; so Doyle conjures another one: young, hearty Trevor, a counterpoint to Holmes's cerebral solitariness. Then to explain how they come together, he invents the dog and Trevor's friendlessness. The real Watson would be better, though.

The first attack: Interesting that Trevor Senior has received threats from poachers. What relevance has that to the story? None to the plot, really, but perhaps it illustrates the theme of threat: the threat to the respectable. Also, how ironic that the former criminal (Armitage/Trevor) now encounters danger by enforcing the law. It's all part of the motif of transformation or social mobility: someone can go from criminal beginnings to a position of punishing criminals.

The danger of knowledge: In "The Stockbroker's Clerk," we saw the limitations of (Holmes's) knowledge. Here, at least at the beginning, Holmes dazzles Trevor Sr. by being able to know so much. But this dazzling also contains within it some fear and suspicion. It is as if Trevor sees Holmes as some sort of wizard, ferreting out secrets – and given that he has an especially guilty secret, this makes him very uneasy. Even those without such secrets might be made uneasy by a man with such powers as Holmes displays. He is the man with very useful talents that at the same time could be very dangerous if turned in the wrong direction: he's useful to use against someone else, but what if he uses his powers on us? Hence we have Holmes as a dangerous instrument, a two-edged sword, and thus someone rather apart from the respectable people he is so often called in to aid. (Does he ever aid the non-respectable?)

Villains and villains: Both Armitage/Trevor and Prendergast commit fraud, but the latter seems to have been engaged in a whole course of it, while with Armitage/Trevor it was a one-time thing, and associated with "a debt of honour," which typically would be a gambling debt, but still to use the word "honour" … Our hero was guilty of an understandable indiscretion; it is important to distinguish him from true villains like Prendergast, who not only carries out multiple frauds, but who is blasé about committing mass murder. Armitage/Trevor shrank from that. This is all part of the theme of respectability: the point seems to be to defend those who hold respectable positions now: don't hold some youthful peccadilloes against them; they're not hardened criminals like Prendergast.

The Musgrave Ritual

V.R.: Victoria Regina, i.e., Queen Victoria. It's interesting that Holmes's patriotism takes this idiosyncratic turn (blasting bullet holes in the wall). Never the conformist, Holmes does still dedicate himself to upholding the law and supporting the social system. In this, we may contrast him with Brunton.

Double, double: Interestingly, this particular story has attracted the attention of academic critics who see it as almost post-modernist and want to apply various theoretical approaches to it.

One thing they mention is the similarity between Holmes and Brunton. Both are middle-class professionals able to see the secret of the Musgrave catechism when the Musgraves themselves, those foolish aristocrats, cannot. There's a doubling here, and yet I would see an important difference between Holmes and Brunton. Although it is Brunton who is literally a servant, it is Holmes who truly serves: he uses his wits to help the Musgraves; Brunton never told his master anything about what he was doing. Holmes helps deliver the crown to Reginald Musgrave; it seems highly unlikely Brunton would have done so.

A Little Learning: Is a dangerous thing, as Pope said. Reginald Musgrave says the butler was poking his nose into things that did not concern him, having developed an excessive amount of curiosity. In "The Gloria Scott" we saw the dangers of Holmes's superior knowledge, that is, the danger to others. But there can be danger for the dabbler in knowledge too, as we see here. Brunton tears the secret out of the Musgrave catechism and loses his life as a result. He overreaches himself, a bit like Adam and Eve eating from the Tree of Knowledge, or Dr. Frankenstein trying to create life: never a good idea.

The Female of the Species: Not only does Brunton tempt fate by reaching above himself, but as the critic Nils Clausson says, he is so much devoted to intellect, he doesn't seem to understand emotions: for instance, that the woman he jilted might harbour ill will to him and thus take the opportunity to do him harm, which she seems to have done – though the critics note that we don't really know this for sure; it's all Holmes's rather uncharacteristic speculation inspired by notions about Celtic passions. All very Gothic.

Mysteries: We don't really know what happened in the black hole. Did Rachel deliberately kill Brunton? Did she let him die after an accident? Was she even there? Holmes solves the riddle of the catechism, but the mystery of Brunton's death and Rachel's whereabouts remains. (This is one of the things that lead the critics to call the story post-modernist: it doesn't resolve everything.)

It has also been noted that this is an odd sort of mystery since it ends with the discovery of a body rather than beginning with it – so in some ways it seems less a mystery than a horror story. Gothic romance and all that. But there's mystery and detection too. A nice melange with little frissons of eeriness. And someone is buried alive: very Edgar Allan Poe.

Watson the Bohemian: Once again Holmes narrates. Watson has no role except for the prefatory interchange and the description of Holmes's untidiness, in the course of which Watson claims "a natural Bohemianism of disposition." Watson? A Bohemian? Good old solid respectable Watson? But come to think of it, there must be something of that in him, or how would he agree to go along on all these adventures?

The butler did it: Or it was done to him. Anyway, this seems to be one of the earliest instances of associating a butler with a crime.

The Reigate Squires

Title: What is the correct title of this story? It's appeared as "The Reigate Squire," "The Reigate Squires," and "The Reigate Puzzle" (in America, where some say people don't know what a squire is or are prejudiced against such titles). The Oxford English Dictionary says a squire is a country gentleman, especially the principal landowner in a district. So is that Acton? Cunningham Senior? Junior? One commentator (Joseph Kestner) focuses on the elder Cunningham and finds it disturbing that this squire who is also a Justice of the Peace entrusted with defending order is actually a criminal violating that order.

I will note that as is characteristic in the canon, the condescending squire types (especially the younger Cunningham here) get their comeuppance and are treated with some hostility. In other words, Holmes (and Doyle) are far from succumbing to the prejudice in favour of the landed gentry which blinds Inspector Forrester to the truth; rather the reverse.

The date of Malplaquet: The date on the house would thus be 1709, and the reference is to one of bloodiest battles in British history to that point. It would be a bit like referring to Verdun or Dieppe. Something bloody is afoot.

A fresh weapon: Is this fresh weapon of Holmes's the handwriting analysis? He does go on and on about it, and why? It seems superfluous to the solution of the crime. But where something seems superfluous you may be sure it is highly important. The whole point seems to be to establish that two men collaborated on the note, two men in a close relationship in which one is in charge, forcing the other to go along.

Like Watson forcing Holmes to rest in the countryside? Aha. Doubling again. We have the two Cunninghams replicating the Holmes-Watson relationship, which actually seems inverted in this story: usually Holmes leads the way, but here Watson's doctoring is to the fore, and when he says "the case was hopeless," he means the medical case in which Holmes is his patient, not the criminal case that Holmes is about to embark on.

Holmes's illness: Watson's doctoring actually seems most inept. He doesn't seem to realize that a new case (criminal variety) is what Holmes needs. Holmes remains torpid with nothing to do; it's a new puzzle that brings him to life. It thus seems less that he was worn out by the Netherlands-Sumatra case than that, with that case solved, he has nothing to do – except perhaps contemplate the thousands of congratulatory telegrams. Holmes doesn't want congratulations; he wants work.

Male couples: As in "The Stockbroker's Clerk," there are male pairings and not a woman in sight, except for the mysterious Annie Morrison. Holmes even insists on being installed in a bachelor establishment. And thus the story may perhaps be said to be a teasing out of the antagonisms that arise when males are deprived of female company. The junior Cunningham bullies his father – or at least that is what Holmes surmises. Perhaps it is not true at all; it is just based on the handwriting analysis. Perhaps it has more to do with Holmes feeling bullied by Watson into resting and not taking part in an investigation. A woman's presence is needed, but all we get is the tantalizing reference to Annie Morrison.

The battle against crime: Watson's description of Holmes's "life-long battle" makes it sound like a moral crusade when really doesn't the canon show, doesn't this very story show,

105

that it's less morality that engages Holmes than puzzle-solving? (The American title may thus be apt.) For Holmes it is a game, a creative exercise, perhaps a bit like writing a story. Is there morality in stories? There shouldn't be any politics or topicality, if we believe Watson – but who can believe Watson?

Holmes's methods: The lengthy denouement gives Holmes room to explain his crime-solving technique. First, you have to distinguish the vital facts from the incidental. Second, you can't have any prejudices (for instance, don't go thinking squires are beyond suspicion). And you have to follow where the facts lead, and do so "docilely." Hard to associate docility with Holmes actually; he seems more apt to leap intuitively (and talks about the importance of intuition in other stories) – what's needed perhaps is a respect for the facts combined with intuition.

More methods: We see another aspect of Holmes's technique early in the story when he asks what the coachman was doing at the house. The Inspector tries to explain this oddity away, but Holmes seizes on oddities, like a terrier with a bone, worrying them to death – and thus arriving at solutions. Focus on the strange and try to understand what it's doing in the story, the crime, the world; you will get further into the heart of things then.

Joke? Being intuitive and worrying at the unusual can often make the more "rational" regular people laugh at you. We need to get the note out of the criminal's pocket, says Holmes. The Inspector laughs at him: if we could get at his pocket, then we'd already have him, he says. But not so, it turns out. Holmes does get at the pocket before getting the criminal.

Forensics: Holmes can tell from the absence of powder burns that the victim was shot from a distance, not at close range as the Cunninghams claim. CSI, eat your heart out. And once again note the method: following the facts, checking the body. Watson asks if there was any doubt about the cause of death. "It is as well to test everything," says Holmes. Indeed.

Reputation: Once again, as often in the canon, the motive for a crime is to protect someone's reputation, though this time it's not some ancient sin from a faraway land that has to be covered up, but the burglary at Acton's. And the point of that burglary was to frustrate a lawsuit that threatened the Cunninghams' property. One might say this means the story is about greed, but maybe it's just another form of protection: protecting what one has against those who would take it from you, Acton in this case: is Acton the true villain? Or the lawyers? Perhaps there is morality here after all.

The Crooked Man

Women: After a womanless story ("The Reigate Squires") in which the lack of women seems to produce male-on-male antagonisms, we get a story in which a woman is the centre of things, the cause of the crime, if there is a crime. (And what is the crime here? If we believe the medical examiner, Barclay died of natural causes. The real crime is what Barclay did years ago, sending Wood to destruction, or at least capture and torture.)

So what is Doyle saying? If there is no woman, there is antagonism (and of course crime); if there is a woman in the case, then it's the same. In any case, here we have a reaction against the male-only environment of Reigate (and Stockbroker).

Elementary: "I have the advantage of knowing your habits, my dear Watson," says Holmes, in explaining his deduction about how busy Watson is. "Excellent!" says Watson. "Elementary," says Holmes. This may be the closest thing in the canon to the famous "Elementary, my dear Watson" misquotation.

The past: As so often in the canon, something hidden in the past is the motive force for events; something horrible happened there. The past is a dangerous country in these stories, rising up even thirty years later to disrupt the pleasant facade of everyday life.

Of course, disrupting the pleasant facade is what these stories are all about: depicting the dark underside that lurks beneath the life of a "model . . . middle-aged couple." Victorian society is intent on putting on a good facade, on being respectable and proper, but life is full of the improper, and the pleasure of these stories is seeing those improper things break through, causing us to gasp. What lurks in the dark, the dark that scares Barclay? Some ancient crime of his that can rear its head like a mongoose and strike him dead.

Symbol: The mongoose is a snake-catcher, we are told, and the snake in the story seems to be Barclay, who is also a David, the Hebrew king who sent Uriah to his death in battle to get him out of the way so that David could have his wife. It's in Second Samuel, Chapters 11-13 (Holmes's recollection, though rusty, belated and a bit vague, is correct.)

Domesticity: In "Reigate," Holmes wouldn't go to an establishment unless it was a bachelor one, without women. Here he has no qualms about entering Watson's married home, but only as a late-night intruder who spirits Watson away from all that: all that domestic peace which mainly puts Watson to sleep, it seems: he is drowsing when Holmes arrives; he wakes up when there's a crime to solve, an adventure afoot. Here is the clash between domestic tranquillity and the disruptions of crime. Like the clash between past and present.

It is almost as if Doyle's imagination keeps conjuring up an Edenic domestic peace only to subvert it with some Original Sin from the past, a snake in the Garden. But in this case how much more interesting to have the snake to go after, at least if you have a mongoose. Eden is dull and drowsy; the adventure is the thing.

Justice or Puzzle-Solving? "It's every man's business to see justice done," says Holmes. As in "Reigate," we get this motive for his actions, but coupled with his desire to solve a puzzle. The puzzle-solving mania even infects Watson (and us, no doubt). Holmes is in "a state of suppressed excitement," Watson says, "while I was myself tingling with that half-sporting, half-intellectual pleasure which I invariably experienced when I associated myself with him in his investigations."

The game's the thing, and that's why it seems unfair to criticize Watson (as Holmes does at the beginning) for holding back information from the reader. Of course, Watson holds things back: by the time he writes the stories, he knows everything. If he told us everything on the first page, where would be the fun in that? ("There was this man who sent another to his death; then the first man is struck dead by seeing the second thirty years later. Holmes figures it out.")

We are titillated by the puzzle. Also by being in the presence of a brilliant detective, so Holmes's second criticism of Watson's story-telling technique is also off the mark (he says he's not the ideal reasoner Watson portrays). We enjoy being Watsons; that is the brilliance of the stories: we can all be slightly befuddled Watsons in the face of a dark, mysterious puzzle which eventually the great Sherlock Holmes elucidates for us.

What sort of justice? Wood says Providence struck down Barclay. The story does not endorse vigilante justice. Wood says he would like to have done for Barclay. If he had, though, could we sympathize? Would Holmes have let him go, as he sometimes does other criminals? But here we are relieved of this dilemma: Barclay dies of a stroke before Wood can kill him.

Note that the justice at the end is different from the search for justice that Holmes says has set him on the trail. At first, seeking justice means finding Barclay's killer. Later it means passing judgment on Barclay.

Holmes's methods and Miss Morrison: Holmes does not just inspect crime scenes and deduce. He also interviews people, notably Miss Morrison (and later Henry Wood). And very effectively too. But what strikes me is this Miss Morrison: finally a Miss Morrison appears after only being hinted at in

"The Reigate Squires." Is that why there is an Annie Morrison at the end of "Squires"? Because Doyle was already thinking of "Crooked Man"? Or did the mysterious reference to a Miss Morrison in "Squires" inspire him to put one in "The Crooked Man"? The imagination is a mysterious thing.

The text on the wall: "I read death on his face as plain as I can read that text over the fire," says Henry Wood (about Barclay). But what is the text over the fire? Our late Priory Schoolmaster, Peter Wood (no relation), says it was common to have a framed quote from the Bible over one's fireplace, but which one would Henry Wood have had there? "Vengeance is mine; I will repay, says the Lord"?

The Resident Patient

How Soon We Forget: Or at least I do. My battered old Penguin Crime edition of the Memoirs prints the version of the story that includes the mind-reading episode copied from "The Cardboard Box." I read "The Cardboard Box" just a few months before "The Resident Patient," and yet I didn't remember the episode at all, how Watson gave himself away by looking at pictures of General Gordon and Henry Ward Beecher. Excellent, I thought – but obviously forgettable. Clearly, it's not the details that matter, but the sense of Holmes and Watson interacting: that's what I remember.

The Eyes the Mirror of the Soul? The interpolated passage from "The Cardboard Box" includes reference to how the features reflect one's emotions, and in "The Resident Patient" itself there are similar comments. At the end Holmes says, "I can read in a man's eye when it is his own skin that he is frightened for." And Watson can tell that Holmes is interested in this case because his lids have dropped more heavily over his eyes. Also, somewhat magically, because his smoke curls up more thickly from his pipe: or would it do so because Holmes is puffing away at it more excitedly?

The image of excited puffing suddenly puts me in mind of sexual arousal: is this why Holmes is so little interested in women? It's crime problems that excite him?

The Past and Respectability: One commentator sees this as another story (like "The Gloria Scott" and, one might add, "The Crooked Man") in which a respectable character is hiding something disgraceful from his past, but really it's hard to see Blessington as respectable. He seems more shady, with a peculiar scheme about putting Dr. Trevelyan in business: that seems more reminiscent of the peculiar schemes in "The Red-

Headed League" and "The Stockbroker's Clerk": something not criminal but odd is going on. It doesn't have to be criminal to get Sherlock Holmes (or Arthur Conan Doyle) going.

Extortion: The story touches on the travails of a young professional man trying to set himself up in his profession. Do I hear echoes of Conan Doyle's own struggles as a medical man? And then the only way Trevelyan can get set up is to promise to give three-quarters of his income to Blessington: does that say something about the writing business?

Things peculiar: Peter Wood, the Stormy Petrels' late Schoolmaster, wondered in his notes on this story whether Watson was getting in a jab at Holmes by speaking of his "mental peculiarities" and his "peculiar methods of investigation." Peculiar is a peculiar word, though: it has two meanings. The more common now is "odd, strange, weird." But an older meaning is simply "distinctive." Later in the story Trevelyan says Blessington was in "a peculiar state of restlessness" (meaning "odd"?). Later Holmes asks if there was "anything peculiar" about the room Blessington was found dead in (again "odd"?). But later still Holmes notes that some of the cigars in the room "are of the peculiar sort which are imported by the Dutch" (is that peculiar odd or, more likely I think, peculiar distinctive?).

So is Watson just saying that Holmes's methods are distinctive, special, different? Or is he suggesting something odd about his friend? If so, why? Is this some Watsonian resentment breaking through? Or are we misreading him?

Deductions: Watson begins by saying it's difficult to find cases which are both interesting in themselves and which also demonstrate his friend's peculiar talents. But why? If we think about this from Conan Doyle's perspective, couldn't he just make up stories that do both? Is he suggesting this is a hard thing to do? Or is he again having Watson make a jab at Holmes by suggesting that sometimes Holmes's role was not that significant?

Watson says "The Resident Patient" is one of those cases with remarkable facts but not a major role for Holmes, but is that true? It is Holmes who determines that the case is murder, not suicide (by looking at the cigars). Holmes can tell that Blessington is not worried about money but about his own life (from the look in his eyes and from the fact the intruders didn't look for money). He can even tell in which order the murderers climbed the stairs (not that that matters particularly: is this Holmes showing off?).

True, the information on the Worthingdon gang comes from "headquarters" (Scotland Yard?); Holmes just relays it. But Holmes does a lot of detecting here. Perhaps Watson is miffed that his own "brilliant departure" (his theory that Trevelyan was making things up) is something Holmes had already thought of and dismissed (based on the evidence of the footprints). It is interesting the relationship between these two.

Shield and Sword: The shield of British law (a sort of witness protection program for Blessington) fails, in part because he won't tell Holmes what is going on. Holmes says Blessington kept quiet because he was trying to hide and because his crime was shameful, but that makes little sense. I will note that these stories seldom show crimes prevented, seldom show successful uses of shields; it's all about the sword of justice later, catching the criminals. In this case the criminals get away, but perhaps drown on the Norah Creina, so justice is done? Or is the true justice the hanging of Blessington?

"Why should anyone murder a man in so clumsy a fashion as by hanging him?" asks the Inspector. The answer seems to be that this was a judicial proceeding: Blessington

114

was hanged for his crime of informing. Some commentators suggest that that is a worse crime in this story than the murder of Blessington himself, and it is hard to sympathize with the fat, lying, extortionate Blessington, who after all was the worst of the original gang of robber-murderers: are we meant to be okay with his hanging?

And does Conan Doyle need to show crimes being committed and then solved rather than crimes being prevented? Would we read stories about shields? Would we feel dissatisfied, thinking No, show us an actual disruption of the fabric of civilization (an actual crime) and then show us things put right rather than just showing us how such a disruption was prevented?

The Greek Interpreter

Oh, Mycroft! Look, look, Conan Doyle played the Great Game too. I wonder what Holmes's relatives were like, one can almost hear him thinking. What sort of family background did he have? Maybe a brother? How about a smarter brother? That would be interesting.

And so we get Mycroft. And what does Mycroft do for us? (Us the readers, I mean.) Well, he gives Holmes his comeuppance, that's one thing he does. Perhaps a bit like The Woman. After all these stories in which Holmes gets to look down on us (and on our surrogate, Watson) for just not seeing properly, suddenly we meet someone who can best Holmes at his own game.

That artilleryman must have a child, says Holmes, playing his usual parlour tricks.

"Children, my dear boy, children," says Mycroft, one-upping him, putting him in his place. Not such a smarty-pants after all, Mr. Holmes. It's like discovering Kryptonite. Suddenly the superhero has a weak spot. I think it must be pleasing for most readers. It is for this one.

(Not that it makes me think less of Holmes. Quite the contrary, it humanizes him – which I suppose is the motive for the Great Game, no? We want to make Holmes into a real human being when really he's more like a brilliant robot, or android. Conan Doyle seems to have felt this impulse too.)

But what a mess: Aside from Mycroft, though (and Mycroft alone is worth the price of admission, so don't feel too bad) – aside from Mycroft, what on earth is going on in this story? Perhaps introducing Mycroft upset the balance somehow. How could two such brilliant investigators make such a hash of things, causing one man's death and nearly causing another's? Why would Mycroft place the ad that endangered the Interpreter and the Prisoner?

And how odd of Holmes to refuse to allow Mycroft to pursue the answer to the puzzle of who the sister is. No, instead of looking up J. Davenport, Holmes insists on rushing to save Melas and Kratides. Not usually his priority at all, but maybe he has to take the other side from his brother out of rivalry. Not that it helps much: Kratides still dies, but it's true they rescue Melas, after which one might expect them to track down Davenport – but no, they let it go, they don't find anything out for sure, and we end with conjectures, and it is Watson's theorizing that is left to stand as the explanation for the case.

Reasoning from an armchair: If all you needed to be a detective was to reason from an armchair, says Holmes, Mycroft would be the best. But, says Holmes, you also need energy, ambition, and an ability to go out and prove your theories and work out the practical points ... I wonder. I wonder especially if someone like Rex Stout, and even Agatha Christie ... I wonder if they were inspired or challenged by this notion. What if we invented a detective who stayed in his armchair and just used his little grey cells or sent off his man Archie to do the legwork? What if you were Nero Wolfe or Hercule Poirot? I wonder.

Holmes the lawbreaker? Though they waste time getting proper authorization to get into the home where Melas has been taken, in the end Holmes has to break in. "It is a mercy that you are on the side of the force," says the Inspector in this case.

I wonder again: a contrast seems to be drawn between following the bureaucratic procedures (something Mycroft the bureaucrat would surely do) and just breaking in. Is there some push here to contrast the two brothers, making Sherlock even more the outsider, almost an outlaw, to distinguish him from the governmental Mycroft?

Now I think of that Star Trek episode where Kirk is split in two: his good but weak side versus his energetic but brutish side. Has Doyle split off his law-abiding side into Mycroft so that Sherlock must be more outside the law?

In Star Trek, Kirk has to be recombined to function properly. Is that what's needed here? Do Mycroft and Sherlock fumble so much because really what we have is a splitting in two of things that need to be together in one person?

Or is it just that too many detectives spoil the broth?

A Fairy Tale or ... The story of the prisoner made me think along fairy-tale lines. Once upon a time there was a man from a distant place who was taken prisoner and made to stay in an out-of-the-way mansion until he would sign over his fortune. But fairy tales usually have happy endings. The woodchopper arrives to kill the wolf and save the girl. Of course, here the girl doesn't need saving, apparently; she saves herself later (maybe). But the prisoner dies. It is a failure. Is this a story about failure? Isn't Mycroft himself a failure? Here's a man with even greater powers than Sherlock, and yet what does he do with them? He audits government books? Is that all? (I know, I know, in a later story Mycroft will seem to be the most powerful person in the government; he perhaps is the government – but in this story he comes across as totally ineffectual despite his great potential. It is rather sad in a way. Such a waste.)

And that is all my musing on this story for now – except that I will elaborate on the splitting off to say that perhaps it's the energy and the brilliance that have been separated. The brilliance is now in Mycroft, leaving Sherlock with only the energy. Well, Sherlock does make some deductions, it's true, but not wanting to pursue J. Davenport, that's odd. There is weakness and failure here, that's what comes from making someone even smarter than Sherlock.

The Naval Treaty

Roses, roses all the way: The longest story in the canon, I am told, but it just flies by, whirling through a phantasmagoria of free association. I was especially struck by the passage in the middle when Holmes suddenly apostrophizes roses. What have roses to do with anything? The others think he's gone mad. Shouldn't an editor have told Conan Doyle to forget about the roses and get on with solving the mystery of the naval treaty?

Thankfully, no editor did, or if they did, Conan Doyle ignored them. But it does raise the question: what are the roses doing in the story? Holmes says they are a sign of the goodness of Providence, so perhaps that means Conan Doyle is pausing to say that the little universe he has created is a benevolent one. Is it, though? He's created a universe of crime – but it's true that mostly the crimes get solved, and sometimes justice is done. Holmes lets the criminal escape in this case, but he restores the reputation (and the job) of poor Percy Phelps.

Holmes also says that roses are an extra, an embellishment. They aren't necessary to life, we could get on without them, and yet wouldn't our lives be the poorer without them? Wouldn't our lives also be the poorer without the 60 stories of the canon? Are they roses themselves?

Wild and Whirling Words: Within moments of the roses comment, Holmes is on to talking of the Board Schools as a beacon of the future (reflecting Conan Doyle's belief in the power of education to help build his benevolent universe?) and then wonders if Phelps drinks and says he is in deep water and it will be hard to get him to shore, a metaphor recalling the metaphor of the beacon or lighthouse. Once talking about lighthouses it is perhaps only natural to speak of deep water and the shore. It is interesting to watch Holmes's mind jump from idea to idea, reflecting the restlessness of the inquiring mind, or the outpourings of genius – which of course is closely allied to madness. And it all somehow reminds me of *Hamlet* – Hamlet's "What a piece of work is a man" is perhaps echoed by Holmes's "What a lovely thing a rose is!" And Hamlet's madness/genius seems to be echoed in this passage generally – was Conan Doyle dabbling in some Shakespeare at the time? "I suspect myself ... of coming to conclusions too rapidly" seems very Hamletian somehow.

And then there is the sudden asperity when Holmes thinks Watson is too busy with his own cases to help on this one, followed by the instant return to good humour when he realizes that Watson is saying the opposite. More of the lightning-quick shifts of genius. Or has he been indulging his cocaine habit?

But back to the education business. Is there any connection between the ode to schools and helping poor Percy Phelps? Does someone need a better education? Or since these are specifically the Board Schools, for those who haven't the right connections to be in the posh schools, is there some suggestion that salvation must come from below? From ordinary people, not perhaps the higher-ups among whom Holmes so often finds himself?

Noble is as noble does: Following up this point, how striking a line is the one given to Watson this time (for Watson must get his innings too) about the nobility or lack thereof of noblemen. Watson comments that Lord Holdhurst "seemed to represent that not too common type, a nobleman who is in truth noble." What a way to praise a particular noblemen while tossing a zinger at the class as a whole – a point of view often found in the canon, where the upper classes often come off not too well at all (unless they be royalty). Hence perhaps the celebration of the Board Schools and the hope that something good might come from the ordinary people: "the wiser, better England of the future," as Holmes says, sounding now less like Shakespeare than a Fabian Socialist.

Good old Watson: Speaking of Watson, how telling that in beginning this story he associates it with the time of his marriage and says that the most memorable things that happened then were three cases he worked on with Sherlock Holmes. How could a mere marriage compete with solving mysteries? We see the preoccupation of the canon – it is not with love and domesticity, except to the extent that Holmes's deductions can preserve domesticity, and also reputations – this is once again a story about reputation threatened, though in this case not by some distant hidden deed that must be hushed up, but by something here and now, a moment of carelessness, but still to the same effect: reputation is a very fragile plant, easily destroyed. Look how a mere accident can do it.

Problem-Solving: Speaking of solving mysteries, that again is what the canon is mostly about, and when (in my view) it is at its best. Here Holmes turns away from a "very commonplace little murder" (who cares about those?) and is much more intrigued by the case of a missing document. It makes my archivist's heart beat proud, but the point is that it's not violence or the horrifying nature of the crime that is the motor of these stories and what gets Holmes going; it is the drive to solve a mystery.

Leftover questions: Why does the fiancée look Italian? What's the point of that? Is she an exotic rose? It makes no sense, since her brother seems quite ordinarily British, so what does it signify? (A late thought: is it because the treaty is between England and Italy? Is there some unconscious symbolism there?)

Why does Holmes think it of enormous importance that the clock chimes 9:45? Or is it that the door was shut but not locked? Holmes says, "That is of enormous importance" – but what does the "that" refer to?

What are the seven clues that Holmes saw? He never tells us. (Those who don't like it when Holmes shows off will be annoyed, I fear.)

New blood? In Joseph Kestner's book on Sherlock's Men, I see that the discussion of the Naval Treaty focuses on the weakness of Percy Phelps: his shrieking and fainting, and his brain fever (when did a man ever have brain fever?). I connect this with the criticism of the nobility in the story and also the hope for salvation from below, from the Board Schools (note that when Holmes and Watson see them, Holmes and Watson are above, looking down on them: the beacon of the future is literally lower down). And is another hope from exotic blood? From the Italians? Is it a necessary thing that the English enter a treaty with the Italians? Is that why Miss Harrison looks Italian?

The Final Problem

Begone with you: Poor Conan Doyle, burdened by his most famous creation (though I was bemused to read, in Wikipedia, that his Professor Challenger is also popular: I'd never heard of Professor Challenger, but perhaps others have). In any case, as every schoolboy knows, Doyle was fed up with Holmes and resolved to kill him off, something easier said than done, it turns out – but in this story he seemed to have succeeded, provoking anguished outcry (though the story of people putting on black armbands in mourning seems not to be true: one of those stories that ought to be true, but ...).

I've been working on an article on A. A. Milne (whose first published work, oddly, was a Sherlockian pastiche). He too was beset by one of his creations (the famous Pooh Bear). It is salutary to compare what Milne did with his unwanted creation: he did kill him off (in a manner of speaking) and unlike Conan Doyle, Milne never brought Pooh back: did that get readers to shift their attention to Milne's other works? What, you say, A. A. Milne had other works? So there you go. It didn't work. So it's just as well that Conan Doyle brought Holmes back; that's what he was going to be remembered for anyway.

Death of a Hero: But a death it is, however temporary. And what sort of death? Nothing ignoble or demeaning here. Tired as he was of his hero, Doyle resolves on a noble death for him – and what could be more noble than a death at the hands of a worthy antagonist, a very Napoleon, a clever intellectual character in some ways a mirror image of our hero, who will grapple with him at the edge of a terrifying waterfall: there's Holmes's chance to study Nature, as he says he would like to do.

It is curious that two such intellectual figures should end with physical combat, in a sort of duel, like jousting knights of old. It seems fitting and yet odd. As if this question of intellect, of mind, can only be settled by destroying the vessel that holds the mind. As if, unable to defeat a computer with advanced programs, you resorted to smashing it to bits. Perhaps that is the only way Doyle could see to rid himself of this superior brain: by sending him to his death. Then he could never come back, could he? (Ah, but he left himself a sort of out, as we shall see.)

The Death of Detection: There is an interesting article on this story by Michael Atkinson ("Staging the Disappearance of Sherlock Holmes") that notes that the story is in many ways the inverse of the traditional Holmes story. There is no mystery here; indeed this is almost an anti-mystery: the solution is announced at the beginning: there is one man, Moriarty, behind it all. And by all Holmes does mean all. It turns out that half the crime of London can be laid at Moriarty's door; he and his vast shadowy network arrange everything.

How odd, how jarring even. How after all can this be? Can we explain the disappearance of the naval treaty this way? Did Moriarty steal Silver Blaze? Did he set up the Red-Headed League? It makes no sense. In fact, it takes away from all the individualized detection Holmes has done over the years. It is to abandon the fox for the hedgehog, to adopt a grand unified theory, to pronounce a Key to All Mythologies.

Oh, well, it will do for a swan song, I suppose. It wouldn't do for starting off in the detecting business, because then you'd have your solution even before you begin, and where would be the fun in that? There'd be no exploring, just saying, Oh, it's Moriarty again.

The whole Moriarty invention seems a radical attack on the canon, which is perhaps fitting in a story meant to kill off the canon.

Absences: Michael Atkinson's article discusses absences in the story, notably the absence or invisibility of Moriarty. But the most important absence is a death scene, and this is where Conan Doyle leaves himself an out. We don't see Holmes die, his body is not discovered; we have circumstantial evidence, and we have clues, and we have Watson pronouncing on what those clues mean, but when has Watson ever been a reliable detective? Maybe Conan Doyle wanted to kill his great detective, but at some level decided to leave it just a bit ambiguous, so that someday it might turn out that ... But we must not anticipate.

That organized network: Holmes is always a bit of a loner, but here he seems a persecuted loner. That whole network of Moriarty's is out to get him. Wherever he goes there they are, tossing rocks at him, mugging him, chasing him. It's like a celebrity being hounded by fans, like an author being beset by readers who adore his stories and beg for more ... Oh, wait: this would cast us, the readers, as the network hounding the poor author, Arthur Conan Doyle, something he is perhaps only too capable of rendering into a criminal conspiracy. How we afflict our heroes.

But if we are Moriarty's network, who is Moriarty? Who is Holmes's biggest fan? Watson? Perhaps it's Watson that Doyle should have sent over the falls. Then there'd be no stories, would there? What a chance Conan Doyle missed.

How many wives had Dr. Watson? Some would say as many as six, but I doubt he had any at all. Holmes shows up, and Mrs. Watson is conveniently absent. It's true that Watson says that his marriage has meant he has seen Holmes less in recent years – but since the stories are the only place we see Holmes, and in the stories he is almost always with Watson, and Watson's wife is almost always conveniently absent, it becomes hard to credit her very existence.

When Holmes suggests the trip to the continent, Watson says his practice is quiet (his practice is always quiet, it seems; he is always ready to go off with Holmes; Watson's very life is bound up with Holmes; his practice? Pah). And, says Watson, he has an accommodating neighbour. What does that mean? He will accommodate what? Look after the house? But isn't there a wife? I think not.

Lest you fear I have suddenly succumbed to the Game, fear not. If the story says there's a wife, I am not going to doubt it, but she doesn't seem very real. Watson's practice doesn't seem very real. All that is real for Watson is having adventures with Holmes. It's a Boy's Own world, away from domesticity and adult cares, a Huckleberry Finn sort of world, a world in which you can simply spend your time messing around in boats – and if only there'd been a boat at the bottom of the waterfall.

Fire: They set fire to Baker Street. "Good heavens, Holmes! This is intolerable," says Watson. Indeed: the base camp of adventures under attack. But Holmes himself is under attack throughout this story, so it only makes sense. But how intolerable it really is. No more Holmes, no more Baker Street; it is the end of everything. Conan Doyle pulls out all the stops. It really is intolerable. No wonder people wore black arm bands (even if they didn't).

But hope, or faith: Why must Holmes wait three days? The story about waiting seems so contrived that it must be there for some other reason. I mean an authorial reason. After death will there be a resurrection? After three days? And is it a necessary death? Holmes smiles at the falling rock. Is he going willingly to his death? Perhaps as long as it will take Moriarty with him: that sounds more like Samson than Jesus, actually. Well, there can be all sorts of echoes buried in the death of a hero.

The Hound of the Baskervilles
Part One (the first five chapters)

Let's begin at the beginning: The first chapter title is the exact same as the first chapter title of *A Study in Scarlet*: "Mr. Sherlock Holmes." As if we are beginning all over again, as we are: in terms of publishing history, this is the first Holmes story in close to a decade, so Conan Doyle apparently feels the need to begin with what looks like a new introduction. But we don't really need an introduction, so beyond telling us that Holmes is a late riser (is this new information?),[*] Watson plunges right into the story – well, actually, he plunges right into a typical Watson-Holmes vignette in which Holmes's superior powers of deduction are revealed at the expense of poor Watson, who somehow thinks that Dr. Mortimer is involved in a hunt: which, come to think of it, he is: there are certainly hounds involved, so maybe he's not so far off the mark as that. Well done, Watson – and perhaps this is a bit of foreshadowing bubbling up from Conan Doyle's subconscious.

Sherlock Holmes as God: But even if Watson is on to something, the overt point of the opening vignette is to put him in his place and exalt Holmes, who is back to denigrating his worshipper. And though Holmes urges Watson to apply His methods, Watson clearly can't: can any of us mere mortals? Only the great Sherlock Holmes can deduce in his astonishing way: but wait, is that quite true? Dr. Mortimer says Holmes is second to Bertillon (this pleases Holmes no end, as you can imagine), and then, in a hilarious touch at the end of the fifth chapter, we find there is someone going around masquerading as Sherlock Holmes, someone who actually bests the real Sherlock: what is going on? Is our God not so great? Is he not the only

---

[*] In fact, this contradicts what we're told in *Study*.

God? Can others get the better of him? Well, actually we saw that long before, with Irene Adler. It actually makes our Sherlock a bit more human.

And there are identity questions raised: if there are two Sherlocks ... well, the mind boggles. How can we tell what is real? Can we trust a person's word? The other Sherlock says *he's* Sherlock ... of course, that's less an attempt at disguise than a nice touch at the real Sherlock's expense.

A picker up of shells on the shores of the great unknown ocean: So says Dr. Mortimer of himself, showing a touch of humility or modesty (in contrast with our hero perhaps). It's a nice phrase, suggesting there is much we cannot know, and of course the whole canon is about dealing with the unknown – though not with the supernatural. The supernatural does get a look-in here, but we just know there won't be devils involved: there never are in a Holmes story. The unknown will rather have to do with the mysteries of this world, and there are plenty of them in the opening five chapters: Why do those boots keep going missing? Who is following Sir Henry, and why? How did his uncle die?

Restoring the nobility: Eight years before, in "The Naval Treaty," Conan Doyle wrote of the decay of the nobility and suggested it needed an infusion of fresh blood from below (or perhaps from Italy). Now it is Sir Henry who is to carry on his uncle's plans to restore the glories of the Baskervilles and save them from the depredations of the *nouveaux riches*. So now the idea is not to get fresh blood, but to somehow go back to past glories, though first Sir Charles and then Sir Henry had to venture abroad to do this: so maybe it is a sort of foreign blood that is needed after all, or if not foreign blood, then a foreign adventure which, in Sir Henry's case, makes him sound a bit North American, apparently, at least when he's angry.

Body and Soul: Holmes says he doesn't need Watson for the thinking through of the problem: when there's action, then he'll need him. And later Holmes is able (metaphorically, I think, but who knows?) to leave his body behind drinking coffee and smoking his pipe while his spirit has travelled to Dartmoor to consider the crime. Is Watson the body and Holmes the brains? I sometimes think of Holmes as the embodiment (wrong word) of the creative spirit: he is an artist. He uses facts, of course, but also the imagination. As he says here, he practises the "scientific use of the imagination." It's an interesting tension.

Looks are everything: Conan Doyle is a great believer in what looks can reveal: Dr. Mortimer, for instance, looks pugnacious and there is something about his eyes that tells Watson that he is a gentleman. This is all part of the notion of physiognomy, a popular belief in the nineteenth century that said you could judge character by appearances: faces revealed all (this is why Dorian Gray had to hide that picture away).

Free trade and tariffs: Why an article on free trade? What might that symbolize? The *Devon County Chronicle* was against *nouveaux riches*, the sort who might make their money through commerce, whereas the *Times* attacks the protective tariff and promotes free trade as the way to wealth, new wealth presumably, creating those *nouveaux riches* that the country paper disparages. So here perhaps we have the theme, again, of Old Money versus New. Will this play out later in the story?

Power and Design: That's what Holmes sees at work here. Are we hinting at the supernatural again? Though overtly not, the story seems to be barely able to restrain the bubbling up of something otherworldly. We shall have to see where this leads. Tune in next time.

The Hound of the Baskervilles
Part Two (the next five chapters)

No Theorizing! So says Holmes to Watson as he packs him off to Devonshire, but of course Watson can't resist: when he sees that Mrs. Barrymore has been crying, he concludes that some love intrigue must be going on, when it isn't that at all: it's her brother the convict out on the moor. Watson also concludes, because Sir Henry has pride, valour, and strength in his eyebrows and nostrils (?), he'll do well in an adventure, even a dangerous adventure – well, we'll have to see if that turns out to be true.

Dark Forces: Meanwhile Watson keeps describing the moor as a dark, ominous place where he can imagine encountering prehistoric men more readily than modern-day Europeans. Not that he goes in for the supernatural fears of the locals; no, says Watson, he's nothing if not a believer in common sense. And yet … he feels he's almost left his own age behind when he sees the stone monoliths. Holmes won't be interested in that stuff, he says, but he reports it to him anyway. He can't help himself, he's just Watson after all, prone to false beliefs and with no Holmes there to correct him. The balance goes somewhat askew as we wait for Holmes to return. Even Watson becomes impatient: he needs Holmes back; he's like id without ego, feeling without reason.

Paradoxical Pairs: The Holmes-Watson pairing may be temporarily disrupted, but we have some other odd pairs here, two sets of siblings, perhaps suggesting there is something of a sibling connection between our two usual heroes: brothers in crime (detection)? There's cool Stapleton the naturalist and his dark, tropical sister;* then there's respectable Mrs. Barrymore

---

* Of course, it turns out she's not his sister. Still.

and her criminal brother. How can these things be? How can two people be so close and yet so different? Or is it difference that allows closeness, opposites attracting? Except siblings are two who just happen to grow up together, presumably with the same genetics, and yet ... Conan Doyle seems to like these paradoxes: there is the Italian-looking sister in "The Naval Treaty."

Physiognomy again: As in the first part, we are told more than once how looks reveal the man. The convict on the moor has his sins scored into his face; Sir Henry looks the hero because of his eyes and nostrils; Stapleton's firm lips betray a harsh nature. It's as if everything is there for the looking, if only you know how to see, and yet it's all a mystery. More paradoxes.

Tracking: In the middle of this section there's suddenly a lot of tracking and pursuing. Watson follows Sir Henry to his rendezvous, then Watson and Sir Henry sit in wait and follow Barrymore, then the two of them rush off to find the convict. All of which does not lead to much, but it does provide suspense, along with some unexpected comedy: in the middle of a murder investigation, Watson suddenly worries about intruding on Sir Henry's courtship of Miss Stapleton. Here's another strange mix: of the conventions of Victorian society and the dangerous forces out on the moor.

And another convention: A big deal is made over whether Barrymore revealed the presence of the convict out of free will, in which case it would have been improper of Sir Henry and Watson to go after him. Or was he forced into telling, in which case what Sir Henry and Watson did would be all right. How quaint, one thinks, or how odd to worry about such niceties when there's a murderer on the loose. But these stories are all about the clash of civilization and crime; it's what gives them their frisson.

Speaking of niceties ... As in some of the other stories, not too much store is put in following the letter of the law. If the convict is going to be leaving the country soon, then Sir Henry and Watson are fine with letting him go rather than calling in the police. Of course, they are also helping Barrymore, the Baskervilles' long-time servant. Still ... It's as if the Holmes stories follow some other higher code than the law (if it is higher).

And speaking of comedy, there's old Frankland, who takes everyone to court, thus offering what Watson himself calls comic relief, and who even lives in a place called Lafter Hall. And yet he has a daughter with an equivocal reputation who may be mixed up in the murder. Comedy and drama, light and dark, respectability and criminality ... they're all mixed up together, like life, especially Victorian life.

Black magic? How disconcerting that Stapleton already knows Watson and then knows his connection to Sherlock Holmes. And how is it that Miss Stapleton can be left behind at her cottage, then materialize ahead of Watson on the path? Yes, yes, a shortcut, but it just adds to the unease. Watson is very uneasy. Things seem to be building to a head, but there are no answers. Who is the mysterious figure on the tor? How does LL fit in? It's time we got Sherlock Holmes back to straighten everything out.

And finally a word about anxious Watson, who yearns for Holmes's return, and also for his favour. "You must acknowledge, my dear Holmes, that I have done you very well in the matter of a report," he says of one night's adventures. Poor Watson, always looking for approval, and seldom getting it. Like the child of a stern parent. So perhaps they are not siblings after all.

The Hound of the Baskervilles
Part Three (the last five chapters)

Father and Son: Yes, as I was suggesting in the last set of musings, I have finally concluded that this is the nature of the Holmes-Watson relationship. Holmes is the stern parent and Watson is the anxious child constantly seeking approval. When he finds out that Holmes has been getting independent reports from the boy Cartwright, he wails, saying, Then mine were all useless.

Now, now, says Holmes, don't say that; yours were very valuable too: see how well-thumbed they are? Later Holmes says once again how valuable Watson's inquiries were, but adds that he'd figured it out by himself anyway. Sigh.*

Watson also sometimes wants to hand things over to Holmes. What a relief from the responsibility of it all when Holmes shows up: "… the responsibility and the mystery were both becoming too much for my nerves," he says, happy to have Holmes take over. And the moral is: Don't make the sidekick run the show; it's not good for anyone, including the sidekick.

Speaking of shows and morality, what exactly is going on here? So Stapleton is actually a Baskerville, a throwback to the original Sir Hugo. Lots of throwbacks here, as the critic Joseph Kestner remarks, especially if you consider the primitive huts. Is there some primitive savagery lurking in the breast of this Baskerville descendant harking back to the wicked Hugo? And what about the parallels between Holmes and Stapleton? They are both first-rate minds, worthy

---

* All a man needs, says Holmes, is a loaf of bread and a clean collar: "What does man want more?" Well, appreciation, that's what man wants more.

antagonists, busy on the moor (and don't forget Selden the convict there too).

The moor, the moor: The chaos that lurks next to civilization. And the fog. Though something has gone overboard with the fog: it's a white woolly plain, an ice-field, a dense white sea, a curtain. Metaphors gone wild. Does this suggest the overheated fears of those confronted with the unknown?

Nets: The nets are perhaps more interesting. There's Stapleton with his butterfly net and Holmes with his metaphorical fishing net in which to catch Stapleton (but does he?), and then there's the net Dr. Watson imagines in Chapter 11 when he sees the note about his visit to Coombe Tracey. He the tracker has been tracked. Someone is following him, an unseen force, "a fine net drawn round us with infinite skill and delicacy, holding us so lightly that it was only at some supreme moment that one realized that one was indeed entangled in its meshes."

Watson is imagining the criminal as the force, but it could be all of life's machinery, or the nature of crime, or ... Actually, it turns out to be Sherlock Holmes; he's the one keeping an eye on Watson (like a good parent?). But it's interesting to think of the way heroes and villains can resort to the same tools: Are you being watched for good or for ill? Are you tracking through the moor for good or for ill? Are you using a net for good or for ill?

Hypocrisy: Frankland is always good for comic relief. Here we find him rejoicing over winning a case granting him right of way over someone else's property while at the same time vowing not to let outsiders come onto his property. Ha, ha. But is there more to it than that? Is this what civilization has come to as the new century dawns: petty legal squabbles? Joseph Kestner talks of a moral decay that in the story can be reversed by a return to old traditions of aristocracy. Can the Baskerville estate be reformed, or will we have to be content with Sir Henry leaving the country?

Sir Henry had already spent most of his life outside the country, just as Stapleton had come from another country. North America and South America. Is England being supplanted: will other countries contest for domination? But perhaps this is too much hindsight.

And what about the women? Used and abused? Or willing accomplices? Or a bit of both? And these abortive romances: there's Sir Henry wooing Stapleton's "sister," but it turns out she's already married (to Stapleton). And then the married Stapleton pursues Laura Lyons pretending to be single; of course, she's married too. I think of Conan Doyle's first marriage and his wanting to woo someone else. Or is it broader than that? Is romance a trap that leads you into the mire? Stapleton wants to use it that way, to lure first Sir Charles and then Sir Henry. And why is there no happy romantic ending? Why does Sir Henry go off with Dr. Mortimer?

The client always dies: Or almost dies. It was a close thing this time, and Holmes is suitably apologetic, but really the point is seldom to save a life; it's to solve a crime: if Sir Henry had died, that would hardly have mattered. Though I note here that in this story the final climactic action has nothing to do with solving the crime; that was done in Chapter 12, when Holmes reappears and announces, It's Stapleton. The next two chapters are just about proving the crime: not the same thing at all and perhaps a bit of an anti-climax, though yes, I know, isn't the hellhound exciting (yawn) ... a cheap trick with phosphorus. There is nothing supernatural here (except perhaps for the moan of Selden's soul leaving his body); it's all faux supernatural: no knightly battles, just legal squabbles, and no hounds from hell, just a hound daubed in phosphorus.

Holmes boasting: So Holmes can distinguish 75 different scents, and they tell him in this case that ... a lady is involved. Wow. And he talks about how this case will impress others. Hmm. Time to wrap this up and get him back to work. He needs a case to work on, not one to gloat over. And a whole chapter to explain what happened? Sigh. The author doth explain too much, methinks, perhaps because in reality there are things left hanging: What happened to Stapleton? What will happen to Baskerville Hall? What will happen to the women? Will Sir Henry and Dr. Mortimer get married?

For a story in which things are supposed to be put back in order, things are actually left a little disordered, which Kestner says reflects the doubts afflicting England as it entered a new century and a new reign.

But there are more stories to come. Though Holmes says that what a man may do in the future is a hard question to answer, in this case we know the answer. Holmes and Watson have more than 30 cases still to work on; perhaps they will bring us some order.

The Empty House

Killing Him Softly: *I had seen birth and death and thought they were different,* says the speaker in a poem by T.S. Eliot. "The Empty House" is a sort of birth, a rebirth, and yet how full of death is it. Here is Holmes returned from the watery grave looking as pale as a spirit, giving Dr. Watson the greatest shock of his entire life, but a shock of joy, he says, and yet ... It's a story all about death, isn't it? Reluctantly, Conan Doyle has brought his famous sleuth back to life, but it's almost as if he would like to kill him off again.

The whole story, almost, is about shooting a dummy of Holmes. And how excited Moran is to do it, gripped with enthusiasm, going rigid with excitement, then letting out a little sigh of satisfaction when he's done. But Holmes isn't actually dead – to Moran's great disappointment. For a moment there, Holmes is just an object to be shot at; the focus is on his would-be killer; the point of view is his. We are away from Holmes, as we have been for years; isn't it glorious? But no, Holmes is there, pouncing like a tiger, making his dismissive gibes – at Moran, at Watson, even at the police.

Enough. Wasn't it enough to do two novels and two sets of stories? But no, the public demanded more, and so we have to bring Holmes back, though we do so in a story where we get to, almost, kill him again. Ah, well.

Rebirth and transformation? Holmes has been away, as if on a spiritual journey, as far as Tibet, talking to a lama, then to Mecca, the holy place of Islam, and off to Khartoum, and elsewhere. He's away for years; it's the hero's journey, on which he should return a changed man – but he doesn't.[*] It's

---

[*] I have not forgotten the Cornish boatman who said Holmes came back from Reichenbach a changed man, but he meant in the sense of not being as skilled anymore. I'm talking about character and personality.

the same old Holmes, full of asperity, though minus his parlour tricks, it's true, and not detecting yet. No, this is another thriller: Holmes on the run, as in "The Final Problem," being pursued, though laying a trap for his pursuers.

But why all the trappings of spiritual crisis and development when there is actually none? Did Doyle hope to transform his hero and just fail? Does he want to show that it's the same old Holmes despite the spiritual journeying? Is it all a thumbing of the nose at the conventions, or at the public who forced him to bring Holmes back?

Or is there some great spiritual change that we're missing?

We can look for clues in the books Holmes the bookseller carries: *British Birds*, *Catullus*, *The Holy War*, and most intriguingly, tantalizingly: *The Origin of Tree Worship*. What indeed is the origin of tree worship, and why should Holmes be interested in it? Or why should Doyle give him that book to carry? What does it signify, tree worship? I cudgel my brains: trees produce paper, paper gives us books and stories, Sherlock Holmes stories; is this about worshipping Sherlock Holmes? It seems a stretch. Is it about weird faiths? Like worshipping Sherlock Holmes? Is Doyle mocking those who would idolize strange, undeserving things?

And then Catullus, the love poet, mixed in with birds and war. Love, war, death, birds – and trees, of course. What does it all mean? Maybe nothing, maybe it is empty of meaning. This is the Empty House, after all: maybe Doyle has brought back the mere shell of his man, an empty man, a signifier signifying nothing. (But we know he has some good stories left in him; this is just the feeling of the moment, the feeling that he has to bring Holmes back even though he has nothing left to say through him. Perhaps.)

And the rocks: I almost forgot: besides shooting at him with an airgun, Colonel Moran hurls rocks at Sherlock Holmes. It feels very mythic, like out of an ancient Greek story. And of course it's another way to kill our hero, and in such a powerful way: rocks cast down from above. Punishment from the heavens for daring to survive.

Watson's bereavement: Watson's bereavement, presumably the death of Mrs. Watson, is almost a cheery note. The gesture towards grown-up living, marriage, domesticity – that can all be forgotten now. Watson and Holmes can be adventuring boys again, and will be. So perhaps Conan Doyle is getting into this now, remembering the fun of adventure, and removing an obstacle to it (not that she was a very strong obstacle to it). Holmes and Watson will be able to take up lodgings together again, just like old times.

Just like old times, Holmes suggests in hoping he can still amaze Watson. And even though he's amazing him through creating a lifelike dummy rather than in apparently reading his mind, maybe there is a hint that the good old Watson-Holmes interaction will be back, and perhaps even Conan Doyle can appreciate that.

Holmes as a dummy: Now there's a joke at Holmes's expense; the brilliant detective becomes a dummy. More of Conan Doyle's revenge, and yet of course Holmes is back; there may yet be good times ahead.

The Norwood Builder

The Curious Incident of the Physician in the Dark: Which I suppose could refer to either Dr. Watson himself or to Dr. Verner, who is given money by Holmes to enable him to buy Watson's practice, all to enable Watson to move back in with his old companion. Holmes talks of there being two singular incidents in this story, but really this is a third: why does he go to such lengths to get Watson back to Baker Street?

My first thought was to think what reason Holmes might have to do this. To ensure the stories get recorded? To get an admiring audience on hand? But he can always win applause from the police; he has no need of Watson. And he doesn't even want the stories published; or so he says from time to time. Maybe it's for companionship or to have a lesser light to shine in comparison to, or maybe Watson's bumblings inspire him ...

But I began to think I was looking at this the wrong way. Maybe it's not so much that Holmes needs them to be together; maybe it's the stories that need them together. Holmes and Watson in Baker Street; that's the iconic arrangement. Conan Doyle needs them back together, and he even seems to need to emphasize the importance of this by introducing the far-fetched story of Holmes paying Verner to pay Watson.

And another curious incident: Sherlock Holmes gets discouraged in this story. When was Holmes ever discouraged before?[*] And why should he be so discouraged? The facts are against us, Watson, he says, but are they? McFarlane's mother hates Jonas Oldacre: is that a fact proving murder? Of course, Lestrade thinks the facts are on his side too. Look at the motive, look at the opportunity: isn't it obvious? "A trifle too

---

[*] Well, he does get a bit discouraged, briefly, in *The Sign of the Four*.

obvious," says Holmes (before he gets discouraged). Now, this is Holmes the believer in facts, details ("I pay a good deal of attention to matters of detail," he says, and there's no reason not to believe him).

And yet here he feels his instincts going against the details. And the details seem overwhelmingly to support the other side (Lestrade's side), or so Holmes says, though I don't believe him. So again why? Why does the story set things up this way? Surely to emphasize the importance of instincts. Doyle seems to want to create a situation in which you have to trust your instincts (or Holmes has to trust his instincts) against the apparent evidence. This is not the same as theorizing without evidence, I don't think. It's not like that silly theory about a tramp or any of the other five theories Holmes says he could produce; it's not about sitting down rationally and coming up with an alternative to the obvious explanation. It's about following one's instincts, being an artist, one might say, knowing when the obvious is a trifle too obvious, letting one's active sense of disbelief have full play.

Like an artist: Holmes essentially calls Oldacre a failed artist, not knowing when to stop, adding just one final touch to his masterpiece and thus undoing the whole thing by trying to make it even better. Holmes is the true artist here, even in his discouragement, maybe especially in his discouragement as he agonizes over the disconnect between what he knows in his bones to be true and what the facts seem to tell him.

Holmes and Lestrade: When Lestrade bursts in ready to seize Holmes's client, I thought, Oh, like something out of Nero Wolfe: private detective versus the official police, antagonism, the whole school of hardboiled private eyes and hostile officialdom. But Lestrade quickly gives way; they are quite cordial, really; these stories belong to a different school. There is of course rivalry between Holmes and the policeman, but a friendly rivalry, and in the end Lestrade is most appreciative, like a child before a teacher ... (wait, I thought that was Watson's role; well, maybe Watson is the child before his father; Watson is the son, and Lestrade is the pupil).

Anyway, Lestrade is appreciative, and not just at seeing a good trick, but because his reputation is barely saved. Reputation, reputation, reputation: it is a driving force in these stories, usually for the criminals, but in this case we see that even policemen care about it.

The great god Moriarty is dead: And what a loss it is to poor Sherlock: where will he find crimes now? In the past, he says, he could see Moriarty's hand in everything, as if everything criminal stemmed from him, but now ... nothing, and London is much more boring. One might think that a criminologist would want to abolish crime, but of course: no more crime, no more crime-solving, and crime-solving is what Holmes lives for. Abolish crime? Not he. Luckily, then, it turns out there can still be crime after Moriarty (just as it could never have been true that all the previous crimes of the canon had been orchestrated by that foul spider: an interesting notion, to be sure, comforting in its way: now we can explain all criminality, just by reference to Moriarty, but life is seldom so simple, nor canons either).

Do you need to relax? Have a cigarette: At least that's Sherlock Holmes's prescription for frantic McFarlane. The times were rather different.

And the real motive: Sexual jealousy. A spurned lover. Hell hath no fury like an Oldacre scorned, that ferret-like little man; you can tell he was evil just from his looks (there's that physiognomy again).

Parlour tricks: Some would dismiss the Sherlockian identification game (I see you are a bachelor, a solicitor, a Freemason, and an asthmatic), and true, even Watson can see how it's done now, and after all how does it help solve the crime? But it makes Holmes look like a genius, that's the point. Usually in comparison with slow-witted Watson. The contrast is essential not to solving crimes but to setting up the yin and yang of the stories, the Holmes-Watson partnership, which Doyle is at such pains to re-establish here. We only know it's Holmes because he can do such things; the rational mind might object, but the instincts know the parlour tricks belong.

It's the same with deducing that the will was written on a train: what does it matter, except to show Holmes's genius? Well, perhaps it also shows Oldacre came up with this at the last minute, which shows that the murder plot was an afterthought, and yet so deeply motivated. A paradox.

The Dancing Men

Simple Remedies: Could just put the farm lads in the shrubbery, says honest, noble Hilton Cubitt, and beat the dark creature when he comes to deposit his notes. "I fear it is too deep a case for such simple remedies," says Holmes, though he proposed a simple remedy himself early on, suggesting that Cubitt simply ask his wife what is going on.

Of course, at the end, with his wife in a coma, it's impossible to ask what's going on, so it is up to Holmes to decipher the Dancing Figures ... and why dancing? are they really dancing? They look like hieroglyphics out of ancient Egypt, suggesting ... well, what? Or they are just children's stick figures, and this is all just a childish prank, but it terrifies poor Elsie, the silent woman in the story, who gets to say just one word: Never.

Never: We're in the land of love triangles again, though that only becomes clear at the end. This is Conan Doyle's love triangle period, no doubt reflecting the agony of his being married to one very ill woman while falling in love with another. He does tend to turn the triangles inside out, though: two men and one woman rather than the way it was in life. And the woman here says Never! She will be true to the man she married, though we can note that she was also engaged to the other – and broke that off. Well, I suppose marriage is more than engagement, but it's hard being betrothed to two. Still, if only she had spoken up.

Failure to communicate: That's what we have here. If only Elsie had spoken, but she couldn't somehow. The critic Alastair Fowler blames the English system of secrecy (though of course Elsie was not English) or Hilton Cubitt for his pride in his honour, which Elsie didn't want to jeopardize. And of course the telegram is delayed in coming from America, and Holmes delays ...

Oh, Holmes, why did you wait? If only he had acted, or communicated! Instead, not for the first time, he fails to prevent a crime. He solves it, it's true, and isn't this what these stories are all about? If the crimes were prevented, would there be a story left to tell? And if the crimes were prevented, would the stories grab us as they do? There's dark tragedy here, but perhaps that is the point. This is the universe according to Doyle, and the best we can do is a post-mortem after the fact. There are no simple remedies; there is no direct answer; it's just a mysterious fog which we only pierce when it's too late.

And discover what? That a Chicago crook/grieving lover/stalker is the one behind all this. The most dangerous crook in Chicago, we're told, but still: rather an anti-climax. But then aren't all climaxes like that? It's the journey that matters, and the mystery. When you explain the mystery, it seems rather ho-hum, like explaining how you can tell that Watson has decided not to invest in the South African gold fields. When you have just the mystery, it's, well, mysterious. How can Holmes know? But when it's explained, as Holmes says, it's seen as mere child's play. Ah, the world.

Hilton Cubitt's fault? Shoot first, ask questions after. A very American credo which, oddly, is what Cubitt follows here, much to his own detriment. Ah, well, to know all may not be to pardon all, but it might save a few murders. But it might also kill the mystery of life: and when we're in the midst of life, maybe it's all one big mystery. Which would be why we enjoy these stories, which plunge us into mysteries – and then solve them for us. Yes. Though leaving us thinking, Is that all there is? Is that all there was to it? Maybe we'd have been better off left in the dark. Or not.

Friend Watson: Has anyone speculated that Holmes was a secret Quaker? Twice in this story he addresses his companion as "Friend Watson," and once he refers to him as "my friend, Dr. Watson." So they're friends now. Though at the very beginning of the story Holmes lectures Watson like a professor. And in earlier stories I suggested there's a father-son relationship here, and professor-student would be similar, but then suddenly it's "Friend Watson." Not that they're the sort of friends who share secrets: at least Holmes won't share his secrets with Watson. He likes his little mysteries.

Out of America: Always something dark out of America. If it's not Mormons, it's Chicago gangsters. And if not America, then Australia or who knows where? Our placid English countryside gets disrupted by old crimes from the New World. Very odd that. Old England, with its pure fresh air (though in decline: those lonely churches speaking of glories now past). Sometimes foreign lands seem to send fresh blood: Italians with their naval treaties. But sometimes they send destruction. Maybe they're just dark and powerful, and can be for good or evil. The Dancing Men can be put to good uses, Holmes demonstrates; fire can be good or evil (as we learned in "The Norwood Builder").

And the countryside: Doesn't Holmes say that the countryside harbours more crime than dark foggy London? Well, here's another example. Perhaps London is inoculated, so the innocent country people are the ones more likely to fall victim. And perhaps Holmes has to come from dark foggy London, knowing crime, so as to be able to ferret it out. Set a thief to catch a thief, and all that. Not that Holmes is a thief, of course, or a criminal, and yet ... You need someone who knows the criminal world to catch criminals. Detectives and criminals, doctors and germs – they are all one.

Boastful or humble? I've written scores of monographs on ciphers, says Holmes, vaunting a bit, and yet he also says, when Inspector Martin expects him to have new evidence, "I have only the evidence of the dancing men." It sounds almost plaintive (Hilton Cubitt was plaintive too in wishing his wife would trust him enough to talk to him about the goings-on, but all we have is the Dancing Men). And yet that is enough in a way. The world keeps things from us, but perhaps gives us enough to let us figure things out. Though one wishes it would let us prevent some tragedies too.

The Solitary Cyclist
Adultery and the Solitary Cyclist[*]

"Then there was the curious incident of the fiancé in the story."
"But the fiancé did nothing in the story."
"That was the curious incident."

Indeed. Why is there a fiancé in "The Adventure of the Solitary Cyclist"? What is the purpose of Cyril Morton? Why did Conan Doyle put him in the story? Why not make Violet Smith unattached?

Or perhaps that's the wrong way to phrase the question, assuming that such decisions are conscious. Why, then, should the story have occurred to Conan Doyle as being about an engaged young woman? Why did she have to have a fiancé, yet one who does nothing?

Cyril Morton, the fiancé in question, is mentioned early in the story, when Violet explains her odd situation of being regularly pursued by a deferential or bashful – but certainly mysterious – cyclist. However, does she turn to her fiancé for assistance in this matter? No; she goes to Sherlock Holmes. Once things are settled, Violet returns to her fiancé and marries him; but prior to this he is off in Coventry, doing nothing. Sent to Coventry, as the expression goes, you might say: exiled.

Is this because Conan Doyle has something against fiancés? Two other stories in the canon come to mind: both "The Speckled Band" and "The Copper Beeches" contain fiancés who are away from the main action; in the latter case the young man in question does step in and save his young lady at the end, although this is not the focus of the plot. Of

---

[*]   Long before I started my Musings, I wrote this essay for the Spring 2007 issue of the Petrels' magazine, the *Petrel Flyer*. It was republished in *Canadian Holmes*, the magazine of the Bootmakers of Toronto, in Summer 2007 under the title "The Mystery of the Missing Fiancé."

course, in order for the Sherlock Holmes stories to work, it's necessary that Holmes do the rescuing. There can't be eager young fiancés around saving the damsels in distress, or what will there be for Holmes to do? There is, however, more to it than that in "The Solitary Cyclist."

It is useful to look at what actually happens in the story in order to get a clue as to what might be happening deep below the surface. Violet Smith is hired, in mysterious circumstances, by Bob Carruthers, who falls in love with her and proposes marriage. At the same time she is virtually assaulted by a friend of Carruthers', Jack Woodley, who makes unwanted advances towards Violet and finally forces a kiss on her before subjecting her to a forced marriage. In the meantime, Holmes himself seems smitten by Miss Smith, taking her hand on the flimsiest of pretenses, praising her spiritual-looking face, and remarking how natural it is for a woman such as her to have admirers. Watson, too, appears to be under her spell, speaking of how beautiful and graceful she is, and the two men literally run to her defence when Woodley threatens her. Yet Violet Smith is, throughout all this, engaged to be married, so cannot accept even the proper advances of Carruthers, still less the violent ones of Roaring Jack Woodley, or the more suppressed feelings of Holmes and Watson.

At one level the story seems, in fact, to be all about suppressed advances or desires. A Jungian psychologist would have a field day with Roaring Jack, who is reminiscent of another dark creature from the late Victorian period, Edward Hyde, the incarnation of all the dark instincts Henry Jekyll has long suppressed. When Jekyll looses those instincts, letting Mr. Hyde emerge, he does indeed come out "roaring."

In any case, what emerges in "The Solitary Cyclist" is a study in frustration and male desire, with Conan Doyle examining the two sides of that desire in Jack Woodley and

Bob Carruthers. Woodley is the violent brute forcing his affections upon women, and the forced marriage at the end of the story seems a euphemistic presentation of a rape. Carruthers, in contrast, is the polite face of male desire, all propriety and protectiveness; yet even his protectiveness leads to him seeming threatening when he mounts distant guard on his bicycle, frightening the woman he wants to protect to such an extent that she feels the need to consult someone, although that person is a detective, not her fiancé. The latter is out of the picture – at least on the surface – but his background presence is what prohibits even a proper expression of male desire, just as the presence of Conan Doyle's first wife prevented him from expressing fully his desire for the woman who would eventually become his second wife.

Out of these murky psychological depths comes the notion that any male desire must somehow be tainted. Carruthers protests his love for Violet Smith, but Watson correctly notes that his love was selfish. Carruthers agrees in a way, saying that love often goes together with selfishness: an odd view to take, unless one is feeling so guilty over an illicit love that any love seems selfish.

What appears to be going on in the story, then, is that Conan Doyle is exploring the varieties of male desire, while at the same time suggesting that while there is, of course, some difference between the brutish advances of a Jack Woodley and the polite ones of a Bob Carruthers, in some ways all male desire is the same, all love is selfish, all men – even when trying to be protective – look like dangerous bearded brutes.

This is not to say that this view of male desire is true, or even that Conan Doyle always believed it. But at the time he wrote "The Solitary Cyclist" – a time when his desire for one woman was frustrated by his marriage to a wife who could not be a wife – this seems to have been his feeling. All desire, or all new desire, is forbidden, the story seems to say, because the object of that desire is committed elsewhere to a fiancé who may not be able to act the part, but who still has a claim which may not be challenged.

This is why the fiancé does nothing in the story. It is his role to be a doer of nothing who is important only because his existence prevents others from doing what he should be doing: loving and protecting a woman. Cyril Morton in "The Solitary Cyclist" is thus a strange representation of Conan Doyle's first wife, whose presence prevented him from expressing his romantic desires for another woman. Once put this way, of course, it seems so obvious as to be elementary.

The Priory School

Musings of Dr. Sheldon Goldfarb, BA, MA, MAS, PhD, etc.

Priory? First of all, what is a Priory School? I've looked up "priory," and it means monastery or convent, but that can't be what we have here in Victorian England. Perhaps it means there used to be a monastery on the spot? And it is a boys' school, so a bit monastic perhaps: and with lurid goings-on as in an old Gothic, like for instance *The Monk.* But still.

And who is the Priory Schoolmaster? A question of moment to me since I have assumed the title. In the story both Thorneycroft Huxtable, that pompous fool, and the German master who gets murdered have the title of schoolmaster applied to them. Not sure either is a good role model to follow. I will certainly not go speeding across moors on my bicycle. (Not that I have a bicycle or know where the nearest moor is.)

Moors and Bicycles: Common motifs at this point in the canon. Doyle does like to take us to barren places, and lately he has become interested in cycling. Not sure if that means anything.

Nasty Aristocrats: That's another common motif, though the Duke at first seems pleasant enough, more so than his secretary, though of course the secretary turns out to be his illegitimate son, and thus from the same class, just a bastardized version of it, you might say. (Who was his mother, by the way? Oh, dear, I'll be turning into a Great Game Sherlockian soon.)

But at the end certainly the Duke is rather nasty in wanting to hush up his illegitimate son's involvement in the kidnapping of his legitimate son, and also in that murder of poor Heidegger. Poor Heidegger. But why did he set off after the young heir? He didn't even know him. Not a good thing to be a Good Samaritan, apparently. This story is full of questions.

Names: We don't have to worry about Heidegger the German philosopher because he's twentieth century, but Wilder is an apt name for the illegitimate son (as Joseph Kestner says). Wilder than whom, though? His father? The legitimate heir? And the legitimate heir is named Arthur! How many Arthurs are there in the canon?[*] Poor Arthur, kidnapped and never seen, just like the unseen presence behind Holmes and Watson. How often does an author name a character after himself, and what can that mean? Certainly, Holmes's main concern at the end is to protect young Arthur. Beyond that he is content to let James Wilder go free and hush up the involvement of the Duke. But we must save Arthur, though from whom? Reuben Hayes is under arrest, James Wilder is on his way to Australia; all that's left at the Inn is the kindly wife of Hayes. But one can imagine that someone named Arthur would want to protect someone else named Arthur: save him from harm and get his parents back together.

Money: Holmes doesn't usually care about money, but here he seems eager for it. Is that just a way to get at the Duke? He won't report him to the police, but he'll take his money. Hmm. Odd.

---

[*] More than I thought, actually. Donald Redmond says there are eight. Most of them are quite positive characters, either heroes or sympathetic victims (or both, like Arthur Cadogan West in "The Bruce-Partington Plans" and Arthur Holder in "The Beryl Coronet"). There's also the falsely accused Arthur Charpentier in *Study in Scarlet*. The most prominent villain among them is Arthur Pinner in "The Stockbroker's Clerk," but I note that Arthur is not his real name.

The gypsies did it: No, of course they didn't. It's never the gypsies (or the butler).[*] Some critics say the Holmes stories reflect fear of the foreign, but sometimes they mock that fear. In "The Naval Treaty" there's almost a celebration of things Italian, and here the "foreign" gypsies are perfectly innocent, while the German character is the well-intentioned victim. We need foreigners to help us, but here we go bashing them over the head. Is that what the story is saying? Be kind to foreigners? It's the hereditary Duke and his illegitimate son who are the dangers, and also Reuben Hayes, none of whom I think are foreign, though the name Reuben is suggestive: Old Testament after all, but still I think we have homegrown villains here, especially aristocrats. They're often the villains in the canon.

Children: That's uncommon, though: the focus on a child. There's even a reference to a children's game: Holmes talks of getting warmer or colder when leaving or approaching the Inn, "as the children say," says Holmes. Are there other children in the canon? Not that young Arthur quite makes it into the canon, being unseen and unheard throughout the story. Still. A concern for children. Quite unusual. I once reproached the author of a Sherlockian pastiche for writing a story in which Holmes is very concerned to rescue boys at a school: Holmes never cares about youngsters, I said, but I'd forgotten this story.

And there's the grimy stable boy. For a moment I thought he might be young Lord Saltire in disguise, and now I pause to think: why after all is the stable boy there? Is it to suggest the sort of thing the young lord might be forced into? The horror, the degradation. Is that what Holmes thinks young Arthur needs rescuing from, the decline into servitude? The

---

[*] Well, it is the butler in "The Musgrave Ritual." But it's never the gypsies. Sometimes it's foreigners, but other times they're just innocents wrongly accused.

canon after all is full of stories about respectable people fearing they will be dragged down by some disreputable secret from their past. Is this story expressing a fear that a young lord could be dragged into the muck by the disreputable past activities of his father?

The past: Yes, there is something to dwell on. Some unfortunate passage in the Duke's past life has produced a serious threat to young Arthur. So it is the standard canonical motif after all. You may be a lord now, young Arthur, but someone could come along to snatch you away from all that and maybe deprive you of your inheritance. In other stories it is this threatened character who is likely to turn murderer or murder victim; young Arthur is lucky to get off with a kidnapping, while it is the German Good Samaritan who dies trying to save him.

Moving on from the past: So we have a priory school, conjuring up the monastic past, and an old aristocratic title, and a schoolmaster who writes about Horace and who ends up collapsing in the parlour at Baker Street. How the mighty are fallen, how the past has decayed, how worrying about inheritance leads into crime. Is this the message? And maybe it's time to transfer money from the decaying aristocracy to the self-made men of the middle class, the detectives, for instance. And finally remember to protect the children, especially the ones named Arthur.

Black Peter

Another Curious Incident: This time the curious incident of the interesting client. But there is no interesting client in "Black Peter." In fact no client at all. And that is the curious incident. How many stories in the canon lack a client? In this case the police summon Holmes. Does that happen often?

It's not quite the same as a distraught or puzzled client throwing themselves at the feet of Sherlock Holmes, begging for help, though I suppose Inspector Hopkins does something similar. In earlier stories I talked of a pupil-master relationship between Watson and Holmes; here it's quite explicitly stated that there is such a relationship between Hopkins and the Master.

But Hopkins is an uppity pupil at times. We didn't need you after all, Mr. Holmes, he says when he thinks he has cracked the case on his own. But he's wrong. In the end we need Holmesian deduction and brilliance: mere mortals can't compete.

Doubles: Peter Carey and Patrick Cairns: two PC's, two seamen. Why? And note the doubling of motives: young Neligan and old Patrick both are after Black Peter because of what happened with Neligan Sr. And in both cases there's something disreputable in the past that's come up in the present: the banker absconding with the stocks and the whaler killing the banker. It's common in the canon for scandal to rise up like this, but two scandals?

Hoist with his own ... I note that Black Peter is killed with his own harpoon, and then left pinned to the wall like a beetle, a biological specimen, for us to conclude ... what? Those who live by the harpoon will die by it? Not that he killed Neligan Sr. with a harpoon. Still, a violent end for a violent man. Do we usually see that in the canon? And it's almost as if he's killed himself, or been killed by his mirror image: the dark side of human nature collapsing upon itself perhaps, while meek and mild Neligan Jr. does ... well, what?

Young Neligan: He should have been the client, so unsure of himself, and then perhaps suspected; that would fit the pattern. But instead we just have Hopkins at the start, and Holmes and Hopkins venture out into the world trying to solve the problem, with Hopkins settling on the weak man as the probable culprit while Holmes says, How could such a milquetoast have driven a harpoon through a man and into a wall? No, you need someone powerful, another harpooner, a spare harpooner ... Yes, we have the main harpooner and a spare. It does turn out to be the powerful dark forces that produce the criminal: is that always the way in the canon? The weak are the victims or perhaps the detectives ... Besides the doubling of the initials PC, there is a tripling of H's in the story: Holmes, of course, plus Hopkins plus John *Hopley* Neligan.

Hopley-Hopkins-Holmes: What can that mean? Versus Carey-Cairns. Weak versus strong? And where does Watson fit? Hapless Hopley wants to clear his father's name. Greedy Cairns wants to profit from the situation, as Carey had already profited: I presume he profited, except if he didn't sell the securities until recently, how did he buy his house and cabin in Woodman's Lee? But if he did sell some years before why didn't the Neligan family notice then? Ah, well. Greed gets punished, and the banker's name – well, it's not even mentioned at the end; it was all rather a red herring: two motives for the crime, but only one was acted on, the other just being the distraction that led Inspector Hopkins astray. And might have led Holmes astray too, but luckily he didn't have that notebook to begin with and concentrated instead on stabbing pigs with harpoons. There were two opportunities, and two motives, but only one means: the harpoon and the strength to wield it, so even after learning of the notebook Holmes could not accept John Hopley as the guilty one.

And the moral? Two motives are better than one? No, that can't be it, though Holmes almost says so in talking of the need to look to alternatives – but he doesn't mean both motives produced the crime.

And Norway? Why does the banker flee to Norway? What does Norway signify? The land of the Vikings? And he seems to have encountered a Viking (Black Peter) on his way. And why will Holmes go to Norway? There's nothing left to find there, surely. The banker drowned on the way, the tin box of securities is back in England ... To retrace the banker's footsteps? To seek out more "Vikings"? Perhaps Holmes is always seeking Vikings and trying to thwart their crimes, or at least solve them afterwards.

Keeping us in the dark: Well, perhaps it's fitting that we end with mysteries and Holmes keeping things from us. At the beginning, too, he keeps things from us (and Watson). Of course, all the stories do that, but in this case we don't even know what case Holmes is working on till Inspector Hopkins shows up. Even Watson is in the dark, and says he doesn't like to pry. (Some detective, not wanting to pry, but I suppose Watson is not really the detective. Still, he and the readers usually know about the crime from the beginning: because a client shows up to explain it, only here there is no client: who exactly is Holmes working for? Oh, the police, I suppose. Still, it all seems wrong, and then he has to run off to Norway. With Watson, apparently. Perhaps they seek for new worlds to conquer.)

Holding onto one's theories: Hopkins does so want Neligan to be the guilty one. Not because he has anything against Neligan, but because it's his theory. He resists giving it up until it becomes clear that Holmes is right.

Savage animals: Like hunters at a water-pool, says Watson, they wait for their prey. Will it be a tiger? No, it is Neligan the mere jackal. The tiger shows up later looking for harpoon work. Of course he actually did his work earlier, turning the victim into a beetle, though he began as a tiger too. Tigers become beetles and jackals become ... well, who knows?

Charles Augustus Milverton

Love and war: Why is there a bust of Athene, also known as Athena, in the apartments of Charles Augustus Milverton? Does it signify anything? Is it important that in Poe's famous poem "The Raven" there is also such a bust? Doyle was a great admirer of Poe; was he smuggling in a reference here? A reference to love that is no more, like the loves destroyed by Milverton? Is Milverton a sort of raven?

And what does Athena signify anyway? Wisdom, usually. Is Milverton wise? Knowledgeable, certainly, but certainly not wise, if morality has any part in wisdom. Athena is also a warrior goddess, and goddess of justice. Is there justice in this story? There is certainly war.

Justice: Commentators certainly like to discuss law and justice in this story. Holmes and Watson take the law into their own hands, breaking and entering, fleeing the scene of a crime, obstructing justice ... But that's the law's justice. Revenge against a blackmailer, even if taken vigilante style, is that justice? Or at least justifiable? Do we feel comfortable going along with Holmes and Watson on their little venture into criminality? Do we even feel the zest Watson feels as he and Holmes go out disguised as respectable gentlemen but with housebreaking clothes on underneath?

But wait, they ARE respectable gentlemen. So is the suggestion that under the cloaks of respectability, under our law-abiding exteriors, lurks a desire to break free, or at least break in? Do we sympathize with Holmes as criminal? But aren't all these stories about fighting criminals?

Set a thief to catch a thief, the old proverb says. If I were a proper Sherlockian, I'd speculate on some previous unknown history of Holmes as a criminal. Is that why he can catch them so readily, because really he is one of them? I won't pursue this literally, but detectives and criminals – they're both out on the frontier, on the fringe of respectability, defending our respectability perhaps (at least the detectives may be), but not entirely respectable themselves. Is one aspect of modern society the fight that goes on at the fringes of our consciousness between the forces of order and the forces of crime? Most of us steer well clear of the police and criminals: let them fight it out so that we can have a peaceful time. In that way, is Holmes just a mirror image of the criminals he fights? And especially of genius criminals like Moriarty and now Milverton? Detective, criminal: what's the difference? Men with guns ...

Not your usual story: You will note that the typical opening of a Holmes story comes at the end here. There's a murder to solve, says Inspector Lestrade to Holmes: can you help? This is usually where we come in, but not this time; this time it's the end, and Holmes refuses the case, saying he sympathizes with the criminals – not surprisingly, since the "criminals" are Holmes and Watson! But what other story begins with Holmes refusing a case? Of course, as I say, this story doesn't begin with that; it ends with it. There's no detection; it's all about confronting a criminal whose crime is well known. It's not in the mainstream of the canon, then, but in a sort of sub-genre within it: action, fighting, like the Moriarty stories. It's less about puzzle-solving than about smashing locks.

And women: Them too. Often absent, here they are central. Are all the blackmail victims female? Why is Charles Augustus Milverton picking on women? Are there no men with secrets? But this seems to be a story about damsels in distress, with Holmes as St. George ready to slay the dragon (the safe containing the incriminating letters is even referred to as a dragon) – but note, the dragon is slain not by St. George this time, but by one of the fair ladies. Conan Doyle as proto-feminist, empowering women. Perhaps.

And cats: There's a cat in this story. When Holmes and Watson break in, something rushes at them, giving Watson a start, but it's only the cat. Is this the only cat in the canon? It doesn't even have a name. Ah, poor cat; it rushes out and is not seen again. Some commentators wonder where the avenging lady goes after pumping Milverton full of bullets. Good question, but no one I think has ever asked what happened to the cat.

And reputation: Many of the stories turn on reputation; it's a frequent motive for crime in the canon, but here's a story that focuses directly on the issue. Milverton makes a business out of ruining reputations, or threatening to. What a society Holmes and Watson live in, where everyone is so fearful of the besmirching of their names. Have we moved on from that? Is this just a quaint Victorianism? It certainly animates things in Holmes's world.

And poor Agatha (the housemaid): Courted under false pretences by Holmes in disguise. Some commentators say it's odd that though so concerned to protect fair ladies in this story, Holmes sees nothing wrong with toying with the affections of a serving girl. Is it a class thing? Are we supposed to not care about serving girls? Or is Holmes in the wrong? Watson does have qualms. Watson in fact has qualms about all the dubious things Holmes gets up to in this story, though that doesn't stop him from enjoying some of them (that zest I already mentioned). And he can indulge in philosophical justifications for their law-breaking – but what about the breaking of that poor girl's heart? She'll find someone else, says Holmes.

Breach of promise: One Victorian law was breach of promise, breaking an engagement. There's even a trial over this in *The Pickwick Papers*, and this story compares Milverton to a benevolent Pickwick – except Pickwick is a jovial, friendly type, and Milverton is nothing like that. What an odd comparison, really, except that if you can imagine a criminal Holmes, why not an evil Pickwick? Mirrors and doubles everywhere, and of course the breach of promise: the breaking off of the promised marriage to the housemaid, which parallels the breaking off of the engagement of the woman who comes back to kill Milverton. Will Agatha come after Sherlock (or after Escott the plumber)? Is Holmes no better than Milverton, then? But he doesn't ruin anyone's reputation, so perhaps it's different. Holmes doesn't betray secrets; he protects them, for instance with that bonfire near the end or with his shushing of Watson after that. Still, poor Agatha.

The Six Napoleons

Foreigners: After a couple of stories in which we seem to be told that a declining England, especially a declining British aristocracy, needs an infusion of new blood, perhaps from an Italian treaty, suddenly Italians are the enemy, or perhaps all foreigners, those outcasts who live beyond London (the marvellous London of theatre, fashion, seapower, and the like). Now where there were once rich City merchants there are tenement houses reeking and sweating with ape-like creatures like Beppo.

But is it really about foreigners? Lestrade thinks the Mafia is behind the crime. Then there's Morse Hudson (good English name that: why, it's the same as the housekeeper's) ... Anyway, this solid English citizen, the bust retailer, blames red Republicans, Anarchists, Nihilists, foreign political groups. It turns out that Hudson and Lestrade are wrong; this is not a political crime (and even the Mafia for Lestrade is a secret political society); this is about a stolen pearl. But even so, what a story we have here about dangerous, unpleasant foreign elements in conflict with good upstanding Brits, taking over from solid City merchants ... Why, it's as if the theme of the story was Make Britain Great Again. Actually, that is the theme of several of the stories, as I have suggested, but in other stories the solution seems to lie in what's foreign: here what's foreign is the cause of the problem. It's as if Watson and Conan Doyle were channelling their inner Donald Trump.

And what about those busts? The busts are foreign too, aren't they? And I don't just mean that they are produced at a sculpture works managed by the German Gelder. (A German Gelder? Has he come, as the critic Joseph Kestner suggests, to geld the poor British?) But never mind that or the fact that the sculptor (Devine) is French. Who are these busts of? Yes, yes, it turns out to be a red herring the idea of monomania. Watson as usual is wrong in his theory (that the criminal has a hatred of Napoleon). For the purposes of the plot, as one critic notes, all that is needed is a bust, any bust, in which to secrete the pearl. I suppose it could just as easily have been busts of Shakespeare or Henry VIII.

But it wasn't: No, it's busts of Napoleon, the arch-enemy of England a century before, the foreigner who might have invaded England and created, well, something foreign there. And yet look how popular Napoleon had become. There's Dr. Barnicot, the enthusiastic admirer who purchases two Napoleon busts – though Barnicot: what sort of name is that? Is he French? For that matter what sort of name is Lestrade? These foreigners are everywhere. Is there a hidden xenophobic streak running through this story?

False idols: Holmes notes that there are hundreds of statues of the "great Emperor" in London. Why is that? What is all this fascination with Napoleon? Is he some sort of new cult figure, a god? These particular busts are made by Devine, it's true: are they divine as well as Devine? Well, we can't tolerate the rise of such a false religion: we must turn iconoclast (in the original sense of smasher of idols) and smash the false gods to bits – which indeed the story does, which indeed Sherlock Holmes does most vigorously to the last of the evil six, though only after purchasing it for what its owner feels guiltily is an exorbitant price. Little does he know. But the point is how honourable Mr. Sandeford is: a good honest Brit who must confess that he only paid 15 shillings for the statue. Perhaps not such an honest Brit is Sherlock Holmes himself, who takes care to have Sandeford sign away all rights so he won't have a claim on the pearl. And is Holmes going to keep the pearl for himself? In his safe? I presume he has just taken temporary possession of it for safekeeping, but others have thought otherwise.

Does this mean that once again the respectable have to entrust their safety to someone not totally respectable himself? Perhaps. But oh, those foreigners, they're the main problem. Such an unexpected turn at this stage of the canon (though harking back a bit to *The Sign of the Four* or "The Engineer's Thumb").

It couldn't have been monomania, by the way: More in Dr. Watson's line, says Lestrade, when the thought is of mental disease. But how could it have been a Holmes story then? If we were going to have a casebook of Dr. Watson, it could fit in there. Has there been such a thing among the pastiches? Perhaps something like the TV show House?

Food: There's parsley and butter for you, which has provoked much discussion over whether parsley sinks in butter, and connects to Holmes's view that the trivial is very important.

Violence: There's a crowd, so there must have been violence, Holmes deduces: and what does that say about human nature? Sigh.

Vampires? Poor Horace Harker having his own life's blood sucked out of him. The journalist who's scooped on his own story about the murder on his own doorstep, inexplicably telling the story to other journalists who write it up first, stealing his very essence. But really if your name is going to be Harker, what can you expect? For Harker is the name of two of the victims in Bram Stoker's *Dracula*. Did Conan Doyle draw on his friend's story for this? If only Robert Eighteen-Bisang were here to tell us.[*]

Watson the detective: Though his theory of the case is wrong (of course), Watson at the end is able to "detect" (his word) uneasiness and expectation in Holmes as he awaits the arrival of the final bust. Is the one thing Watson learns in the canon the nature of Holmes, the man behind the mask who actually does have feelings and desires applause? But did he know Holmes would so eagerly strike Napoleon a blow? Well, the eagerness is for the pearl; still, it's important to fight Napoleon and all the other false gods and foreigners, it seems, in order to preserve our England. Or so the story seems to suggest.

---

[*]   Robert Eighteen-Bisang was a member of the Stormy Petrels who specialized in studying Dracula and other vampires. He edited a collection of Conan Doyle's vampire stories.

The Three Students

The rule of three: The Petrels' former schoolmaster, Peter Wood, in his notes to this story pointed to the *three* of the students, like the three little pigs or the three bears in fairy tales or, I might add, the two nasty stepsisters plus Cinderella, or Lear's three daughters, or the three caskets in *The Merchant of Venice,* or for that matter the three-card trick Holmes mentions.

But the thing about all these cases is that there are always two wrong answers and only one correct, or two bad sisters and one good – but here there are two good and one bad. A bit of a reversal. Two of the students are innocent; only one has cheated. And which one?

After the rather anti-foreign excursion in the Six Napoleons, it was a relief to learn that the Indian student is not the culprit. Nor is it the brilliant though wayward McLaren (a sort of Holmesian double? and a Scotsman?).

No, no, it is the solid scholar-athlete, the son of Sir Jabez Gilchrist, a knight and presumably a landed gentleman, who however did manage to ruin himself on the turf (i.e., by gambling on the horses).

This is more in line with previous stories in this era of the canon. It's not the foreigner who's the problem (often quite the contrary); the problem is in some old English family, like that of Sir Jabez Gilchrist.

Another reversal: Often in the canon someone has lived abroad and done something discreditable there, and then there is danger of it coming to light. Here our "hero" has done something discreditable in England and is going to take off for abroad, to purge himself perhaps. Off to serve in the Rhodesian police: hmm. Will that truly improve him? Holmes hopes so: Gilchrist has fallen low but now may rise high. Is this what the sons of the English gentry need to do? It does remind me of the Baskerville family. Reinvigorate yourself by going away. Sounds a bit like the archetypal journey of the hero, and this tale of *three*'s is perhaps a bit in that way.

More three's: Three slips of paper, three pyramids of clay. Pyramids, hmm. Why pyramids? They're really just clumps from the jumping pit, no? Called balls sometimes. But pyramids: very exotic, mystical, distant. Or is it the Knights Templar? There is all this fairy tale stuff around the fringes of the story, though the story itself seems very rational and hard-headed, full of Holmesian deductions (and arrogance).

Did Conan Doyle like puns? Now I will make a slight excursus to wonder why this story has a staircase and a Bannister. I suppose a bannister is something to hold onto if you are in danger of falling, and this particular Bannister does help young Gilchrist when he is in danger, so ...

Good old servants: Yes, the servant Bannister is all right; are servants usually good in the canon? It's their masters to watch out for.

Irritable Holmes: Insulting Watson (well, that's nothing new) and also Hilton Soames. Because he's away from Baker Street. And why are they not in Baker Street? (And yes, not being at home can make one irritable, though one can be irritable at home just as well.) They are off because some combination of events has led them to one of the universities, whose identity must be disguised even in Watson's telling, for fear of scandal, just as Hilton Soames fears scandal at the time. Everything so secretive, hidden, like an eye in a pyramid (I really must stop talking about pyramids). But secrets. A lot in the canon turns on secrets and the need to preserve them. Here we will quietly send Gilchrist off to Rhodesia and no one will know that there was nearly an exam scandal.

An exam scandal? It doesn't really seem like a big deal. There's no murder here. Maybe some money for a scholarship, but really. Perhaps, though, it's the reputation of the college that's at stake. Reputation is a big deal in the canon. To preserve reputation one must preserve secrets. Preserve, repress, hide, keep down. Is this a repressed story? Or a story of repression? Of cheating, yes, and I keep wondering about Miles McLaren, that dissipated card shark and brilliant student, the only one who won't open his door. Up there on the top floor (you'd expect him rather to be on the bottom, in the basement, the mad scientist, the suppressed id), but no ... There he is on the top floor, and when the knock comes, it provokes a torrent of bad language. Go to blazes, he says, I have to study.

Good student. Maybe not as dissolute as all that, whereas Gilchrist has been out at the jumping pit. But yes with a bad temper, perhaps a Holmesian temper: well, Holmes doesn't pour out bad language, but when Hilton Soames first appeared, Holmes told him to go away. More politely than McLaren, of course: perhaps McLaren is a younger Holmes with not even a pretence of civilization about him, whereas Holmes can do a few of the niceties, but underneath is impatient of our slowness when he is so quick to race ahead and find out the criminal. So ...

Things are not what they seem: It's not the foreigner; it's not the rude and angry McLaren. It's good old Gilchrist, of good English upper class stock, who's come from the playing fields of Eton, or the like. It's the good one who's the bad one, so there you go. And maybe, the story may be suggesting, we need to look at those we vaunt up as if good and question whether they are really as good as all that. Maybe we need to get rid of them, ship them off to Rhodesia, and leave our colleges in the hands of the rude and angry brilliant ones and the studious, quiet ones from overseas. Perhaps that's what we need at university, not people who are good at the long jump: those athletic ones, let them become policemen. Holmes at the beginning distinguishes between mental and physical cases. Let the Gilchrists handle the physical, and let the McLarens and Daulat Ras do the creative work that requires brilliance and application (a combination of McLaren and Ras?) rather than expecting it of a long jumper.

The Golden Pince-Nez

Golden?   Okay, so why is the pince-nez golden?   Well, Holmes tells us that it's because its owner is no slatternly type but a lady, though she turns out also to be a revolutionary, a Nihilist, another foreigner. The stories lately seem interested in foreigners. Of course, we don't know that she and Professor Coram are foreign, Russians, till the very end. At first it seems we're being all very British and academic, buried in the past. Holmes even begins the story by looking at a palimpsest from the fifteenth century ...

A palimpsest? Something whose original peeps through from underneath, which could be a symbolic statement of what these stories are all about: finding the hidden, the secret that lurks underneath. And what is the secret here?

It is a very palimpsest of a story, isn't it? On the surface all very proper and English, but underneath the Russian Revolution. (Well, not *the* Russian Revolution, that was a decade in the future, but old style Russian Nihilists out of the nineteenth century; perhaps you've read your Turgenev.) Those foreigners, they're everywhere: are we back in the mindset of the xenophobic Napoleons? But our foreign lady is impressive and noble, commanding and yet admirable.

And then she kills herself: Yes, what? We're moving along, following Holmes in a nice set of deductions in this country house ... Yoxley Old Place, how very British. But as I say it turns out to have a whole long Russian history behind it, and Coram is not Coram but ... well, something else, we don't know the real last name, though the Professor's first name is Sergius, or is that a last name? But Anna, the noble Russian lady, won't reveal his name, she said.

But she kills herself: Yes, I am getting to that. Holmes smokes her out, so to speak, and has essentially solved the crime, the killing of poor Willoughby Smith, which turns out to be no crime but an accident, or is it a crime to kill someone accidentally while you're in the process of committing burglary? And Anna emerges and tells her story, which is odd in itself and in its placement in the story: a very long exposition at the end. But okay, it is interesting, and now we understand, but then ...

She kills herself: Yes, but why? Her original plan was to steal the papers and show them to the Russian authorities to exonerate her lover Alexis. (A touching faith in the Russian authorities, that, but never mind.) When she accidentally kills Willoughby Smith and ends up in her estranged husband's bedroom, her plan is still to slip away once the police have left. But now that they have found her, she kills herself with a convenient phial of poison. She brought no weapon to commit murder, but did bring something for suicide. Odd. Was she planning that all along? Did Anna have to die? Why?

Why does Anna kill herself? If she wants to get the papers to the Russian government, this is a marvellously foolish thing to do. She is forced to rely on Holmes and Watson to deliver them. So why then? Perhaps she does not want to go to jail, because she is an upper class Russian lady who has never seen the inside of a prison – no, that's not right, she's spent years in Siberia.

Perhaps she feels guilty? For killing young Willoughby Smith? But it was an accident. For stealing papers? But they were her papers, and it's in a good cause, to save Alexis, who was innocent of the violence the other Nihilists got up to. Ah, there's the clue perhaps. She and the other Nihilists got up to violence. A police officer was killed. Noble and admirable as Anna is, she was involved in an actual murder: not now, but in the past.

But she served time for that: Yes, but on a deeper level is that enough? Could we let this accessory to murder (and murdering a police officer, an agent of order, of civilization ... note, by the way, that Professor Coram is embarked on a study that will undermine the foundations of revealed religion; he may have betrayed his comrades, but he is still attacking civilization? He's a nasty sort. He's the one who should die. Why doesn't he die? The story is odd, the wrong person dies ...).

So why does Anna have to die? If she hadn't, would she have eventually gone off with her lover Alexis? Wait, Anna was committing adultery, perhaps an even worse crime than murder in 1904. Oh, these adulterous triangles, they torment Doyle so, torn himself between Jean Leckie and Louise. Caught like that, the guilt, the guilt: better just to kill yourself. So Anna's death is symbolically Doyle's own to escape from an adulterous situation? Or it's just because in 1904's England, you can't allow a happy ending to an adulteress who helped kill a policeman?

Or wait, perhaps she feels guilty to have caused Alexis to be imprisoned. If not for their affair, her husband would not have framed him. Or perhaps she even takes responsibility for her husband's actions in betraying the comrades. In the end, it's amazing she didn't kill herself long before: once you scrape off the surface, the palimpsest reveals all. And she is after all a noble, self-sacrificing woman, more ready to kill herself than her husband.

What else? Well, there's Stanley Hopkins (another SH, doubling Holmes? but playing more the bumbling Watson role: "What did you do, Hopkins, after you had made certain that you had made certain of nothing?"). And there's Holmes in an irritable mood, perhaps jealous of Hopkins being on the scene and not calling him in earlier. We had everything there, says Hopkins. Except me, says Holmes. Quite.

And the weather: Nasty, wild, Nature showing she can uproot human civilization? Just like some old Nihilists?

Who's virtuous, then? Not Holmes and Watson. All the virtuous will be in bed, says Holmes, so you get the door, Watson. Our less than respectable agents of respectability who will perhaps go off to the Russian authorities to plead the case of the innocent Nihilist. But should even innocent Nihilists go free? Maybe Anna has to die because she is a Nihilist, and her husband is allowed to live because he has betrayed the Cause? In the end it's actually a bit troubling.

The Missing Three-Quarter

"I thought you knew things": So says rugby star Cyril Overton to our hero Sherlock, who laughs and says yes, but not those things. Not rugby. And we laugh too. You haven't heard of Godfrey Staunton, says Overton? Or me? Me??? Why, I'm one of the biggest star athletes there is. But no, Holmes hasn't heard of him, and we laugh because – well, why? At the vanity of human wishes? At human self-importance? Perhaps.

Vanity: Holmes has his vanities too. His seven schemes to find out who the telegram went to, his superiority to Watson (he's putting him down again), his defensiveness about his profession when Dr. Armstrong questions it. I am a pioneer, he says. Why, he almost sounds like Cyril Overton.

More vanity: Or something. Miserliness, selfishness ... in Lord Mount-James, who is very concerned to protect his precious money, who hilariously says he is sure his nephew wouldn't tell thieves anything about where he keeps it, and oh, I have to move my plate to the bank right away.

Comedy: There's a lot of comedy in this story. As I read the first half of it, I thought, This must be the funniest story in the canon, mostly because of these different worlds that don't understand each other: the world of rugby, the world of detecting, the world of domestic tragedy. Everyone is off in their little world, concerned for themselves, with hilarious results when they collide with someone else's world.

But tragedy: Yes, it all comes to a sudden, tragic end. And not because of any crime. There is no crime. We of course expect a crime. Holmes expects a crime. If you bring a case to a detective, then of course he will seek the crime in it. It would be different if you went to a dentist. But Overton is wrong, Holmes is wrong, we are wrong: there is no crime, just a dying wife, dying of tuberculosis.

Golden lads and lasses must come to dust, as the Bard said. We have all our little vanities and self-importances, about which others can laugh, and then – it's over. Then there's just going out into "the pale sunlight of the winter day." Sigh. One of the saddest endings to a Holmesian story. Not a very Holmesian ending at all. Well, it is in a way: the mystery is explained and now we understand, but what we understand is not some human plot that has been revealed but the nature of life, or death: the fact that we all come to dust.

Sleepy hollows: I note the possible allusion to Washington Irving (the headless horseman story, Legend of Sleepy Hollow). Of course, Holmes could just mean we're in a quiet valley (which I suppose is what a sleepy hollow is), but if there is an allusion, what might that mean? That we're in a story in which it seems something nefarious and even supernatural might be going on – but it really isn't. Like at the beginning, when Dr. Watson worries about the "fiend" of drug mania and wants to bless Overton for providing Holmes with an interesting puzzle to keep him from falling prey to his old vice. Mania, the fiend, blessing – very religious somehow. Are we in that land? And then Holmes has a syringe ... But it's just for aniseed. Things are not that way, though it is true that Holmes needs his stimulation. We need something to energize us, but it needn't be drugs.

Not drugs, not crime: No, none of that, really. Sometimes our imagination seizes on fragmentary bits of information and turns them into headless horsemen when there are really simpler explanations. There's been no kidnapping, no plotted theft, no attempt even to fix an athletic contest (this isn't Silver Blaze). No, it's just life – and death.

And secrets: Yes, those too.   Staunton has to keep his marriage to someone beneath him secret from his uncle for fear of being disinherited.   There's a class slant here, and almost the canonical concern with reputation. But the class thing is all mixed up. Lord Mount-James rides the bus and dresses like a shabby parson. The father of the dying girl can't be pegged down: he is neither gentleman nor workingman. Holmes himself, it is emphasized here, can mix with the humble and win their trust: he is perhaps outside the class system? Watson, too, seems disconnected: so distant from his own profession that he doesn't know Dr. Armstrong, and doesn't even think an illness might be at the heart of things, even when a doctor turns out to be. Watson has become a detective too, far from the regular life of a doctor within the class system.   He and Holmes float through society, pioneers perhaps, guardians, investigators, focused on crime – and thus surprised when they meet a case that contains no crime.

Recognition: They do of course recognize illness when they come right up against it. You can be a famous detective or a great rugby player or a doctor, but you all will be struck down one day.

But after death? I don't mean the after-life or the spirit world. But death is not entirely an end because there are children, new generations – except not for Godfrey Staunton and his unnamed wife.   Joseph Kestner notes that despite Staunton's class transgression, the story makes sure that the inappropriate wife dies, so Staunton can return to his class and presumably father children who will eventually inherit the Mount-James estate. Is the story ensuring that class lines remain in place? Of course, Holmes and Watson seem to have transcended the lines, but is that why they have no children: where would Holmesian and Watsonian children fit in society? Well, I suppose there are always pioneer families, and detectives. Have there been pastiches based on the imagined children of Sherlock Holmes? Sherlock Junior?

Dr. Armstrong: He seems rather fierce. An open and honest antagonist, says Sherlock admiringly; could be as formidable as Moriarty. Hmm. But he's actually helping the poor girl and Godfrey, and becomes friendly with Holmes at the end. Still ... Is the doctor defending the private realm of husband and dying wife from a prying detective? There's a rugby match and a disappearance and a nervous miser of a rich uncle – yes, yes, but what is that to defending the sanctity of a marriage and the love that has to be kept secret? By keeping the love match secret from Lord Mount-James, is the story actually defending the class transgression, contrary to what Joseph Kestner says? Once Holmes makes clear he is not working for Lord Mount-James, it's all right: so the aim is to protect a love match against the class rules that might forbid it. But the wife does die, and we're left with – what? The conclusion that you can't after all fight the rules of society? And pale sunlight.

The Abbey Grange

The Bass Rock: Captain Crocker (or Croker; depends on your edition) transfers from The Rock of Gibraltar to another ship, The Bass Rock. The first suggests solidity and loyalty ("solid as the Rock of Gibraltar"), but Bass Rock? Why, that's an island in Scotland sometimes called the Scottish Alcatraz because it used to house prisoners. Hmm. Is he going to prison after all? But he was acquitted in the Court of Baker Street.

And why two Rocks? Sounds lonely, like the solitary swan that swims in a hole in the frozen pool, which suddenly makes me think of Swan Lake and the Flying Dutchman and stories of horrible curses damning people to eternal loneliness, but after all Captain Croker may come back in a year and be accepted by his lady.

Should he be allowed to, though? Holmes and Watson acquit him, and he does seem to have a reasonable defence of justifiable homicide or self-defence, if Sir Eustace attacked first. And then there's the whole domestic abuse angle (the story is far ahead of its time), reminding me of much more recent cases. Of course, we have only the word of the killer and his two accomplices (Croker, Lady Brackenstall, and her maid), so who is to know? Some have speculated that Holmes has been duped, but the story doesn't really read like that.

Judge and jury: It does read like a story in which it seems okay to take the law into your own hands. Holmes is quite explicit about this, saying he's putting his conscience first, unlike some other time (do we know of this?) when he followed the law and regretted it. This is part perhaps of his sense of superiority, which is highlighted here by Watson talking of his friend's extraordinary powers (Holmes talks about them too). And of course there's Holmes and Watson play-acting as a court; they seem to think that's perfectly fine, and maybe it is. Or is it?

Cat and mouse: If you're superior, I suppose it's always a temptation to toy with people. Holmes seems to toy with Stanley Hopkins by throwing him a hint but not more. Watson acquiesces, saying he trusts Holmes's judgment. (At the end he again follows Holmes's judgment or is he issuing his own? "Not guilty, my lord," he says of Croker. Holmes is the judge, but Watson is the jury.) Not that all this acquiescing spares Watson the Holmesian lash: he is told that he's writing the stories all wrong, and when he comes up with what he thinks is a legitimate question (why is the lady tied up?) Holmes dismisses it.

But why is the lady tied up? What strange little game is that? I know, to help create the burglar story, but hmm ... Captain Croker is lassoing his bird?

Cat and mouse 2: Captain Croker complains that Holmes is toying with him and even uses the cat and mouse figure of speech. And Holmes is toying with him a bit, no? But is Croker a mouse? He's more the fine specimen of manhood, powerful and capable who perhaps thinks himself as superior as Holmes, at least in one area: whether Sir Eustace gets to live or die. "Damn the beast, if he had as many lives as a cat, he would owe them all to me!" Because he's abused his wife, whom Croker loves? Hmm. Lots of animal references, by the way. Cat and mouse, lives of a cat, that swan, the deer heads in the magnificent oak dining room. It all makes it a bit mystical almost, as does the reference to Stanley Hopkins having called on Holmes seven times. Why seven? Oh, and we mustn't forget all the references to Sir Eustace as a devil or a fiend, and

Lady Brackenstall even says that the wicked laws of England will lay a curse on the land. She is the outsider, come from Australia, who can see these things clearly.

Divorce laws: Those are the laws in question, which in those days would not allow divorce for domestic abuse. Conan Doyle was later active in the divorce reform movement, and this is actually a very realistic portrayal of a political situation. Not mystical at all. And yet "these monstrous laws" will bring "a curse upon the land." What sort of curse, exactly? God or Heaven will act: how? By sending a flood? Destroying cities? For a moment Lady Brackenstall sounds like an angry prophet. Or is she just a suffering woman? And a woman who comes from a freer place not so concerned with proprieties ... like the propriety of not committing murder? That God she invokes (or "Heaven" in some editions) is presumably the one that said, "Thou shalt not kill," but she does work to let the Captain get away with killing. Maybe the killing of abusive husbands is the curse she has in mind.

De novo: Starting afresh. What Holmes says he must do after he jumps off the train to return to the scene of the crime. A bit like Dr. Armstrong returning at the end of "The Missing Three-Quarter." Why such returning? Go back, think again – at least that's the motive here. I shouldn't have let my mind be warped by others' descriptions of the events, says Holmes. (Good advice: always check the evidence for yourself first; read the story before the Musings, that sort of thing.)

Art and science: And so Holmes repeats the investigation, this time with an open mind. And we get commentary about how his deductions emerge from his investigations, though he does seem to jump to an erroneous conclusion about who cooked up the burglary story, and his analysis of the wine and its beeswing (a sort of film on old port) has been questioned.

186

Still, he basically figures things out by means of his scientific (or is it artistic?) approach. (He talks of scientific demonstrations, and yet plans to write The Art of Detection. I suppose art and science must work together in such matters.)

The Usual Suspects: The upper classes are villainous again. At least Sir Eustace is. His appearance as a grinning corpse in a foppish nightshirt seems especially unpleasant. And then there's the maid's summation of how he won Lady Brackenstall: through "his title and his money and his false London ways" – oh, the nasty, nasty man. And then there are the haggard faces revealing haggard events: physiognomy rules (whatever happened to the stiff upper lip: or do you look haggard by trying to maintain one?).

The game's afoot: Here is where that famous line appears. And it's Holmes summoning Watson, tapping him on his shoulder while he sleeps, so the two can work together. And they work together well, don't they? It's all good fun, even if we wish Holmes would be nicer to Watson. But then that would be a different Holmes, wouldn't it? Here we have the teacher and the student, as Watson himself puts it. Sometimes a severe teacher, but friendly in his way, and Watson seems to enjoy it (mostly).

The Second Stain

What's going on here? This story bothers me. Oh, it begins all right, with a clients' visit, and there are Holmes and Watson as usual listening to the latest case, which seems a lot like ...

The Naval Treaty: Doesn't it?

But there are ominous noises from Watson about this being the last case he'll write up (liar!), because Sherlock Holmes has retired (tearful sigh) and doesn't want any more publicity – but didn't Holmes say just in the last story that he was going to write up some of the cases himself? Another lie? Oh, well, you can't expect consistency from story to story, I suppose.

Anyway, the story seems fine enough (if a bit copied from "The Naval Treaty") until suddenly there's a murder! What's a murder doing in the middle of a stolen document story? It's just a diversion, says Holmes; the real case is finding the document and stopping a disastrous war. It's an amazing coincidence, says Watson. What, that one of three possible recipients of the stolen document has been murdered? That's no coincidence, says Holmes, and we are of course inclined to agree with him ... until we learn that in fact it was an ...

Amazing coincidence! Yes, Eduardo Lucas, the agent who receives the letter, is murdered, but not because of the letter. It has nothing to do with the letter. It's just that he's been leading a double life; he's also Henri Fournaye of Paris, and his Parisian wife has just found him out in London and is sure he's having an affair with Lady Trelawney Hope (which actually he's not; he's only blackmailing her, so that should be okay; if only he had told his wife ...).

The mad woman of Godolphin Street: So you make your plans, you're involved in international intrigue and blackmail, and then your wife stabs you in the heart with a curved Indian dagger. Of all the rotten luck. And it's not only inconvenient for Lucas, it rather throws a wrench into Sherlock Holmes's lucubrations, though he overcomes the difficulties and retrieves the letter.

But what is going on here? Is this a story of international intrigue, or a tawdry *affaire de coeur*? There have been at least a couple of academic scholars who have looked into it, being interested in the numerous doubles in it (two stains, two husbands hiding things from their wives), and one of them notes that the story is an intersection of the domestic and the political. And you could say, sure, on a thematic level this is a story about how the best-laid (political) plans get derailed by the personal. If only Lucas had explained things to his wife, and why after all was he playing such an elaborate double game (well, okay, he was a spy, I suppose; still ...). And if only Trelawney Hope had explained things to his wife ...

No, wait: Wouldn't it have been more important for the wife to have explained things to her husband? What is this secret she is keeping from him? His honour is so pure, he would never understand, he would lose confidence in her, but would he? She doesn't test this. Holmes tells her to take her husband into his confidence, but she won't.

Confidence, confidence, confidence: Oh, I have lost my confidence. Is that the theme of the story? People won't share things. The Prime Minister doesn't want to tell what's in the diplomatic (or undiplomatic) letter (though he does in the end). Lady Trelawney Hope won't tell what's in the other letter (two letters: another doubling, must be important). And most important of all, and most disturbing, Sherlock Holmes won't tell his clients, especially not Trelawney Hope, what happened to the purloined document. What is this? Since when does Holmes lie to his clients?[*] He's treating Trelawney Hope like a small child. No, no, the document is still in your despatch box; it was there all along; you just missed it. How could you know, says the grateful Foreign Secretary. Because, says Holmes, I knew it was nowhere else.

He knew it was nowhere else? What a brazen, bald-faced ... oh, never mind, but it disturbed me. Still, the main point is to figure out why this story should end like this. No pleasant Naval Treaty land here, with Holmes going on about beacons and lighthouses. Things are dark. There's a madwoman. There's a threat to the peace. There's a threat to the Trelawney Hope marriage. What must be done? Well, above all, we must keep this all very quiet. We're Victorian, you know (well, Edwardian, but ...), and the main thing is to hide disreputable things like whatever was in Lady Trelawney's letter and also to hush up intemperate outbursts like the one by that foreign potentate.

Oh, those foreigners: Yes, we seem to be a bit in xenophobic Six Napoleons territory. There's the intemperate potentate; we don't know what country he's from, but clearly he's not British. I mean, really, old chap, there are things that are done, and things that are not done, and you don't go dashing off intemperate letters threatening the peace of Europe.

And then the Parisian wife, who's not only French but Creole. I mean, well, no wonder she goes insane: at least that's what the story seems to be saying. This is the sort of

---

[*] Well, he withholds the truth from Mary Sutherland in "A Case of Identity," another example of his being patronizing.

thing we have to guard against, the story seems to suggest: this eruption of murderous insanity (and also even the intemperance of the potentate).

Let's just sweep everything under the rug (or into the despatch box): What tries to erupt into this story, somewhat implausibly in the form of the coincidental murder, is not just the personal, but the acting out of unchecked emotion. The story frowns on this and thus goes along with what surely is a horrible sort of cover-up in which the Trelawney Hope marriage is preserved by keeping the husband in the dark. Let's not air the past peccadillo; let's suppress it ... why? Because, oh, the scandal, the threat to reputation; it would be motive enough for murder; in fact it is motive for murder in other stories in the canon, murders that Sherlock Holmes winkles out, not allowing reputation to be preserved by suppressing the past. (Or well, maybe he allowed it before, but here he is a major agent in suppressing Lady Trelawney Hope's past and keeping her husband in ignorance. Is that really a good idea? Maybe if she'd come clean, he'd have forgiven her and they could have had a more honest relationship.)

And was it really a good idea to suppress that international document? Maybe the grievances of the foreign potentate deserved a hearing. Maybe something could have been done about them. By suppressing the grievance Holmes (and Doyle?) think they have averted a war that could have cost 100,000 lives. Well, think again. World War I came a decade later, and it cost more like 17 million. And the story almost seems to know this: you can't suppress things, or it's a bad idea if you do, because then you might get someone insane from the Continent coming over to kill you. That perhaps is the unintended message of the story, though on the surface the point seems to be to cover things up: do that and everything will be all right. That bothers me.

The Valley of Fear, Part One

Watson the Sherlockian? "We have only their word for that," says the good doctor of Barclay and Mrs. Douglas, prompting Holmes to wonder if he's suggesting that everything in the story (Barclay and Mrs. Douglas's story) is false. Let's not accept a word of it, let's invent our own story – but that won't work, says Holmes, it leaves too many things unexplained. So maybe this is a warning not to wander too far from what we're told in the stories. Maybe this is an anti-Sherlockian jab at people who want to play "the Game" and resolve inconsistencies in the canon by questioning the very facts of the stories.

Could that be one thing *The Valley of Fear* is about? Ronald Knox had written his essay about Holmes the year before, the essay credited with beginning the Game of imagining Holmes and Watson were real people; perhaps *The Valley of Fear* is a response …

Or perhaps it's self-parody? The story does tend to go on and on, elaborating on every step in which Holmes solves the Porlock cipher – and why is he called Porlock, by the way? Some see an allusion to the possibly imaginary man from Porlock who, the story goes, interrupted Samuel Taylor Coleridge when he was writing "Kubla Khan" ("In Xanadu …" etc.), but what does that have to do with Holmesian deduction, Moriarty …

Wait, Moriarty? Yes, Moriarty is back. But wasn't he killed in "The Final Problem"? Well, yes, but this story is set back in time, before that. Hmm. But why? Why bring Moriarty back? And then mysteriously have him drop out of the story. At the end of the first part of *The Valley of Fear* he has essentially disappeared: the murder seems to have nothing to do with him. It's about some goings-on in America (there are always goings-on in America). Very puzzling.

Story interruptus: But maybe that's what's going on: things are being interrupted, just like the man from Porlock interrupted Coleridge. This is going to be a story of Moriarty, but that's interrupted to examine the tragedy of Birlstone, which seems to turn on some secret society from America, not Moriarty's nefarious doings. But oh, those nefarious doings, that one poisonous spider at the centre of a web. It's as if there's a longing to give one overarching explanation to everything rather than accept that every case is its own thing, a longing that recurs, and not just in the Holmesian canon. If only there were one simple answer that explained all.

Study redux: And so it will be off to America for Part Two, just like in *Study in Scarlet*, except instead of Mormons there will be … well, we'll have to wait and see about that. A strange way to construct a story, really, but we can't account for it by saying the canon has run out of steam or run aground, since this is how the canon began, with that running off to America, the break in the middle of an English mystery, and perhaps that takes us back to …

Self-parody, or at least repetition. Maybe the canon *is* running out of steam; Doyle has to recycle old structures, and is his heart really in it? Look how drawn out Part One is, look how many detectives show up to discuss the case: what is going on? There are lots of nice aphorisms in this part, including more than one about not theorizing before you determine the facts, but what a lot of theorizing there actually is here. The regular police theorize, Watson theorizes, even Holmes (despite saying not to) theorizes and shows us his work as he goes along, even though he says he doesn't like to do that either. We are with him every step of the way as he deciphers the message from Porlock. At least at the end he solves the mystery of the dumbbell without us, so can dazzle us with the result: that's the Holmes we want and love …

And there's comic bickering: Holmes and Watson going at it in the way we love, with Watson even getting in a few shots. A pawky sense of humour, Holmes says, meaning sly apparently, and he calls him Machiavellian, though that seems to be mockery, and yet Watson does seem Machiavellian in saying no one can solve this cipher, which prompts Holmes to solve it. A little reverse psychology from the good doctor.

And other usual suspects: A decaying manor house revived by someone who's been in America (can you say *Hound of the Baskervilles*?). An apparent romantic triangle. Holmes as artist. A discussion of what sort of knowledge a detective needs: tour guide information about secret hiding places in old mansions, apparently, but not so much eclipses and asteroids: that's Moriarty's field, or ostensible field. Of course, hiding places may connect to eclipses; eclipses hide things. Is Douglas being eclipsed somehow? By the dead man in his study. Or actually he eclipses himself, switches identities with the dead man. And what does that mean?

Playing dead: A good way to escape detection, but it doesn't work here, thanks to Sherlock Holmes. Of course, Holmes himself played dead for a while, and Moriarty is dead, but here we've brought him back. Life and death, such tensions between them. Appearance and disappearance. He's gone, he's back. Holmes was gone, but now he's back. Moriarty was gone, but now he's back. Douglas was gone, but now he's back. And now we'll learn his early story in America, but for that we will have to wait until Part Two.

Love and marriage: Meanwhile what about the Douglas marriage? Or no, marriage generally. A loving wife would not be steered away from her husband's corpse, says Holmes; that leads Watson to conclude that Mrs. Douglas is a murderer and Holmes to the better conclusion that her husband was not the murder victim. But look at the assumption this is built on. One critic (Martin Priestman) notes something similar in "The Blue Carbuncle": Holmes can deduce something based on the assumption that a loving wife would make sure her husband's hat was brushed. Priestman calls this a conservative assumption about the nature of marital relations or society generally. Perhaps a reassuring assumption too, one of many in the canon – an assumption that tells us there is an accepted order to things. We may be in the middle of a disruptive crime, but still we know how things are supposed to be. Or Holmes knows, and can remind us.

But is it reassuring? If you think of yourself as a loving wife, does this make you feel pressured to brush your husband's hat or stay by his corpse? Admittedly, the latter situation may not arise too often; still ... Are the stories forcing certain ways of thought on us? Are they propaganda for a certain point of view? All art is propaganda, some say. And what more likely time for propaganda to come to the fore than with a world war breaking out, as it was when *The Valley of Fear* appeared. Perhaps that is why the novel seems so full of aphorisms ("Mediocrity knows nothing higher than itself ..." "All knowledge comes useful ..." etc.). And full of police too. Time to rally for the fight, boys. But first off to America.

The Valley of Fear, Part Two

We aren't in Sussex anymore, readers: No, it's Vermissa Valley, aka the Valley of Fear. And we don't have some cosy locked room mystery, but a hardboiled detective story, a thriller, a spy story. But there's still deception, even involving the same character: Douglas from Part One turns into Jack McMurdo, who is really Birdy Edwards, an undercover detective infiltrating the murderous Scowrers of the American coal country. Not that we're really fooled, are we? But the Scowrers are, as Detective Edwards plays the part of a cold-blooded murderer.

And who is telling this story? Not Watson. Nor Douglas/McMurdo/Evans, even though Part One ended with Douglas presenting the manuscript as if he had written it. It is an anonymous narrator who speaks to us and who remains outside the thoughts of McMurdo/Evans (otherwise we would know he was an undercover detective right away). The effect is quite different from the usual Holmes story, and of course on top of that, there is no Holmes, and we're in a rough American neighbourhood.

So what is going on? Of course there was something like this in *Study in Scarlet:* a mid-story American digression sans Holmes and Watson. And there are evil groups in both (slurs probably, on first the Mormons and then the Molly Maguires). And a young woman has to choose between suitors, but in this case both her suitors are, or seem to be, part of the murderous Scowrer gang, and though one of them isn't and turns out to be a supposedly good Pinkerton detective, and she even gets to marry him, she dies quickly (at least in narrative terms: a few paragraphs, and then "the light went" from the life of our detective hero). And rather than the Mormons being chased to

197

London and punished for their bad deeds as in *Study*, here it's the detective being chased by the nasty Scowrers, who end up in league with Moriarty.

And what good came of it? Well, nothing, apparently. At the end we have not a triumphant Holmes but an almost beaten one straining to "pierce the veil." The veil of what? The cloud of murder? That's the phrase that Brother Morris uses to describe what hangs over the Valley of Fear. Later, oddly, the "cloud of avenging Law" descends to defeat the Scowrers – but are both sides clouded? Who is good and who is bad? Can we tell anymore? This is after all not 1895 but the beginning of World War I (at least in terms of publication dates).

The Good, the Bad, and the Disguised: The Scowrers are bad, but is Birdy Edwards bad too? He certainly puts on a good impersonation of evil. Of course, this is what an undercover detective has to do. Still … And with the readers in the dark, who are we to sympathize with for the opening chapters of Part Two? We do see from Birdy's point of view, even though we don't know who he really is, so perhaps we sympathize with him. Perhaps this is simply a plunging us into the intrigues of a Mafia-like organization, with Birdy (and Brother Morris) being less bloodthirsty than the leaders.

The American Virus: Some critics see American roughness and violence erupting into a Holmes story, invading peaceful Sussex. Of course, Conan Doyle began with this sort of thing in *Study in Scarlet* and often has his stories turn on some past misdeeds in America or elsewhere far from civilized England. But in *Study* and the other stories, the virus tends to be tamed; England survives, the rough characters are disposed of, and above all Holmes solves everything nicely, we can understand everything and go peaceably about our business. This time in Part Two there is nothing to solve; it was all nicely solved in Part One; what need is there of Part Two? None, except to express uneasiness. Some rough beast is coming from abroad, and worse is combining with that native beast, that Moriarty, leaving us with no mysteries to solve, just terror to shrink from.

Or can we fight it? In the main chapters of Part Two, though we may not entirely realize it because of Birdy's disguise, someone is hard at work combating the terrorism of the Scowrers. It is an interesting portrayal of the infiltration of a gang. Not a typical Holmesian story at all, but an interesting anticipation of later twentieth-century fiction. But it does rather blur the distinctions between good and evil. Now, Holmes you may say goes in for disguise (yes, but not for such an extended period) and even breaks the law at times: but a little breaking and entering hardly seems the same as Jack McMurdo's supposed history as a murderer and a counterfeiter.

Counterfeiting? Interesting thing, that counterfeiting. The false coins McMurdo spreads are actually real, and it's the counterfeiting machine that is counterfeit. But it's all of a piece with the blurring of detective and murderer: what is real, what is counterfeit? Who can know? And where is Sherlock Holmes to put it all right? Not in Vermissa Valley.

And what of the woman? Not one of the stronger women in the canon. Young Ettie can just wring her hands and plead with the disguised detective to flee. At least she doesn't faint or come down with brain fever, but then she just dies and is gone. What was her role? For that matter, what is the role of the sentimental singing the Scowrers indulge in? Human nature, says the nameless narrator, making it so even murderers indulge in music. But what music? Two songs

("I'm Sitting on the Stile, Mary" and "On the Banks of Allan Water") that lament the end of romances and talk of death.

If woman here is mere ornament, and music too, perhaps we are being told this is no time for ornaments. We're in a land of hellish fires (from the coal and iron works); it's a bleak landscape, and no place for gentle things; or even gentle things turn to death and sorrow here, in America's coal land, and not just there, for a bad time is coming everywhere.

And foreigners and class war: Those Scowrers are Irishmen, and perhaps include other foreigners? In any case, the brave newspaper editor denounces them as an "alien" element who have fled the despotisms of Europe and who are now introducing a reign of terror. Reign of Terror? The French Revolution? Why, indeed, there are even references to Danton and Robespierre. But mostly this is a union struggle. The Scowrers denounce the capitalists, and in this story that puts them on the side of disruption. The world is under threat, and who will save it?

And who is that dark-bearded man? The one at the end of Chapter 4 who denounces the Scowrers as "damned murderers" and says, "We'll fix you yet!" He seems as scary as the Scowrers. You become what you fight, I suppose. And so we are left, dissatisfied, like Barker beating his head and clenching his fists in impotent anger. Is there nothing that can be done? No, no, says Holmes, don't give up, I will do something; but it sounds like a hopeless bleat. Ah, well.

Wisteria Lodge

Meet the foreigners: But will they be good foreigners or bad foreigners this time? It's so hard to know what to expect in the canon: good Italian blood in the Naval Treaty or nasty ape-like creatures as in The Six Napoleons? More the latter, I fear. Even the "good" side has a "savage" practitioner of voodoo amongst its members. And are they actually good, these people out to commit a murder? "There may be a hundred crimes in the background," says Watson, but all that matters here in England is what's been done here, and in the case of the Tiger of San Pedro, heinous as his actions may have been when he was dictator, can the courts take those into account?

Well, maybe they can: Inspector Baynes seems to think so, and in the end, when Don Murillo is murdered, Watson thinks it justice. Hmm. Do we even know that the tale told by Miss Burnet, the English governess, is true? How do we know Don Murillo was the bad guy? But the story does encourage us to think so, though at one point Holmes asks Miss Burnet: "How can an English lady join in such a murderous affair?"

Marriage: That's how she got involved, by marrying a San Pedro minister later murdered by the dictator (or so she says). A strange alliance, though, prompting Holmes's question. Or perhaps that's being xenophobic. Why shouldn't the English become less insular and involve themselves in international affairs? Why, they had begun to do that just the year before this story got published, forming the Triple Entente with Russia and France to face off against the Triple Alliance of Germany, Austria, and Italy. And that worked out well, didn't it? Hmm.

Maybe it's actually dangerous to get mixed up in foreign affairs – but somehow those affairs are coming home to us, right in Surrey. But the official view, the police view of Inspector Baynes, and Watson's concluding judgment seem to be saying, Yes, let's choose sides in these international conflicts.

And yet, and yet: We actually end not with Watson's comment about justice, but with Holmes saying the case was "chaotic," followed by a description of grotesque and horrible voodoo. So maybe choosing sides is not such a good idea after all.

But the case is solved: Yes, we see Holmes at his light-footed best figuring things out, "amid a perfect jungle of possibilities." Jungle, hmm. It's a dangerous world out there, what with jungles and voodoo and tyrannical dictators drugging Englishwomen with opium, but Holmes prevails. It is a much more optimistic ending than the one in *The Valley of Fear*, but then that one was several years later when the world scene was even more dangerous.

And not alone: Well, Holmes does work alone, of course, but on a parallel path Inspector Baynes has figured the whole thing out too. Why is that? Doesn't it make Holmes a bit superfluous? Is this Conan Doyle trying again to find an excuse to retire our old friend? (He does retire him, sort of, in the preface to the *Last Bow* collection, in which this story appears, sending him off to a farm near Eastbourne, but you can't keep a popular hero down.)

Even Watson seems to be figuring things out. Not about the case: Holmes shoots down every Watsonian theory about that with his usual tactless glee. But Watson can tell that Holmes is preoccupied with the telegram at the beginning of the story and later knows when he is hot on the scent. If we all become

Holmesian, will we need an actual Holmes? Conan Doyle teases us, I think.

Adventures? Watson at one point says Holmes's ice-cold thinking convinces him to go along with the adventure of breaking into Henderson's house to rescue the governess. This doesn't actually happen, though there is some of this in other stories, and I suppose that would be an adventure. But my real question is the same as the one I asked in my discussion of "Boscombe Valley": Why are these stories called Adventures and not, say, Cases or Mysteries? They're mostly about solving mysteries, aren't they? Not about shooting tigers in India.

But cases sounds too legal. Now we must turn to our legal work, says Holmes, but they don't. Is Holmes ever in a courtroom in the canon? This is not Perry Mason. But they could be called Mysteries, and yet they are not. Adventures. As if to make us feel we're being active when we're mostly ratiocinating. Or maybe that's too rational a term for what Holmes does. He's creative; perhaps he's on a creative adventure. When we journey with him, we adventure that way: into the heart of criminality (if not darkness) or, more precisely, the heart of confusion, chaos as he puts it, to try and set things straight. By which I mean less bringing the evil to justice than just figuring out what's going on.

And it was chaotic: We begin with Scott Eccles, who really turns out to have little to do with things, though it is perhaps common in the canon for some innocent bystander to be dragged into some bizarre situation (a disappearing host, feeling abandoned out in Surrey) which turns into something much more serious: the grotesque becoming horrible. And by beginning with Scott Eccles, the hapless innocent, are we beginning "wrong end foremost," the way all Watson's stories begin according to Holmes?

But that is life, is it not? Or a typical mystery story: you have to begin at the end, with the result, the murder or whatever, and work backwards from that to figure things out. Watson actually does these things admirably. Who would read a story that began with the dictatorship in San Pedro and then flowed neatly to its chronological end? Or that would be a different sort of story, a thriller, a real adventure story.

Respectability: Scott Eccles is not only an innocent; he's a respectable innocent. That's what Garcia wants: a respectable person to give him an alibi. It's a common thread in the canon, the search for respectability. Don Murillo seeks it too as Henderson. And yet in these later stories the common thread has become exotic, foreign. It's not just some ancient peccadillo threatening an English magistrate; it's a whole world of foreignness threatening the British way of life. Nihilism gets mentioned, as in an earlier story; is the whole machine going smash?

Gender: A woman would not have sent a telegram, but would have gone in person, Holmes says. Why? What stereotype is that playing on?

Disrepair: Wisteria Lodge is in a "crazy state of disrepair." This is the typical situation in the canon. Not only are there external threats, but internally things are falling apart. And the servants are underworked and overfed; it sounds like conservative grumbling against wasteful government.

Can passion save us? Miss Burnet, the English governess, has been caught up in "the passion of her hatred [of the evil dictator]." Is that a good thing? She desires revenge. Is that the way to go? Readers may wonder. Will that really help San Pedro? Killing its *former* dictator? Hmm.

The Cardboard Box

No foreigners here: After several stories about external threats, here we are back among the domestic issues of the early stories. Which after all is no surprise because in fact this is an early story, originally published in 1893, but then suppressed until 1917. And why suppressed? Because it was about sex, some report Doyle saying. Can that be true?

Perhaps it was just too gruesome: Those severed ears, you know. Ugh. And what do they represent? Some commentators go on wild Freudian excursions: castration anxiety, they say. Well, there certainly is some sort of anxiety here, residing in the heart of the murderer, Jim Browner, but he's the one who performs the double "castration," so it's not clear how the Freudian approach would work. But Browner certainly has reason to question his situation, as his wife seems to be involved in an extramarital affair.

Or perhaps it was too bleak: Consider the closing lines, where Holmes almost seems to descend to lament, noting the "circle of misery and violence and fear" that humanity seems trapped in. Did Doyle not want this sentiment spread abroad? But he did publish the story again eventually, in 1917, in the midst of a horrific war, at a time when its sentiments may have been more appropriate.

A preposterous way to settle a dispute: War, that is, but also perhaps murder. Holmes voices Watson's thought in the famous mind-reading passage at the beginning of the story (so famous that when the rest of the story was suppressed, Doyle rescued the passage by inserting it in "The Resident Patient").

War and Murder: One tiny appearance of the foreign in this story is Henry Ward Beecher, the American preacher and anti-slavery advocate, whose trip to England on behalf of the North in the American Civil War is what Watson was thinking of. Watson, says Holmes, then went on to think about the preposterousness of war as a means of settling international disputes, a comment much more à propos in 1917 perhaps than in 1893.

Sex scandal: Yes, even in the nineteenth century there were sex scandals, and there was one involving Henry Ward Beecher and some alleged adultery. Some critics say that's why Beecher is mentioned in the story, and adultery certainly is relevant to the story, but after all Watson was thinking of Beecher's public life and war and the preposterousness of resorting to violence, which seems even more à propos to the story's theme than the rumours of adultery, which after all only have to do with the story's plot.

But let's consider the plot: It is a tangled one. There's Browner married to the angel Mary, who turns out to be rather less than an angel; and there's her sister Sarah, who is attracted to Browner herself, creating a triangle that Browner wants no part of. Then there is Alan Fairbairn, whom Sarah pushes on Mary, creating yet another triangle: we move from Browner and two women to Mary and two men.

And what comes of it all? A double murder, a *crime passionnel*, committed by Browner, for which he takes the blame while at the same time laying off some of it on Sarah Cushing. We get to hear Browner's confession at the end, a confession that I think makes us sympathize with him – and yet can we allow people to go about committing murder (or starting wars) even if their cause is just? The last lines of the story, the lament of Holmes, leave that question unanswered. "What is the meaning of it?" he says, voicing the great

Victorian question that troubled the likes of Tennyson mourning the death of his friend Hallam.

Well, what is the meaning of it? The Victorians tended to buck themselves up and somehow still saw meaning. By the time of this story, however, especially the time of its second publication, modernism was in the air: meaning was threatened altogether. And so we can see this story as almost ahead of its time, or at least as being in tune with Doyle's bleakness in *The Valley of Fear*.

But the mystery is solved: Yes, it is. But what does it amount to in the end? A postal error. The reason two severed ears were sent to Susan Cushing was that they were actually meant for someone else, as Susan Cushing herself says. Holmes thinks so little of his solution to this problem that he asks Lestrade not to mention him in connection with it. Is this fair? It is after all a clever solution to what seems like a baffling problem: it baffled Lestrade after all. But if the puzzle can be solved, something larger remains intractable: the passions of the human heart, the love that turns to hate (in both Sarah and Browner), the violence that a man may resort to … Instead of feeling uplifted by the solution to this crime, we feel with Holmes: what is the way out? What does it all mean?

And what else? Watson is the bored one here, eager for a case in the manner we usually associate with Holmes, meaning … Well, who knows? He also gets a "thrill" when he learns there may be more than just a bizarre prank going on. But Watson is us: if he is excited by the thought of "strange and inexplicable horror," what does that say about us? Perhaps that we are the bored ones looking for stimulation? Like Holmes usually, like Watson here? Oh, it is very confusing. Is this the most confusing story in the canon?

Some call it the darkest, and this despite the lack of fog: instead we are in the blazing August heat, but we still can't see because of the glare. The glare hurts our eyes. Is it the glare of reality? The reality that people cannot stand, to paraphrase a later poet? The glare from the human heart? The heart of darkness?

Respectability: Often respectability is a cover for a deep dark secret from the past (or America). Here the respectable Susan Cushing is simply that: a respectable lady with nothing in her past that can account for the crime, for the simple reason that the crime is nothing to do with her. So what is she doing in the story? Just one of those innocent bystander types, like Scott Eccles in "Wisteria Lodge," dragged into things to serve someone's ends? But not even that: she's in it by mistake, by sharing the same initial as her sister Sarah. But wait, there is something there: it is her sister who's at the heart of things. It's not completely accidental, and one of her sisters is a scheming manipulator and the other is an adulteress: can she be as innocent as all that? She even has ears that look like her sister's. How is it that one from the family can be so proper, and the other two ... well ... Hmm. Oh, wait ...

Respectability in the midst of horror: Perhaps we are not Watson and his thrill at horror (or maybe that too), but Susan Cushing, the respectable one, in a world of horror, horror that she generally is able to keep at bay, but which here presses in on her through the agency of the post office. And so it means we thrill to horror and shrink from it and are guilty of it ourselves. Perhaps that's what it all means.

The Red Circle

I heard you can read great things out of small ones: So says the landlady, Mrs. Warren, in bringing two burnt matches and a cigarette end to Sherlock Holmes in hopes that these will help solve the mystery of her invisible lodger.

But Holmes just shrugs and says there's nothing here – because he doesn't want to be used like a trained bear? Because *he* will decide when to use his magic? It can't actually be because there's nothing there, because a moment later Holmes is saying, Oh, wait, actually this cigarette end is rather remarkable: it proves the smoker was cleanshaven – which is not surprising given that we later find out she was a woman (but of course we don't know that yet; even Holmes doesn't know that yet, but he does deduce that there must be two lodgers or a switch of lodger).

Some say that Holmes does little in this case, but he does deduce things (he just doesn't kill the evil Gorgiano, but then deduction is more in his line and he's never been good at stopping criminals before they strike).

I really have other things to engage me: So says Holmes when Mrs. Warren brings him the case. This seems odd. When does Holmes ever turn down a case? Well, okay, he sometimes hesitates when he has some other case he is on, but this time what he's busy with is "arranging and indexing some of his recent material." Far be it from me to deny the importance of keeping your records in order, but still ...

Unusual but nothing more? That is what Holmes seems to think about the secretive lodger at first. Just because it's bizarre doesn't mean there's a crime involved, does there? Wait, has he forgotten all his previous cases, from Wisteria Lodge to the Red-Headed League? That's where crime lurks in the canon: underneath some odd but not criminal-seeming situation. You have to have red hair or wear a certain dress and sit by a window; odd, but not criminal – but in the end it's a bank being robbed or a murder being planned.

Yes, underneath the oddities, there's often something fairly prosaic. Criminal but not exotic: greed, jealousy, or anxiety over reputation are motivating a crime which is covered up by something mysteriously bizarre, and it is the standard result in the canon to show that what seems truly out of the ordinary comes down to common human impulses.

Of course, sometimes there are foreigners: This story, like "Wisteria Lodge" and even like the second part of *The Valley of Fear,* involves foreigners up to no good. Earlier in the canon foreigners (and gypsies) were often the unjustly suspected, and it was good old Brits who turned out to be the culprits. But now we're in the era of international intrigue and danger, and in this story we have a foreign criminal gang, the Red Circle (modelled on the Italian Black Hand). Nasty stuff come to England's shores.

So we can add to domestic motives, the machinations of international syndicates. Which is perhaps a bit exotic, but not truly as bizarre as at first appears. And Holmes figures a lot of it out, though not the international element: that requires the appearance of a Pinkerton detective – shades of the Valley.

Not that it's the Pinkerton who saves the day: No, that's Gennaro Lucca, whose wife Emilia Lucca sings his praises as her protector. Some see this as a New Woman or feminist story, because Emilia takes over the ending, explaining the political backstory while her husband is who knows where. And it is interesting that the woman is present and the man is not, but it's the man who dispatched the Red Circle assassin, not her – or Holmes, Gregson, or the Pinkerton from America:

they were on the sidelines, which perhaps is the safest place to be when foreign entanglements beckon. Perhaps this is an isolationist story. Let the Italians fight it out amongst themselves.

Quotations: "Journeys end with lovers' meetings," says Holmes, slightly misquoting Shakespeare's *Twelfth Night*. And why does he say it? And who does he say it to? Why, to Inspector Gregson. It's not the first time he has said it either: the first time was to the criminal Sebastian Moran ("The Empty House"). Hmm. Is there some suggestion here that Holmes is connected both to the police and to the leading criminals? Perhaps there is. The private detective flits between many worlds.

And another quote: Art for art's sake, says Holmes in explaining why he pursues this case. Not for the fee (is Holmes ever really motivated by money?), but to keep his hand in, for education, he says. Education never ends, he adds, and the last lesson is the greatest: presumably a suggestion that death will teach us more than anything else. A little throwaway philosophy, that, and of course the canon contains many deaths, but those are all seen from the outside. I think here Holmes is talking about what one will experience at one's own.

Oh, and the quote, "Art for art's sake"? It's an old catchphrase, originally from French artists perhaps, but popularized among the late Victorian Aesthetes in England, and it meant art should not serve some moral or instructive purpose; it should be an end in itself. As perhaps Holmes's work in solving crimes is: the game's the thing.

Crime, crime, where's the crime? Though I've said the bizarre often masks the criminal, there isn't really a crime here, is there? Unless you count Gennaro's killing of

Gorgiano, but that seems to have been in self-defence. There is of course what seems to be attempted murder by Gorgiano and the kidnapping of Mrs. Warren's husband, the timekeeper (why a timekeeper? is time important in this story?). But the bizarre situation here (the secretive lodger) is not the cover for a crime as in other stories, but an attempt to avoid a crime: a sort of witness protection situation. So in these later stages of the canon potential victims are picking up tricks from criminals: are we all being infected? Is the whole world becoming a mass of intrigue? One might almost think a World War was coming.

And women: Though we have an important role for a woman at the end as storyteller, mostly what the story as a whole seems to tell us is that women need protecting. Also that you can tell a woman's handwriting from a man's. And that women are persistent and cunning. Not perhaps the most enlightened attitudes (though can you tell a woman's handwriting from a man's?).

And all those precautions: The interesting thing about all the attempts to keep the lodger's whereabouts secret is that they don't work. Gorgiano and his accomplices find the lodgings anyway, the moral being … what? That powerful forces are coming and you can't hide from them? Perhaps. The rain it raineth every day.

And maybe it all fits together: The precautions to stay out of the way, Holmes's saying he's too busy to take on the case, Holmes not even wanting to perform by showing great things from little, Holmes not seeing anything in the case, and at the climax Holmes and the police leaving it all to the Italians to work out themselves. It's all about not getting involved, perhaps because Doyle is tired of these cases and perhaps because we're in a more dangerous international situation where the best course is to stay out of things.

The Bruce-Partington Plans

No politics please, we're detectives: Desperately searching for something to alleviate Holmes's restlessness, Watson knows better than to draw his attention to the news of wars, revolutions, and changes in government. These "did not come within the horizon of my companion" – and yet they soon will. You may not be interested in politics, but politics may be interested in you. The whole British government, in the person of Mycroft Holmes, arrives at 221B Baker Street, and Holmes and Watson are willy nilly swept up into international intrigue and espionage.

Never mind your usual petty puzzles of the police-court: So says Mycroft to his younger brother, thus laying out the real conflict in this story. Not between England and its enemies or its traitors within, but between the ways of the private detective and the forces of government and the international order. Mycroft offers Holmes "the whole force of the State," but Holmes just smiles and says, "All the queen's horses and all the queen's men cannot avail in this matter."

It is always 1895: And in this case Watson says that really is the year. But is it? The publication date is 1908, and the concerns of the Edwardian period are leaking heavily into this account set back in the last years of Victoria. Submarines, international espionage … where are the stolen horses of yesteryear, or the missing rugby player? Simpler times leading us inexorably to *The Valley of Fear* and the stymieing of the private detective.

But not quite yet. It is interesting that in this story, the full British government, or let us say Mycroft, do … what? Essentially nothing. As Holmes (our Holmes) says, the forces of the State are of little use here. What's needed is old-fashioned detective work, ferreting out the significance of points and junctions, determining that Cadogan West is no villain but a hero, or martyr, tracking down the real villains, and even retrieving the stolen plans. It is a miracle. The private detective carries the day, wins the battle (even if a war is coming that will put him in the shade, at least for a moment).

But let's consider government matters … And patriotism. At first Holmes is disdainful of possible rewards for helping the government. The honours list? Bah, I play the game for its own sake, he says. But by the end of the story he's playing the loyal soldier. "Think of Mycroft's note," he says to Watson, "of the Admiralty, the Cabinet, the exalted person who waits for news." And later: "For England, home and beauty." And there is also his suggestion to Watson that if he is at a loss for something to do, he can begin writing the narrative "of how we saved the State."

Perhaps Holmes is speaking a bit tongue in cheek – and yet the country, patriotism, seems to have overcome him, or taken him over. It's a new world in which even detectives have to work for grand causes instead of worrying over orange pips. And don't forget his emerald pin.

Things fall apart: One moment everything is the height of efficiency at the office where the plans were stolen. And now, laments Sidney Johnson, everything is a mess: two deaths and the papers gone. Is there some larger symbolic meaning in this? The international order has disrupted the local; it's the theme of this story, I think.

The two deaths: Cadogan West, of course (and isn't it appropriate that someone whose name sounds like a subway station dies on the Underground?) and also Sir James Walter. "How did he die?" Holmes asks, but we never learn. Was it natural or did he kill himself for shame, Holmes asks? (Or did his brother kill him, I wonder?) But this is simply dropped. Why? Holmes doesn't usually ignore unexpected deaths. Perhaps he is too busy trying to save the State, but still …

Murder vs. Treason: Murder is worse, says Holmes, bringing me up short. It is a "more terrible crime," he says, but if he were really a convert to the importance of saving the State, surely he wouldn't say such a thing. Still a private detective at heart, it seems.

However improbable: Holmes says, "We must fall back upon the old axiom that when all other contingencies fail, whatever remains, however improbable, must be the truth." But this is no old axiom: this is Holmes quoting himself (in *The Sign of the Four*). Oh, well, if things are falling apart, perhaps it's good to hold on to old axioms and to do solid detective work, which is what Holmes does in this story, though he does theorize more than usual and even lets us in on his thinking (partly), so much so that I was wondering where else the story had to go once we had discovered that someone killed Cadogan West and put him on top of the railway car. But then there is the twist at the end, the unexpected bird, the real inside man.

Holmes and Watson: Besides holding onto old axioms, Holmes seems quite close to Watson in this case. "I will do nothing serious without my trusted comrade and biographer at my elbow," he says, and then when Watson reluctantly agrees to the burglary, there is something near to tenderness in Holmes's eye. He does rather spoil the moment, though, by saying that if Watson should get arrested for carrying burglary equipment it would be "a most unfortunate complication." The case comes first, after all, and perhaps we need to fend off excessive tenderness.

A children's party: How many children's parties are there in the canon? Why is there one next door when Holmes and Watson break into Oberstein's? Is the "merry buzz" of the children meant to contrast with the serious task of saving the Nation? There is also the "soft rhythm" of the policeman's step. Again the contrast between everyday life and the greater dangers that are looming, which are perhaps also signified by the "low, harsh murmur" of the approaching train. A loud roar is coming …

The Dying Detective

And now for something completely different: Hardly a detective story at all. Instead, a story about the detective, a dying detective, our detective. A medical story about Holmes, with Watson the one who can take charge, or so he thinks. "A sick man is but a child," he says, but Holmes won't let himself be babied or told what to do. In fact, Holmes behaves more like a difficult adolescent, saying hurtful things to Watson – not to mention misleading both him and Mrs. Hudson.

Mrs. Hudson: Yes, she gets a leading role here, at least in the opening scenes, a bit like Mrs. Warren in "The Red Circle." And like Mrs. Warren, she gets totally forgotten at the end. Not nice. But Holmes (and the whole story) seem not very nice here.

But suspenseful: Yes, there is suspense. Though it's not a traditional Holmesian story at all – no client, no pre-client banter, no parlour tricks. But suspense over what's going on. Is Holmes really sick? Is it some sort of trick? It must be a trick – Holmes can't die here, not again – but then what is going on?

Dying: First there was Reichenbach, then there was the bust in "The Empty House" (another story featuring Mrs. Hudson), and now this. If only Holmes would die so Conan Doyle wouldn't have to write more stories about him. But no such luck. Holmes is just acting, and all to lure a murderer into confessing. It sounds less like Holmes than Columbo.

Coins and Oysters: Okay, what is going on with these? Watson is supposed to balance his coins in his pockets while Holmes rambles on about oysters covering the seabed. We've done our part about them, Watson, Holmes adds. About oysters? Do the oysters stand for criminals? They have natural enemies, Holmes adds. Who? The police? The walrus and the carpenter?

Coals of Fire: And then there are those coals of fire. Culverton Smith uses the phrase when he comes to see Holmes – as if he is somehow forgiving him and thus, in the Biblical way, heaping coals of fire on his head. Is Culverton Smith a good Christian? Or perhaps a bad one? Forgiveness in the Bible seems almost a way to punish your enemies, and Culverton Smith does want to punish Holmes. His forgiveness or good nature seems insincere: is that perhaps why it doesn't work? The coals of fire end up heaped on Culverton Smith instead, and the vengeance enacted is Holmes's, not his.

Vengeance: Is this a story about vengeance, then? Perhaps a settling of accounts. A bringing of a criminal to justice, the end of an earlier case not presented in the canon. It's almost as if this is the mere second half of an unwritten story. Or the back story to something we don't have: the murder of Victor Savage, Culverton's nephew. Or it's a bit like the second half of "The Red Circle" or "Wisteria Lodge": some deeper past story that explains the present – except here there is no present, except for the dying detective. Very strange. And short. Is this the shortest story in the canon?*

We could add to it: suppose the story opened with a client coming to Holmes talking the strange death of Culverton Smith. Holmes would nose around and eventually discover that the killing was a revenge killing for the death of Victor Savage. That would be more Holmesian. We could even throw in a few parlour tricks. I see that you are thinking

_____

* Actually, "The Veiled Lodger" is the shortest.

of tropical diseases, Watson. Something like that. But never mind.

Never have I had such a shock, says Watson, when the supposedly ill Holmes leaps out of bed. Never? Not when Holmes returned from Reichenbach? Not when that old man turned out to be a disguise for the supposedly dead Holmes? Methinks the doctor doth protest too much. To pump up the story because he fears it is dying too? And why two hours locked in a room? And why the pictures of celebrated criminals? Aren't they the enemy? Would Wellington have a picture of Napoleon in his room? Well, maybe he would.

Strange how the brain controls the brain: What does that mean? The delirious side controls the rational? Are there two brains, two sides of the brain? Some very modern neurological thinking emerges from Holmes's delirium.

Smug and demure respectability: How odd for a house to be smug and demure, but perhaps this is synecdoche or metonymy: it stands for how its inhabitant (Culverton Smith) is: a supercilious type, dismissive of Watson until he learns he comes from Holmes. Snobbery, thy name is the outsider from Sumatra trying to put on airs.

Non-conductance: Holmes says he's like a battery pouring energy into a non-conductor. This is the opposite of the problem he has when he has no cases. Then he lacks energy. Here he has energy but can't harness it, or so he pretends, because of his supposed illness. Actually, it's Watson whose energies are frustrated: stuck in the room, locked in, for two hours before he can go for assistance. And then he is full of conducted energy, pushing past the butler and getting Culverton Smith to come. He is an excellent messenger, as Holmes says, but perhaps he aspires to something more? It's not entirely clear what, though. He is always loyal Watson, writing up his tales of his remarkable friend. Perhaps Mrs. Hudson is not the only one in awe – though perhaps the awe is undercut by presenting us with Holmes's bad behaviour. A little ambiguity to season the veneration. The great man who irritates so. Such is the canon, at least in its later passages. Journeys end with lovers bleating.

The Disappearance
of Lady Frances Carfax

Wait, didn't we just do this story? There's the bearded man pursuing the young damsel. He's forgotten his bicycle this time, and she's maybe not so young, but … And he turns out to be a good guy, not the villain – except some commentators ask, What kind of good guy is this? More like a stalker. And Holmes and Watson leave him alone with the chloroformed damsel – stop.

So is this a rewrite of The Solitary Cyclist? In some ways. There's the "savage" bearded guy who isn't really a villain (just a stalker, ha ha). And then the really threatening guy, Dr. Shlessinger, this story's version of Roaring Jack Woodley. Except Roaring Jack was, well, roaring, and Dr. Shlessinger is studying the Biblical Midianites. (Descendants of Abraham, by the way, and there's an old Abrahams in this story – and that Biblical subtext just sort of peters out. But let's see, the Midianites were enemies of the Israelites, the Chosen People, so that suggests … I don't know, that Dr. Shlessinger is one of the bad guys?)

No adultery here: One can see an adulterous subtext in "The Solitary Cyclist": the damsel is engaged but has to fight off various suitors. Well, maybe that's not quite adulterous, but it does seem to reflect Conan Doyle's quasi-adulterous situation at the time of the Cyclist. Now, though, times have changed, there's no offstage fiancé, Lady Frances is totally unattached – a big deal is made of that, in fact. She's the solitary one, a stray chicken in danger of being eaten up by foxes.

Male chauvinism? Leslie Klinger sees male chauvinism in this depiction, a reaction perhaps to the New Woman of this period, the early feminists, suffragettes, and so forth. Such women are dangerous, Holmes says, but when he goes on to explain, it seems the danger is mostly to them, so I'm not sure the story is painting women in a negative light, except that it's perhaps suggesting they can't manage on their own and need protection.

Protection, protection, protection: Actually, if anyone is portrayed in a negative light, it's men, isn't it? One of them is a bearded savage, and the other is a con man after Lady F's jewels who is willing to go as far as murder. What kind of world is that for a woman to have to deal with?

Or for a Watson: Poor Watson. He's feeling old and rheumatic, and look how Holmes treats him: Go to Lausanne, track down Lady Frances, keep me informed – But then I'll show up unexpectedly and tell you you've done everything wrong (but has he? most commentators say no). And for good measure you'll get beaten up by the savage stalker, who I'll then tell you is the good guy. And the apparently good guy, that reverend studying the Midianites, turns out to be the bad guy. What a nightmare Watson finds himself in. Is this story a picture of a world gone nightmarish – or Turkish?

Turkish bath: A Turkish bath – what's that doing here? Of course, it could just be a Turkish bath; they were common enough. Still, it makes me think of associations with the word "Turk": for instance, the old slang sense of Turk meaning a barbarous man who treats people, especially women, badly. That does seem to be a motif in this story: barbarous men treating people badly. The Honourable (Honourable!) Philip Green, the nefarious Dr. Shlessinger, and the unfair, bullying Sherlock Holmes mistreating Watson, as the other two mistreat (or seem to mistreat) Lady Frances.

Who's the client? At first it seems to be Lady F's old governess (Miss Dobney, another unattached woman), or is it the family? But what family? Holmes says Lady Frances is "the last derelict" of what used to be a "goodly fleet." Very naval, but doesn't it mean there's no one in her family left? It's the disappearance of the aristocracy, that old foil for Holmes, but now is he, is Doyle, missing them? Perhaps they come back with the Honourable Philip Green, who is called the client at the end of the story. What is going on? Is it Miss Dobney or Philip Green? The unattached woman or the savage beast?

Multiple unattached women: Perhaps I should mention Rose Spender, the 90-year-old from the workhouse. An old nurse of Dr. Shlessinger's wife, or so Dr. S says (but do we believe the story?). But maybe the point is to remind us of the Brixton Workhouse: is that where unattached women end up? Oh, the dangers: the aristocracy is vanishing, women are on their own, and bearded men assault Dr. Watson. What is the world coming to? And when you try to make sense of it and send off your findings to your "illustrious friend," what do you get? Bizarre requests for information about Dr. Shlessinger's left ear and then a general upbraiding for making "a very pretty hash" of things. Ugh.

Holmes's blunders: Or so Dr. Shlessinger (aka Holy Peters) calls them – but they're not blunders either. Not really. Holmes expects to find Lady Frances in the casket; he does not, at first, but only because he is premature: she will be in there eventually. So it's only technically a blunder, and technicalities are being used to mock those who are essentially right, in this case Holmes. First we saw Watson unfairly accused of blundering; now it is Holmes. It can happen to the best of us; so there. But does that provide comfort? It still leaves Lady Frances undiscovered, at least for a moment. But then she is found and revived, so all is right with the world, except the Shlessingers escape, and Lady F is left with the man she was trying to escape from. Ah, well.

And more Turks: Philip Green is the son of the Admiral who fought the battle of the Sea of Azov in the Crimean War, the war in which England was on the side of the Turks. How can that be, England allied with Turkey? A sign of the disruption of the times, and perhaps of the fact that it is a perilous thing to leave Lady Frances with the Honourable, since he's the son of a Turkish ally. Oh, well, perhaps we need to find comfort in religion (smiting the Midianites) or solidarity with the workers (as Holmes demonstrates by dressing up like one). Or perhaps we should just resign ourselves to feeling old, or go for a Turkish bath (ha ha), something to alter our situation, an "alterative," as Dr. Watson puts it, and who better to prescribe for us than the old doctor?

Silent Women: These women are not only unattached, but silent. In fact, the silence of Lady Frances is what triggers the detective story. But her maid, Marie Devine (aha, more religion?) is silent too, though her lover gets a word in (well, we hear a summary of Marie's ideas from Dr. Watson, but it's not the same, is it?). Only Annie Fraser, Dr. Shlessinger's wife, speaks dialogue. Women are endangered and silenced in the story. Such Turks we are to them.

The Devil's Foot

Divorce: Conan Doyle, president of the Divorce Reform Union, here gives us a story all about the evils of the marriage laws. If only Leon Sterndale had been able to divorce his absent wife, he could have married Brenda Tregennis, and everyone would have lived happily ever after.

Well, but wait, Mortimer Tregennis would still have wanted to kill Brenda anyway, so maybe divorce wouldn't cure everything …

Mortimer Tregennis: What a name. Sounds like he should have been an evil wizard in *Harry Potter*. Meanwhile Leon Sterndale seems like Aslan out of the Narnia tales, not just a hunter of lions but a lion himself – though tamed by Holmes. What a strange crew we have here: lion and lion-tamer, evil wizard and his howling brothers (true, only made to howl by the evil wizard, but still …)

And the landscape: Bleak, sinister, on the Cornish coast, where the people speak a dialect somehow connected to ancient Chaldeans, or so Holmes thinks. Which connects back to our leonine Leon, godlike in an Old Testament vengeful way. Or not.

And beyond the landscape all the horrors of the universe, as perceived by Watson under the influence of the deadly drug, the devil's root, a devilish thing out of Africa, brought back by the imperialists and thus proving what? The dangers of Empire? Hmm. Actually, Holmes is the one called "the devil himself" … The canon frequently hints at other-worldly forces, and yet in the end we have perfectly natural explanations for everything. It shows great restraint on the part of the spiritualist Doyle. Or perhaps he wasn't truly a

Spiritualist yet, and these hints at the supernatural, beginning much earlier, of course, for instance in *The Hound of the Baskervilles*, are merely signs showing where his interests were moving.

Speaking of The Hound, isn't this story a bit reminiscent? Those bleak moors, and apparently devilish things afoot. And the horror! Which also puts me in mind of *The Sign of the Four*, not to mention Conrad's *Heart of Darkness*, which takes us back to imperialism and – but I'm not sure that gets us anywhere.

Gods: I suggested Leon Sterndale somehow seems like an Old Testament God, in appearance and desire for vengeance, but we all know who the true God of our canon is; after all, it's his canon. Thus when Holmes seems to clumsily knock over a watering pot, who among us thought, even for a moment, that he was actually clumsy? Of course, he did it deliberately to better see footprints.

Present Tense: I'm not sure I've seen this before in the canon: a moment when we seem to be observing things as they happen. I don't mean a crime; all the crimes are safely in the past and in Watson's notes. I mean those notes themselves. I mean Watson writing this story based on the notes. Holmes sends a telegram suggesting this story, and Watson is eager to get it written before Holmes changes his mind: "I hasten, before another cancelling telegram may arrive, to hunt out the notes which give me the exact details of the case ..." Why, here we are with Watson, hunting down his notes: and where does he keep these notes? Does he have an Index? How did he keep his files? Where did he keep them? Perhaps some Sherlockian has investigated.

Good Old Watson:
> *"You perceive our difficulties, Watson?"*
> *"They are only too clear," I answered with conviction.*

Ah, Watson, always convinced of the difficulties, always unable to see the truth. It takes our Holmes to do that.

Motive: One of the difficulties Holmes is speaking of is the apparent lack of motive. We eventually learn the motive, but it's almost an afterthought. Most of the focus is on the means: how was this done? As to why, shrug. Something about tin mining.

Back to Divorce: Or at least to singlehood. I was struck by the lack of marriage in the story. All the Tregennis siblings are single; so is the vicar. Holmes we need not speak of. Watson – well, was he married at this point? There's only Dr. Sterndale, and he doesn't want to be married; his unhappiness stems from it. Is this a paean to singlehood? But of course there is close friendship between Watson and Holmes here, though maybe that's not so good either because it nearly kills Watson. But it's true that this near death experience does evoke deep feeling from both our heroes, and so after all the ideal may be the Watson-Holmes relationship. What doesn't kill it makes it stronger.

Speaking of killing, the opening passages describe a bay that appears inviting, but is really a death trap, something that appears inviting but lures sailboats to destruction, and something that was well suited to Holmes's "grim humour" – does this mean humour in the sense of the comic or humour in the sense of Holmes's nature? Either way it paints a grim picture of life, one that perhaps fits the horrors of the story and the horrors Watson sees in his drug nightmare. And by the way, who is that "unspeakable dweller upon the threshold, whose very shadow would blast [Watson's] soul"? Is *that* the

Devil? Of course, that creature is just a drug-induced hallucination; still it must draw on something in Watson's brain: where would he get such a notion? Or is the suggestion that we all have these horrors inside us?

His Last Bow

What is this? My first thought was: Where's Baker Street? Where is the Holmesian parlour game and the repartee? Where is the client knocking at the door, let in by Mrs. Hudson? Where above all are Watson and Holmes? Can this be them atop the chalk cliffs? There are two, and one of them looks like a wandering eagle – that could be Holmes, no? But no, they are …

Germans: Germanophobia, says Joseph Kestner about this story, but I don't know. Of course, this is taking place on the eve of World War I, and was written during the conflict with the Kaiser's Germany, and yet … At the end Holmes is sympathetic to Von Bork: you played the game, done the best you could for your country. Pip, pip, tally ho, and all that. And yet supposedly this story marks a break with all that; the east wind is bringing something new, something to produce a "cleaner, better, stronger land." Is the war a good thing, then?

But it's the most terrible August ever seen, or so the unnamed narrator tells us at the beginning of the story. Who is this narrator? Why is Watson not narrating? Is it to universalize things, as Kestner says? But how does it do that? I keep coming back to …

Doubles: Von Bork and the Baron doubling Holmes and Watson. Smoking their cigars together. True, the burning ends look like the eyes of a malignant fiend, but still, Is there something of Baker Street about the German duo? They are trying to undermine England, it's true, and Holmes and Watson would never do that. Except hasn't Holmes all along been very un-English, even in his service to England? Watson of course is the quintessential Englishman, but the cocaine-injecting loner Holmes, I don't know.

American: And now he plays a caricature of an American. He is the master of disguise. That is partly what I thought at the beginning: is this German eagle really Holmes in disguise? Holmes can be anyone, an old bookdealer, an old woman, who knows? And an eagle, that sounds Holmesian.

Protagonist/Antagonist: Of course, Von Bork and the Baron are plotting something, taking the initiative. When you come to think of it, Holmes and Watson seldom do that. They sit at home in comfy Baker Street waiting for crime, waiting for criminals to initiate something that they can put right. So Von Bork and the Baron are the very opposite of Holmes and Watson. Or should we say mirror images?

A strong and secret central force: Moriarty? No, no, the German spy network. That's what Holmes has been lured out of retirement to fight. Sounds like Moriarty, though. Always this push towards one overarching enemy instead of believing in the individuality of evil.

Subverting the strong and secret central force: Holmes has completely undermined the spy network, has he not? Captured Von Bork, sent five of his agents into captivity, and so the German threat was ended, and there was no war after all.

No, wait, that's not right. So what is the power of Sherlock Holmes? Not much in the face of international militarism, as we perhaps also saw in *The Valley of Fear*. And yet this story is not gloomy the way that one was. It is written later, when the conflict is underway, and there is hope from that east wind, terrible as it may be.

But is it a degenerate world? Jacqueline Jaffe says this is an unusual description in the canon, but surely not. We see this sort of thing in *The Hound of the Baskervilles*, "The Naval Treaty," etc. There is decline that must be put right somehow, with the infusion of new blood – except now that's changed to the shedding of blood: the casualties of the war will somehow make us free?

But we see nothing of those casualties: Not in this story, set on the eve of the war, though written right in the middle of it. In the story we hear of British somnolence; the Brits are slumbering, or they were before the war, or so the Germans thought. Were they wrong? Holmes was at work, but was that enough? Is the point of the story to tell the British to wake up to the German threat? But it would have been pointless to say that in 1917, when the story actually appeared.

Was it to point fingers and say, You were slumbering in 1914; you should have been awake? Or were the Germans wrong? The British were not asleep; they had Holmes on the case. But why then the need for an east wind to make things clean? How indeed does the east wind fit in with Holmes? What use for a private detective in a public war? Maybe he should go back to his bees.

Honour: And is honour gone from the world, as the Germans say? Is it in fact outmoded in this "utilitarian age"? Is the east wind sweeping it away? Or bringing it back. Such confusion. It is a "changing age," though, or so Holmes says, but with Watson as its one fixed point. Except that fixed point is Watson's inability to understand that Holmes was speaking metaphorically about an east wind. So there's something solid, but lacking in perception in Watson – and in the British generally? Except for Holmes, of course, the opposite of solidity and the very definition of perceptiveness. But if a Holmes is not enough, perhaps you need an east wind.

Money: A story that begins with talk of the disappearance of honour ends with Holmes wanting to cash a cheque. He may be joking, it's true, and after all despite the supposed disappearance of honour, England did honour its treaty obligations (which of course meant going to war, so is honour such a great thing? more confusion: perhaps we need less honour, not more). Oh, well.

Start her up, Watson: For it's time that we were on our way. So says Holmes in almost the last words of the story. A farewell benediction? Is it the end of Sherlock Holmes? We will not see him after 1917 (chronologically, this is the last story in the canon), but of course there is a whole Case-Book still to come.

And I note the vehicle our heroes depart in: no more carriages for them, but a newfangled motorcar. A changing world indeed.

The Illustrious Client

"In the mud with my foot on his cursed face": That's how Kitty Winter would like to see Baron Gruner. And I thought, Wait a minute, we've seen something like that before: Lady X grinding her heel into the face of Charles Augustus Milverton after shooting him. Grisly stuff, female revenge on the male. Is Conan Doyle just repeating himself?

Not entirely: For instance, in the earlier story a lady does the shooting and the heel grinding. In this one Kitty Winter is no lady; she's what? A force of nature? A whirlwind, a flame, a she-devil, a leprous female Shinwell Johnson found in the "garbage" of the underworld? She lives in "Hell, London," but wishes Gruner in a deeper one. And she doesn't in the end go in for shooting and heel grinding, but for tossing acid in a man's face. It seems almost more horrifying.

And what man? Baron Gruner, a suave aristocrat from the Continent, from Austria. The Austrian murderer (perhaps), but civilized, handsome – except for a murderous mouth (oh, Conan Doyle, how you still believe in physiognomy: the face tells us all). But if we're looking at faces, there's Shinwell Johnson's coarse, scurvy-looking one, and Kitty Winter's ... we have delved into the underworld, the dregs, though Kitty Winter has a certain attractive liveliness about her. Maybe she represents the dark energies that we need to harness to avoid turning into frozen ethereal Violet de Mervilles. But still ...

Aristocrat vs. Aristocrat: So what we have here is our heroes reaching into the gutter to find a weapon with which to attack the aristocratic Baron Gruner on behalf of Colonel Sir James Damery and his illustrious client (the King?) who has taken an interest in the prospective marriage of Violet to the Baron.

Now, earlier in the canon, aristocrats are not a favoured species. In "The Naval Treaty" we are told that it is uncommon for a nobleman to act nobly. But here the first nobleman we see is quite appealing. (Well, he is not a nobleman perhaps, only a Colonel Sir, but Watson calls him an aristocrat.) Anyway, Colonel Sir James Damery seems quite appealing. Pleasant, honest, delicate.

So for a change the English upper classes seem to come off fairly well here, but the German baron …

German baron? Okay, Gruner is Austrian, not German. We did have a German baron in "His Last Bow," a story that is somewhat surprising for its lack of animus against the Germans. It was the middle of World War I, with Germany at war with England, but Holmes's attitude (and Conan Doyle's?) seemed to be, Pip, pip, good try, old boys, you've played well, only we have played better.

Austrian baron: The attitude to Baron Gruner is quite different. He is someone who must be stopped at all costs, even burglary and acid-throwing. And for what? What crime is he committing? Charles Augustus Milverton is in the midst of blackmailing when his life is brought short. Holmes wants to stop him and destroy his papers to save various marriages. In this story everything is inside out. Holmes wants to save papers (the "lust diary") to prevent a marriage.

But again, what crime is the Baron committing? He simply wants to marry Violet de Merville.

Ah, but what will he do? He's a murderer, we're told. He killed his previous wife, so action must be taken now to prevent another wife-murder. Is this about that past murder, Holmes asks? No, says Colonel Sir James, this is not about revenge for that, but prevention of a repetition. (And a repetition here in our blessed England, one might add.)

Symbolism: It suddenly struck me that this desperate attempt to use the lower orders to attack a foreign aristocrat might actually have something to do with international politics. The leaders of Germany had fought one war with England. Was there fear they might launch another? Is this what lurks beneath this story? A return of the German threat?

Revenge? But in the early 1920's was there such a threat? Maybe this is about revenge after all; maybe what is driving this story is what we might have expected to see in "His Last Bow": anger against Germans. (Yes, I know, Baron Gruner is Austrian. Still …)

Ethereal Woman: And what are we to make of Violet de Merville? So angelic and remote, not realizing the danger she is in. It annoys Sherlock Holmes: you have to see the danger of the Baron, why can't you? If I were to pursue the political allegory, I might see Violet as representing the wilfully ignorant leaders of Europe, not recognizing the dangers of a second European conflict.

Or is she just Woman? Women are the Other here: mysterious creatures no male can understand. Who can fathom their motives? Though Holmes (and Doyle) seem confident that a lust-diary will kill their interest. Maybe acid disfigurement too, though Holmes says that wouldn't have been enough.

Secrecy: Then there is the theme of secrecy. Holmes doesn't like Sir James's secrecy surrounding the client, but he is quite willing to be secretive himself, even to Watson, which of course is sometimes necessary for the sake of the story, but is secrecy good or bad? Holmes is actually quite open and unsecretive towards Baron Gruner: he sends in his card to him and tells him exactly what he wants. Is it more important to keep your friends in the dark than your enemies? Maybe there are things your friends are better off not knowing.

In Milverton the idea is to protect secrets, the secrets of good people who've committed indiscretions. Here the idea is to expose secrets, the secrets of a bad person who poses a threat. Secrecy is neither good nor bad, but a tool? After all, Watson is always secretive to us: he knows the solutions when he sits down to write, but he keeps them from us till the end so we'll be entertained.

And finally, insects: Why is Baron Gruner described as having "little waxed tips of hair under his nose, like the short antennae of an insect"? Is this an attempt to dehumanize him? What do antennae do anyway? They are feelers, sense organs? Baron Gruner's "quivered with amusement" when he listened to Holmes. It seems quite monstrous somehow; is he being portrayed as a monster to justify the acid attack to come?

He's also called an affable cat contemplating mice, and "some people's affability is more deadly than the violence of coarser souls."

In this story the threat is not from coarser souls like Shinwell Johnson. Shinwell Johnson can be used as an agent; Holmes uses him as an agent. The true threat is this smooth-talking foreign aristocrat who loves Chinese pottery. I was going to say it's not 1895 anymore; there are snapshots and telephones. But even in the earlier stories the threat is from where? Not the lower classes. And here it's creatures from below who can be used to fight the real threat – except maybe they get a little bit out of control. Maybe it's dangerous to set a Kitty Winter loose. The result makes Holmes recoil in horror – and do we?

The Blanched Soldier

Our Man Godfrey: Godfrey, Godfrey, haven't we had a Godfrey before? No, not the one who married Irene Adler … (by the way, in the Hollywood movie *My Man Godfrey*, Godfrey marries an Irene too; I wonder if the screenwriter read "A Scandal in Bohemia," but that's another story).

Another Godfrey: The one I was thinking of was the one in "The Missing Three-Quarter." In fact, he is the missing three-quarter. So a missing Godfrey there and another one here. If you want a missing man, he has to be a Godfrey, I suppose (though originally it was going to be a different name, I learn from Klinger).

But why? I don't mean why does the name have to be Godfrey, but why do each of these Godfreys go missing? I note a similarity in the two stories: in both cases Godfrey has a good friend who is looking for him. So is "The Blanched Soldier," like "The Missing Three-Quarter," about friendship? I think so. In both a good friend goes looking for the missing Godfrey. In "The Blanched Soldier," as if to bring home the point, someone else has gone missing: Watson. Watson has deserted me for a wife, says Sherlock Holmes. In "The Missing Three-Quarter" that Godfrey has also deserted his friend for a wife. In this story, though, the latest Godfrey has deserted for – well, because of illness. A skin condition. Leprosy (maybe).

Leprosy? Or maybe it's not leprosy, maybe it's only pseudo-leprosy. Now, the first story this one reminded me of is the one just before, "The Illustrious Client," in which Kitty Winter's face is described as leprous and Shinwell Johnson also has a skin condition – not to mention the bad skin condition Baron

Gruner ends up with. Is Doyle suddenly obsessed with skin conditions? And horror? Is this some sort of delayed reaction to World War I, as some suggest?

Horror: The blanched soldier at the window, like something out of *Wuthering Heights*. And leprosy. But it isn't leprosy (probably). So, wait. In "The Illustrious Client," the problem was that a real danger was being ignored (Violet is blithely going to go ahead with marriage to a predator), but here what seems like danger isn't. Well, that's okay then, we can just relax. Maybe we need to read these two stories in tandem: don't ignore real dangers, but don't get upset over false ones?

And danger from whom? Godfrey has been to Africa. Always something bad out of Africa? Though note that it's a Boer hospital that he stumbles into, where he sleeps in the leper's bed. Don't go sleeping with lepers (people did think leprosy was sexually transmitted – though of course Godfrey didn't have sex in the bed). And Boer lepers, not native Africans, but Dutch, another set of rival Europeans. Is there danger out of Europe? That's what I thought the message of "The Illustrious Client" was. But here the danger turns out to be illusory. In fact, it's thinking there is a danger that is the danger: if you think you're going to come down with an awful skin condition, you will. If you think there is danger, you could create it with your thinking: sounds a bit like how World War I came about: if you mobilize for war out of fear of war, then you'll get war.

But back to friendship: Chris Redmond's father says the absence of Watson means we lose the usual Holmes-Watson interchange. But do we? James Dodd seems to fill in nicely, first by being amazed at the standard Holmesian parlour tricks (You're from South Africa, the Middlesex Corps, etc. etc.) and then by getting in a Watsonian jab when he plunges into his story midstream and in response to Holmes's bafflement says, But I thought you knew everything.

So a friend can be replaced? But Holmes does seem to miss his Watson, and perhaps the point of the story is to tell us that the two should not be separated, certainly not for a marriage. James Dodd won't give up his friend to illness. Should Holmes give up his to marriage? Is marriage an illness? Of course, in this story what we seem to have is a pseudo-illness. Perhaps Watson's marriage is a pseudo-marriage?

When you have eliminated all which is impossible: That old quote, recycled from *The Sign of the Four*, but not so convincingly deployed here. What's so impossible about Godfrey being insane or even a criminal? No, the dice are loaded here in favour of leprosy, because it is somehow important to get leprosy into this story, as in the story before. The strange obsession I have already noted.

Still, Holmes deduces well here, though it is a bit of a misfire to ask about the newspaper which, if it had been the *Lancet* or the *British Medical Journal*, might have told him something. But instead it was the *Spectator*. So why bother even telling us about it? I suppose to let us know that that would have been further proof that the "keeper" in the garden was a medical man. But Holmes knew this was a medical man without that proof; was the deductive theorizing enough in this case? That would seem to go against all of Holmes's usual emphasis on the facts. Oh, well, I suppose there just had to be leprosy, or pseudo-leprosy.

Bleached skin: One of the symptoms of the disease. And the disease, or something, has turned Godfrey Emsworth, a "frank, manly lad," into "something slinking … furtive … guilty." If "The Illustrious Client" showed us a predatory masculinity in Baron Gruner, here we have something much weaker. Is this a danger Conan Doyle sees, upstanding manly Brits being laid waste by foreign diseases? But it's just a pseudo-disease, so maybe not.

But where are the women? There's a phantom whom Watson has married. There's Emsworth's mother and the butler's wife. In "The Missing Three-Quarter" there was an important female presence at the end which explained all: the dying wife. The men in that story are trying to save her. Here there's no woman to save; the person who is sick is not the wife of the missing man; it is the missing man himself, and perhaps even though the illness is waved away at the very end, the story is betraying some anxiety about the health of British men. It is the missing man in this case who needs caring for or rescue, and who is indeed rescued more than once: by the doctor in the leper hospital and now by more doctors, along with Sherlock Holmes and his friend, and even his gruff but protective father.

Once upon a time, it was Godfrey who could do the protecting, saving his friend Dodd in battle. "He was a fine man," says the butler, but now … One critic I've read (Joseph Kestner) sees postwar anxiety in the later stories, reflecting a dissolution of "patriarchal structures." Is that what's going on? Is it the end of patriarchy that this story foresees? Though if it is, it's strange that there are no women around to pick up the pieces.

The Mazarin Stone

Consider the furniture! So says Holmes to prevent violence at 221B. The furniture? Really. Earlier he points Watson to his customary arm-chair, and says it's good to see you back in your old quarters. And we agree: it is good. Why did he ever go away? Don't talk to me about marriages; how can Watson keep deserting his good friend: what deep dynamic is at work there? Is it the nature of all relationships: the pulling away and the coming back together? Or is that dancing? Still, the whole series began with the two of them finding lodgings together, one of the most famous lodgings ever, and yet Watson keeps leaving (but then coming back). Is it actually Doyle at work, trying to get Watson away? If he can't kill off Holmes, then at least get rid of Watson?

Speaking of killing Holmes, here we are with airguns and bad guys trying to shoot him, so that he has to resort to a dummy. But this is nothing new. Even Watson says, "We used something of the sort once before." Yes, to thwart Sebastian Moran in "The Empty House," and in fact the play upon which "The Mazarin Stone" is based (*The Crown Diamond*, a now forgotten effort of Conan Doyle's) had Moran returning as the villain, but in story form the character has been renamed Count Negretto Sylvius, which translates as Little Black Wood. Joseph Kestner says this is a little jab at *Blackwood's Magazine*, but I can't quite see the point of that. It made me think more of Germany's Black Forest, and thus might play into Conan Doyle's interest in things German in this postwar period (the story is from 1921), but I'm not sure where that takes us, and in any case the Count is supposed to be half-Italian, not German.

But back to the furniture: It's just a little joke, I suppose, but are we come to this? Is this all that's left? The furniture? It does seem to be a story in which the furniture of Holmes and Watson has been reassembled, but the spirit has gone missing. Told in the third person, in not very convincing fashion, it shows us Watson returning to an old haunt, as one would to a place once important but now neglected – and in fact that 1921 date may be significant: it marks the first new Holmes story in years. Though it is placed third in *The Case-Book*, it was the first written after "His Last Bow," which appeared in 1917, and it is the first in the postwar period. Let us pick over what has survived the War to End All Wars: perhaps that is in part what is going on here – and in *The Crown Diamond*, which Doyle subtitled "An Evening with Sherlock Holmes," as if to give a little encore for the Great Detective who had already made His Last Bow … so what was this? A little something to give to the public, like *The Hound of the Baskervilles*, that other restarting of the canon (well, there were several, weren't there).

This isn't one of the best, though, is it? Almost more like a pastiche, I thought as I read it, and *The Sherlock Holmes Book* says the same thing. Heavy-handed and "hammy," to use their word – and written in the third person. Who is this third person? Who is the narrator? Hilariously, I thought, this is just about the only story Leslie Klinger and the traditionalist Sherlockians are willing to attribute to Arthur Conan Doyle. It's not very good, you see, so it couldn't be by Watson, the usual author. Ha, ha.

I suppose Doyle resorted to third person because the original was in play form, but surely he could have worked on it a bit more to make Watson the narrator and to restore us some Watson-Holmes repartee. But no, this is more Watson returning to pick over things and a rehash of "The Empty House," mixed in with a diamond theft.

It's the stone I want. So says Holmes. He has already snared the evil Count and his sidekick (Holmes and Watson versus Sylvius and Merton, hmm: doubling, sidekicks, meaning ... I don't know: sometimes I think Doyle just likes to go in for doubling). Anyway, Holmes has his shark and his gudgeon (a small fish), but he wants the gem, the Crown jewel, the Mazarin stone, named after an adviser to Louis XIII, a great yellow thing, signifying what? And why is it more important to get the stone than the criminals? Holmes is ready to let the criminals go if they will give him the stone, even though arresting them would make the world a better place. But he must have the stone. Because the government wants it? The King? Because of patriotism, symbolism, not letting a foreigner steal part of England's heritage? Who knows?

Lord Cantlemere: Not in the theatrical version of the story, the Lord appears here to play the role of disbelieving client, doubting the powers of Sherlock Holmes, and also representing something rather out of date, with his mid-Victorian whiskers. Holmes, in contrast, has moved with the times and uses a gramophone (in the play version he uses as well an elaborate electrical apparatus). Cantlemere also plays the part of foil or butt of Holmes's practical joke in planting the reclaimed diamond in his overcoat, a sleight of hand that I'm thinking Doyle might have learned from his new friend Harry Houdini (the two became acquainted in 1920).

Practical joke? Since when does Holmes go in for this sort of humour? Or do his various disguises count? We certainly see several here: well, actually we don't see them; we just hear about them, first of all from Billy the Page. This is Billy's most extended appearance in the canon, as Bob Coghill has pointed out, and Watson makes a point of saying that Billy is unchanged, but it is hard for us to judge because we have hardly ever seen him before. So even this comment about things being unchanged is more like showing us that something has changed. It's the era of gramophones and electricity now, not gaslight and horsedrawn carriages.

Disguise: And what about the disguises? Joseph Kestner thinks dressing up as an old woman indicates blurring of gender, but maybe it's just a disguise, part of the deception in this story. Both the Count and the Lord get fooled: The canon does like to make fun of aristocrats, and Holmes remains imperturbably in control. He knows everything, as Billy says, though not perhaps the future. Or perhaps he knows the future only too well. When the Count starts talking about death, Holmes stops him by saying these anticipations of the future are morbid. Intimations of mortality? And what are we to make of Holmes's comment that "we all have neglected opportunities to deplore"? So many things we might have done, but … Ah, well, we can still make a few last turns in the old quarters, and as it turns out "The Mazarin Stone" would be just the first of the last dozen stories Doyle wrote about the Master before finally laying down his pen.

The Three Gables

I shall not appear in the matter: So says the mysterious Isadora Klein, remaining artfully in the background after setting her minions to work to terrorize poor Mrs. Maberley. Holmes thinks she has miscalculated, but though she disagrees, he is somehow able to convince her to pay 5,000 pounds: as hush money? Has Holmes turned blackmailer? A sort of Charles Augustus Milverton, holding compromising letters over his victims? But all Holmes has is the last page of a bad novel. Still, it somehow does the trick and will lead to some solace for his client, who can now get away from it all on a round-the-world journey.

Hmm: It doesn't seem quite right somehow. Commentators have said the story doesn't fit together, and indeed you have the opening comedy, a sort of minstrel show involving the black boxer Steve Dixie (which has inspired charges of racism against Holmes, Doyle, and Watson). Not to mention the "huge awkward chicken," Susan the squawking or wheezing servant who is also in Isadora's pay. All that comedy mixed in with the anguish of Mrs. Maberley, the perhaps greater anguish of her dead son Douglas, spurned by Isadora for a better marriage, and the mention of "the belle dame sans merci," an apparent reference to the haunting poem by John Keats. What can it all mean?

Echoes? People compare it to "A Scandal in Bohemia" and "The Illustrious Client." I see an interesting connection with the latter: instead of an Austrian baron, you have a Spanish-German adventuress using the lower orders to deal blows to good old English people. Isadora's people beat up Douglas Maberley and burglarize his mother's house. Is Doyle returning to his foreign danger motif?

If only he had a poker: In the opening scene Holmes faces down Steve Dixie with icy cool, but what really saves the day, it seems, is Watson making a clatter with a poker. You can get more done with icy coolness and a poker than with icy coolness alone, as Al Capone might have said. At the end, though, it's Isadora with the poker, pushing at the "calcined mass" of the burned manuscript. And in opposition to her villainous ways all we seem to have on the other side is bumbling idiocy. It's Violet de Merville all over again. Have your lawyer stand guard, says Holmes. And Mrs. Maberley doesn't even do that. (As if a lawyer would be any use against burglars anyway.) Holmes and Watson depart, knowing that the answer is probably in the recently arrived trunks from Italy, but they do not bother to open them themselves. We'll call again tomorrow, Holmes says.

Villainous? I've called Isadora villainous, but some say we are meant to sympathize with her. Or that Douglas Maberley is in the wrong for trying to possess her. I come back to Keats, though, and his poem about the poor knight languishing by the lake where no birds sing. (Is this why we have a squawking chicken in the story?) The poor knight has been rejected by an alluring woman, much as Douglas Maberley has been. Don't we sympathize with him? (But there are readings of the Keats poem that tell us to sympathize with the woman, so who knows?)

Gables? The story gets its name from the "feeble" projections atop Mrs. Maberley's house. They're a feeble justification for naming the house, and perhaps even more feeble for naming the story. What do the gables have to do with anything? They're triangular, and perhaps one can see a love triangle here (Isadora-Douglas-Lord Lomond?), but ... By the way, writing Isadora-Douglas this way makes me think of Isadora

Duncan, the famous dancer notorious for her love life: did Conan Doyle have her in mind? And Lomond reminds me of the song about "me and my true love" never meeting again – and again by a lake, as in the Keats poem.

Disappointed love: So we have a disappointed lover (Douglas Maberley) whose love turns to hate and a novel. But is a novel any better at fighting off ruffians than a lawyer? Are we lacking the proper tools to fight villainy now in the 1920's? Although again on the issue of villainy: what exactly is the crime Isadora has committed? Holmes talks of compounding a felony for accepting money to cover up … what? The burglary? The earlier beating up of Douglas M? The anguish caused to Mrs. M? The first two might be felonies, I suppose, but at least no one died – except of course poor Douglas. But that was from pneumonia, contracted while abroad, in Italy, where he imbibed the cruel Italian spirit, according to Isadora. Something in the air, she says: well, did that cause his pneumonia? Or did he really die of a broken heart? Is Isadora to blame for that? But he was the cruel one, she says. Ah, who can settle these things?

And how in the end does it all fit together? The minstrel show and the poem by Keats. Pierre Nordon thought the story much too changeable. Chris Redmond sees an uneasy mix of raciness and elegance, but maybe life is an uneasy mix of raciness and elegance. You have knockabout minstrel show moments of comedy and times when there is anguish and disappointed yearning turned to hatred. All mixed with a little scandal, courtesy of Langdale Pike. And where does the scandal lead? Not to the squawking chicken and the black bruiser, but to the Spanish beauty. The bullies beat Douglas Maberley up, but is it the woman who kills him? As Baron Gruner might have killed Violet de Merville?

But no vitriol here: No one destroys Isadora's looks by throwing acid in her face, but her looks are going all the same. She prefers to be seen in the half light. Age comes to us all, I suppose, but at least if we age and die, we leave children behind – except the one hope for that, the one lively son in the story, has died too, leaving only his aging mother in a rundown house with three gables, whose only pleasure now will be to escape on a trip around the world. Refined and cultured Mrs. Maberley is reduced to that. And how, come to think of it, did she end up in a rundown house? Who are these Maberleys? Is this what England is reduced to? It used to be refined and cultured, but now it is poor and depressing? Chris Redmond, contrasting this story with "A Scandal in Bohemia," says the latter channels the high art of opera while this one is racy and low, like a cheap novel.

And yet there is life in this story. Passions. Holmes laments the fact that nowadays one is unlikely to find buried treasure because people bury their treasure in the post-office bank. "But there are always some lunatics about," he adds. "It would be a dull world without them." And lovers too and poets.

Even comedians: Commentators are unhappy with Holmes's sneering at Steve Dixie and the servant Susan, but the better comedy in the story turns, as so often, on the Holmes-Watson relationship. There's the suggestion that Watson's fiddling with the poker may have had more to do with scaring the boxer off than Holmes's icy coolness. And then there's Holmes's comment that "Dr. Watson agrees, so that settles it." Sarcasm? But it's the Holmes and Watson we love. So some things remain.

Dainty hands: "Have a care!" says Holmes to Isadora. "Have a care! You can't play with edged tools for ever without cutting those dainty hands." Is he smitten by her dainty hands? Is that why he lets her off easy? And what are the edged tools? Her hired ruffians? Or the men whose hearts she breaks? Is it dangerous to recruit from the shadows? But Holmes will do it himself with Shinwell Johnson and Kitty Winter in "The Illustrious Client." So many questions.

The Sussex Vampire

Asking for a friend: Oh, Watson, did you really not realize that Ferguson was talking about himself? But what did Holmes mean when he said, "There are unexplored possibilities about you, [Watson]." This is just after he's said, "I never get your limits, Watson." Does he want to explore those limits? It would be only fair, since the whole series began with Watson enumerating what Holmes did and did not know about: all aspects of crime detection, yes; the arrangement of the solar system, no. Though with Holmes it's more that he's wilfully decided to ignore some areas of human endeavour to focus his powers. With Watson, well …

Still, what exactly are those unexplored possibilities in Watson? Is Holmes just joking? Even if so, I am curious now: what might we find in Watson? What limitations? He does rather take things at face value, I suppose, and hence in this story he tries to see how the facts might accord with stories he's heard of vampires who were not dead people.

Rubbish, Watson, rubbish! That's what Holmes has to say about all this vampire talk, which is odd in a way, given his creator's growing interest in Spiritualism. Of course, Spiritualism is not quite the same as Vampirism (at least, I hope not), but Conan Doyle knew about vampires too, through his friend Bram Stoker. Of course, Stoker was writing fiction (I hope). In any case, the Holmesian universe remains resolutely rational. Holmes won't believe in a supernatural agency here, and he's quite right. Ferguson's nameless wife is no vampire.

But why is she nameless? It makes her perhaps more mysterious, foreign, alien? This is yet another story in the canon touching on foreignness, and as in "The Priory School," it comes down on the side of the foreigner. She may seem like a vampire – and after all, blood on her lips, the wound on her infant son's neck … who wouldn't think something very wrong is going on? Who wouldn't lock her up? But exactly who did the locking? We learn the wife won't see the husband: did she lock herself in?

And is it racist to suspect her of evil, as the critic Sampo Rassi says? Or is it even more racist to proclaim that there can't be any vampires in Sussex? Vampires in Sussex, who ever heard of such a thing? Maybe in foreign parts, but in England?

Good foreigners and bad: Is it the Latin ones that are good and the Teutonic bad? But in Priory School, the German is a good character. Maybe there's more an ambivalence in the whole canon: sometimes what comes from abroad can be very helpful, sometimes less so. It makes me think of nitrates. Robert Ferguson met his Peruvian wife because he'd had business dealings with her father "in connection with the importation of nitrates." Nitrates, eh? Les Klinger connects this to bat guano (a sort of manure), but the interesting thing for me is that nitrates are used both for fertilizer and explosives: this foreign material can help things grow or blow things up. Beware! Beware!

Vigor, the Hammersmith wonder: Who (or what?) is that? Donald Redmond notes that Vigor was an actual surname and notes that another commentator says the phrase is an allusion to a mechanical horse. My interest, though, is in the meaning of the name. In a way, this is a story about vigour, or the lack of it. This lack is most prominent in young Jacky, who has an injured spine and frankly seems quite spineless. I mean, really, attacking his helpless baby brother with Peruvian poison? Not to mention the dog.

England in decline: England seems always to be in decline in the canon. As far back as *The Hound of the Baskervilles* we get this sense and of the need to infuse fresh blood into the Old Country. Here we are told of the "odour of age and decay" that pervades Ferguson's crumbling mansion, typically (for the canon) containing an ancient core with more modern wings. Perhaps the new wings are an attempt to reinvigorate, but really what we need is fresh blood from Peru, it seems. Ferguson himself is not what he was, having lost much of his hair and his former athletic physique. Watson isn't much better.

And Ferguson's first son, from a wife who was presumably British, is a feeble coward. But the new son is a wonder (there's that word again) or at least "a wonderful mixture of the Saxon and the Latin" (which actually makes me think of the English language). If only we can unite Saxon and Latin, then we can be rejuvenated, reinvigorated, be a wonder again.

More explosives: "One forms provisional theories and waits for time or fuller knowledge to explode them." So says Holmes, and it seems a reasonable approach: how can you proceed without at least a provisional theory? But no, it's a bad habit, he says. One should proceed without theorizing at all? Well, that is in accord with his prescriptions elsewhere, but …

And what is the provisional theory that's been exploded here? Holmes doesn't say, but he makes the remark after being told that only one of the Peruvian wife's attacks on Jacky occurred at the same time as an attack on the baby. That complicates things, says Holmes. Does it? Surely he has already figured out that the wife is attacking Jacky because of Jacky's attacks on the baby, and that turns out to be the truth.

This reminds me of "The Blanched Soldier," where Holmes hopes to see the mystery man in the garden reading a medical journal to prove his theory that he is a medical man.

In both cases, the facts don't quite fit, but the theory is right anyway. Hmm. Is this a backdoor way of smuggling Spiritualism in anyway? Well, not all the facts fit, but the theory is quite right …

Holmes says he is less scientific than Watson has made him out to be. Perhaps he is right, but not in the way he means. It seems perfectly scientific to develop a provisional theory, but to hold onto it when it is exploded, no. And yet that is what Holmes does here (and in "The Blanched Soldier"), and the stories vindicate him. Sometimes you just know you're right, even if the facts are against you, I suppose. I suppose.

So why did she hit Jacky twice? If only one attack was provoked by an attack on the baby, what was the reason for the other one? We need more information, I think, but we are abandoning facts now in the later stages of the canon. We have vampires and exploded theories instead. Not to mention a dog that knows when it's being talked about and who can survive an attack of Peruvian curare. (This is like testing the sheep in "Silver Blaze," where of course there is another famous dog, who does nothing. This one perhaps does too much.)

It is life and death to me: So says Robert Ferguson, pleading with Holmes to realize that the case is more than just an intellectual puzzle. But surely the whole point of the canon is for Holmes to solve intellectual puzzles. Is Doyle thinking that Holmes's approach is actually a bit callous? But we shouldn't discount the power of intellectual puzzles, the true power of the canon, which dips us into danger and, even more disconcerting, mystery – and then rescues us. What could be more life and death than that?

Return to normalcy: That closing letter to the lawyers. How odd, except that it returns us to the everyday world after our plunge into the weird and unknown. Very Jungian in a way. The hero's journey over, we return to civilization, perhaps rejuvenated from our experiences with "vampires."

The Three Garridebs

Comedy? What a wonderful opening paragraph: "It may have been a comedy, or it may have been a tragedy ..." It reminds me of something, I'm not sure what. Dickens in *A Tale of Two Cities*? ("It was the best of times, it was the worst of times ...") Or something.

But how is it a comedy? Where is the element of comedy in this tale of Garridebs, real and phony? One commentator (Barrie Hayne) says it is in the portrayal of the "absurd" Nathan Garrideb with his collection of antiquities, and also in the search for people with the odd Garrideb name, but are these things really funny?

Another commentator (Sherloki1854) says comedy here is used in the Shakespearean sense of happy ending, and the happy ending in this story is the declaration of affection between Holmes and Watson in what the commentator calls the gayest story in the canon.

Gayest? Well, there certainly is affection here between Holmes and Watson, but what does that prove? Chris Redmond is ready to go down this path, though, seeing homosexual imagery in the story, notably in the attack on the cellar by the phony American Garrideb. Shades of "The Red-Headed League" – and certainly there are lots of similarities between the two stories, such as the outlandish fabrication (about redheads or Garridebs) meant really just to lure a Jabez Wilson or a Nathan Garrideb away. Many have noted the parallels, but perhaps we should look at the differences.

Differences: In "The Red-Headed League" Holmes and Watson are engaged because Jabez Wilson has lost his sinecure, his little gift of extra money for nothing (well, for copying encyclopedia articles, which is a benefit in itself,

257

Sherlock Holmes says half-seriously, because it has provided him with "minute knowledge ... on every subject which comes under the letter A").

In "The Three Garridebs" Nathan Garrideb is still seeking his bonanza; he doesn't get anything from it, and the disappointment of not getting it drives him mad. Is that comedy? "The Red-Headed League" is much funnier.

Greed and Benefaction: Jabez Wilson is basically motivated by greed; he can get something for nothing. Nathan Garrideb wanted the money to add to his collection of curiosities, but not for himself: he hoped eventually to donate his collection to the nation, to become the Hans Sloane of his age (Hans Sloane was the benefactor who essentially started the British Museum). Well, perhaps there is vanity in this, but still: instead of personal gain, Nathan Garrideb aims at philanthropy and adding to the national treasure.

But it all comes to naught: There is an old proverb that says God laughs at Man's plans. Is that the comedy here? But what an unhappy comedy it is: derisive, mocking us. We want to do good; look, a chance to do good, but it's all a sham; what can you expect? Can we do good in this world? Is anything like that possible? Or will a lifetime of collecting merely end with the collector in a nursing home, and his collection – well, what happens to it? Was it worth anything to begin with, or is it just a vast clutter?

Pray allow me to clear these bones: Well, there's some good-natured comedy: Nathan Garrideb has to clear bones away to allow Sherlock Holmes to sit down. And then Watson has to move a Japanese vase. It is a bizarre mixture of oddities in this homemade museum. And it all signifies what? The mess of civilization – or of the entire universe? (Watson is much taken by the "universality" of the collection.) And where is it all going? "They degenerated greatly towards the end," says the museum keeper, referring to one of the coins in his collection. And the museum collector himself has degenerated: he has "a cadaverous face with the dull dead skin of a man to whom exercise was unknown." He is amiable enough, but hopelessly ineffectual. He never goes out; he knows nothing of real life. He is in desperate need of rejuvenation, though he doesn't seem to know it. He would like nothing better than to keep cataloguing life instead of living it. Ah, well.

Death and Bachelors: Is it any accident that Nathan Garrideb lives near Tyburn Tree, the ancient place of executions? True, the area looks golden and wonderful, but that is because it is picking up the rays of "the setting sun." The sun never sets on the British Empire, they used to say, but now it seems to be doing just that.

And bachelors: Jabez Wilson was a bachelor and so could not propagate the red-headed race – which is just a bit of a joke. Nathan Garrideb is a bachelor in a house of "Bohemian bachelors." Which is odd. The Bohemian part, I mean. Anyone less Bohemian than Nathan Garrideb would be hard to imagine. Is he wild and roving? But he is perhaps unconventional in the sense of not having married. And his bachelorhood means he is not propagating either, and here it seems less of a joke and more of a lament: the poor old Garrideb, polishing his Syracusan coin, with no one to pass on his collection to.

More differences: Consider what the phony Garrideb is after, compared to the target in "The Red-Headed League." John Clay, in the League, wants real gold from a real bank. John Garrideb (alias Killer Evans) wants a counterfeiting machine and counterfeit money. This is somewhat reminiscent of the ironically phony counterfeiting machine in *The Valley of Fear*, where the point is you can't tell the difference between real and counterfeit. Here we seem to have gone even beyond that to saying that even what the criminal is after is counterfeit. Is there anything solid we can rely on? At least John Clay was going to deal in legitimate currency; Killer Evans would put phony notes into circulation, causing a great danger to the public, as Dr. Watson says. Everything will be undermined.

But it's not: Holmes and Watson save the day, the criminal returns to prison, and all is perhaps right with the world. Perhaps. Holmes and Watson even express their mutual affection. Is that the message, that we cannot depend on money or collections, but there is friendship. And the counterfeiting is thwarted, so society will live on. Is it a happy ending? Not for Nathan Garrideb, I suppose – and I wonder what he did in Birmingham, wandering around looking for the non-existent third Garrideb. And Watson could have been killed, and was indeed wounded, but is it a comedy?

Is the danger from the States? Is this another foreign danger story? But not from the Continent this time. It's from the "Wild West," a rather out-of-date term by this time, but the one Holmes uses to describe the killer from America, who has an American accent but no other eccentricities of speech (ahem), and who misspells words – well, as Holmes puts it, he writes "bad English but good American." Oh, those Americans, not quite quite, as they say. Prone to violence too. So if only we can stick to our English ways … but then we end up like Nathan Garrideb, decaying in his museum. Is there no third way? The way of Holmes and Watson? Friendship? Or is there something else? If only there'd really been a third Garrideb.

Or maybe Holmes and Watson stand in for him, combining English culture with a bit of American violence. Perhaps.

Thor Bridge

Wife found dead – bullet to the head,
No weapon found – perhaps it drowned.

Once upon a time there was a Gold King who was unhappy with his wife. And he encountered a lovely new young woman and wished to be with her. But the young woman said no, that would not be right, and Sherlock Holmes said you were evil to try to ruin such a pure thing, and the pure thing stayed on as a mere guiding light or moral compass, teaching the Gold King to be generous and good. But his wife was very angry.

So there you have it: Doyle must have found the story in the Brothers Grimm. Or perhaps he was reading *Jane Eyre*. The mad woman in the attic (well, there's no attic here, but a pond and lakes or something and a bridge of course, named after a Norse god) and not Grace Poole, but Grace Dunbar playing the role of Jane. And Neil Gibson is Mr. Rochester. And Bertha Mason of course is Maria Pinto, one of those "tropical" beauties from Latin America, whose beauty unfortunately has faded and who seems to have gone insane.

Whose side are we on? At first we don't much like Neil Gibson; he is brutal to his wife: he defends this by saying he is trying to kill her love, but surely there must have been a better way – and in any case it doesn't work, or it turns her feelings into "perverted love" and hatred, leading to her fiendish plan to frame the innocent governess by killing herself. Bertha Mason in *Jane Eyre* similarly kills herself, but at least doesn't try to frame Jane. Her death does, however, open the way for Jane to marry Rochester, just as Sherlock Holmes envisages a union, now that Maria Pinto is gone, between Grace Dunbar and the Gold King.

Is that okay, then? Grace (a very religious term, I note) marrying the Gold King, who she will presumably reform (she may have already reformed him). But he was so brutal; can we approve? Perhaps, because in one of the most surprising moments in the story, when Sherlock Holmes upbraids Neil Gibson for immorality, what he is talking about is not his brutality to his wife but his near ruining of the innocent governess: a young girl would be considered ruined, you know, if she had sex before marriage: *autre temps, autre moeurs.*

That was the problem in Jane Eyre too: Rochester wanted to marry Jane, but he was already married, so that would have been bigamy, but once his wife is dead, everything is fine. And here too? One critic (Joseph Kestner) shakes his head, and calls the story conflicted and deplores the ethnic prejudice against the South American wife. I do note that we just read a story where the South American wife was the hero, so it's not a continuing prejudice; there does seem to be a continuing obsession with creating Latin characters, though, especially women, from the Spanish Isadora in "The Three Gables" to the Peruvian wife in "The Sussex Vampire."

Speaking of Isadora, how is it that there is a man in this story with that name? Isn't it a woman's name? Do we have some gender bending? And I also was amused to note the thought experiment Holmes begins by saying, "Well now, Watson, suppose for a moment that we visualize you in the character of a woman …" Hmm.

But mostly I want to talk about eggs: There's a new cook and she's ruined the eggs, letting them boil too long because she was distracted by a romance story in a popular magazine. Ah, romance, so disruptive. If only people didn't fall in love or fall out of love or marry one person and fall in love with another. It's such a nuisance.

This is a story about disruption, isn't it? As Joseph Kestner says, you get that sense starting with the wild October morning and the leaves being whirled off the plane tree in the backyard (wait, 221B has a backyard?). And then there's poor Isadora, driven mad by some mysterious worm in a matchbox: irrationality intruding into everyday life, as the critic Barrie Hayne puts it. And what could be more irrational than this love story mixed with murder and revenge? If only everyone could have been rational about it: then Mr. and Mrs. Gibson and their lovely governess could have worked something out. Hmm, well, maybe not.

But we're supposed to learn something from this. Or Neil Gibson is. From "the schoolroom of Sorrow." And what is that Sorrow exactly? That his wife died? That she tried to frame his girl-friend? Maybe more the latter. And what is he supposed to learn? To be nicer? To not think he can get everything with his money and bluster? But he'd learned that already from Grace. What does the Sorrow teach him? That he shouldn't have married the tropical Brazilian woman? That he should have sent Grace Dunbar away? Grace does say that she should have left because her presence caused unhappiness (for Mrs. Gibson). But that's not where the story takes us; instead we head towards a union of the Gold King and the ethereal Grace. Which means what? That it's good to get out of a bad marriage and into a good one? Hmm.

Mixtures: We have the usual Tudor and Georgian house in the story, and maybe the point is that the rough and powerful Gold King needs to acquire a little grace (or Grace). Meanwhile Holmes is positively brilliant here, conjuring up a deduction out of an orgasmic frenzy, and yet he is surprisingly self-deprecating, saying Watson's account will not show him in a good light; he was too sluggish. Why does he say that? He's not sluggish at all; he sees what no one else can. Where others just shrug off the chip on the bridge or the clutching of the note, he notes their strangeness, and explores that until the actual explanation emerges. This is a Holmes at the height of his powers, and a bit surprising perhaps since this is his first appearance after the disaster of "The Mazarin Stone." Here is the real return of our Sherlock after the hiatus following "His Last Bow," and perhaps it is the fact that this is his first real case in years that leads to the modesty and humility.

And the length? This must be one of the longest of the stories: it had to be published in two parts. Did Conan Doyle have so much pent-up Sherlockiana in him that he had to write at such length? Not that I'm saying it's too long; it holds your interest to the end, even if the plot is so memorable that you remember it from the last time you read it.

But back to mixtures: Often in the canon there is talk of the need for foreign blood (Italian, American, even South American) to revive an enfeebled England. Often England seems to be in decay. But here, despite a reference to an autumnal panorama (which is in any case said to be "wonderful"), there's no sense of autumnal decline. Disruption, yes; decline, no. And to bring order to the disruption what is necessary is to bring in the English qualities of Grace Dunbar to tame the rough-hewn Gold King. Conan Doyle has certain recurring motifs, but he comes at them in various ways.

And so they lived happily ever after, except of course for poor Maria. Ah well, is that what life is like? Someone always suffers even if others prosper. Do they *have* to suffer so others will prosper? In a story with a Maria and a Grace, is somebody dying for everyone else's sins? Or to be less Christian about it, is it simply that life moves on, people move on, and unfortunately sometimes someone gets left behind.

The Creeping Man

Monkey glands, Watson! Or is it lumbago? No, not lumbago. You are so flat-footed, Watson. You have to think outside the box, or in this case inside the box. What is in that box? Some mysterious injectable drug. Cocaine? No, that was my drug. This is Professor Presbury's drug, which he is using to, well, you know, become young again so at the age of 61 he can properly function as the fiancé of a young woman – if you know what I mean.

And maybe he's ready to function, but he's only the fiancé, not the husband, and in those days fiancés didn't get conjugal rights, did they? But he has to work off his energies somehow, so he climbs the ivy and peers in his daughter's bedroom, even seeming about to push in the window of the bedroom in order to … well, what? Is this turning into some lurid incestuous fantasy? But Sherlock Holmes says that climbing to the daughter's window was mere chance because the monkeyfied professor enjoyed climbing.

He certainly did that, and was quite agile about it. Maybe he is still quite agile about it. Holmes doesn't stop him from taking his monkey serum, does he?* Does anyone? Does he marry his colleague's young daughter and show her some of his monkey tricks? Would that be a bad thing?

Well, of course it would be a bad thing, a scandalous thing, an "excessive" thing, as the family says, and as Holmes reinforces. And this is not even considering the monkey drug; it's the idea of an old professor marrying a young girl. Where did he even get such an idea? Perhaps from studying

---

* Well, he tries to by cutting off the supply, but does he succeed?

Comparative Anatomy? Or does that just take us back to monkeys?

But wait: As a couple of recent critics have suggested, doesn't the monkey serum actually make the Professor come more alive? And it doesn't dim his mental faculties as Holmes at first expects; he remembers things very well and is able to give brilliant lectures. He has even more energy than before, his assistant and son-in-law-to-be says. So what's the problem? Well, it does mean he gets rather irascible, pervertedly spies on his daughter, and tries to torture his own dog, who finally slips his leash and attacks back, perhaps reflecting the transgressiveness of his master.

And it's all a great threat to humanity, says Mr. Sherlock Holmes. All this playing with science to go against Nature. It will mean encouraging all the sensual, physical types to prolong their lives, especially their, ahem, sexual lives, turning Darwin on his head and ensuring the survival of the unfit. Though as the critic Virginia Richter says, are we sure those are the unfit? If they're so strong and all, aren't they after all the fit? But true, they're not spiritual types who are ready to give up this life on earth for "something higher," as Holmes puts it. Would that be the better way? To just give up? You're 61, you've had your innings, let the young people play now.

Retirement, that's the thing, and after retirement, well, you know. Holmes thinks maybe it's time he was moving on to "that little farm of my dreams," and Watson lets us know that in fact by the time of publication he has done it. The critic Sylvia Pamboukian slyly notes that though Holmes seems eager for retirement, that's not the path his creator chose for himself: Conan Doyle embarked on his new career of promoting Spiritualism and kept on writing, even writing these

Sherlock Holmes stories about retirement, and of course he remarried just like that aging Professor and even produced some more children. Was he using monkey glands?

Older men pursuing young women: This features a lot in the *Case-Book,* Pamboukian says. Check out "Thor Bridge" and "Sussex Vampire." Are these good things? But Holmes and Trevor Bennett disapprove, and they are proper Victorian gentlemen, so shouldn't we believe them? Maybe not, says Pamboukian. She says this story, which lacks an actual crime and seems on first reading to fizzle out into implausibility and obviousness, may actually be a quite serious study of the problem of aging.

And what does Sherlock Holmes have to say about aging? Well, really, you know, this is not exactly the detective's area. If you've lost your racehorse or your naval treaty, he can help you. But to retrieve your youth, ah, well. So what is one to do? There seem to be two choices: either you gracefully slide into retirement and, well, you know. Or you resort to the back alleys of science and find some questionable means to prolong your life and rejuvenate your essences. But that second path could undermine all our social norms, our civilization, the boundaries of what is proper. Is there some middle path? Lawn bowling?

Fresh blood: Several of the stories talk about the need to reinvigorate England by drawing on the Continent or North or South America, but this one goes a step further and talks about actual blood, or serum. Perhaps that is taking it too far? But who knows?

Meanwhile, the most entertaining part of the story, unless you really enjoy professors acting like monkeys, is the opening, in which Watson explores the nature of his "alliance" with the Master Detective. I'm sort of a plodder, Watson says, but useful for all that, as a sort of whetstone that helps produce sparks. But is he beginning to resent his role? Dorothy Sayers, as reported by Klinger, seems to think so: why else does he complain about being dragged away from his work to hear about the problems of the professor's dog? When has Watson ever been reluctant to abandon doctoring for an adventure? But maybe he's growing old too; maybe our old friends have reached the age when soon they'll just be creeping along. Will they become creeping men?

But no, no, no, that's not what the story means by a creeping man. Professor Presbury can leap large buildings in, well, not a single bound, but in perhaps several. Bounding, that's what he seems to be able to do, or skipping as Watson puts it at one point. He doesn't crawl on hands and knees; he goes on all fours, hands and feet. So it's bounding or, perhaps, bouncing. And his knuckles, we are supposed to notice his knuckles: they have grown thick and horny, as they would if you were knuckle-walking like an ape. No, creeping is not at all the right word for the Professor, unless it is to suggest that his actions are creepy; he is certainly creeping the other characters out, to use a much later idiom. But he is bounding along, really, not creeping. Full of energy, not sluggishness. The title of the story seems unfair to him, as if written by the other characters who fear his new powers, though I suppose to have called it "The Skipping Man" might not have conjured up the right sense either.

Some huge bat: That would be the Professor again, now reminding us of Dracula. And earlier all that talk of dates and the phases of the moon, not to mention the wolfhound, can make you think of werewolves. But no, it's monkeys all the way, and not something supernatural, but out of the realms of science, or at least science fiction: something to scare us about science gone wild and creating a race of bestial men. But at the end we put it all behind us, and go off to the Chequers inn, where the linen is above reproach and one can get a nice cup of tea. Holmes carries us back to civilization, leaving The Monkey-Man behind. (Now that would have been a better title, though it would of course have given the game away.)

Ah well, an end to these experiments with rejuvenation or with solving the problem of 61-year-old men who seek after young women, and let us return to the natural current of life, carrying us inexorably towards our end.

The Lion's Mane

It don't belong to Sussex: The Lion's Mane, that is, the killer
jellyfish that somehow finds its way into a tidal pool and kills
poor Fitzroy McPherson. Is it foreign, then? Is this another
story about the danger of foreigners? Or is it something else?
The critic Joseph Kestner sees it as an intrusion of something
female into an essentially male world, just like Maud Bellamy,
the lovely young woman who attracts the interest of both
McPherson, his fellow teacher or academic coach, Ian
Murdoch, and even perhaps, Sherlock Holmes.

And Watson? Yes, Watson would no doubt be interested too,
but he's not here. This is another Watson-less story, like "The
Blanched Soldier," narrated again by Holmes himself. This
time, though, there's no Watson-substitute like James Dodd in
"Blanched." Or there's a whole host of substitutes, all the
boys of the coaching academy, the various coaches like
Murdoch and McPherson, the solid Sussex constable, and
perhaps most of all, Harold Stackhurst, the head of the
coaching establishment, with whom Holmes becomes friendly.

It's not the same, though, is it? We miss the usual Watson-
Holmes interaction. As Holmes himself says, he can't by
himself produce the same effects we get when Watson is there
as an amazed observer. Stackhurst does try, but all we get is
his appreciation of Holmes's ability to deduce that he's going
swimming because of his "bulging pocket." What is in that
bulging pocket anyway? I'm surprised the commentators who
like to see homosexual suggestions in the stories haven't
mentioned it. Probably just his towel, I suppose. Or bathing
trunks? But Joseph Kestner says they were swimming nude:
can that be?

Skin problems: Some commentators have noted the awful disfigurations in the late stories, from the leprosy or pseudo-leprosy in "The Blanched Soldier" to the horrors of Kitty Winter, Shinwell Johnson, and the acid-struck Baron Gruner in "The Illustrious Client." Here we have what at first looks like torture inflicted on McPherson and later Murdoch, as if they'd been flogged. Horrors indeed. Reflecting the agonies of World War I? The anxieties of the postwar world? The realities of aging? The aging Holmes is in retirement now, alone with a housekeeper and his bees. Lonely, he says, without his Watson, and all the other men in the neighbourhood can't make up for it.

And what is he reduced to now? Attacking a jellyfish. The man who fought Moriarty, who disentangled the most complex of problems, now has to come to terms with the fact that sometimes a death is just natural. Or at least accidental. He looks for a motive, but there is no motive for killing McPherson; it was not a conscious, malevolent act; it was the natural action of a poisonous jellyfish, something that Holmes blames himself for being slow to recognize. In "Thor Bridge," when he upbraids himself, it seems odd: he actually did excellent work there. But this time the self-criticism seems valid: he was slow, "culpably slow," as he puts it. But even that is to take too much credit; it's not as if his "culpability" cost anyone their life, as in some earlier stories. It's just that he was slow to exonerate Murdoch.

What about Murdoch? The aloof, quick-tempered math instructor focused on surds and conic sections who could throw a dog through a plate-glass window and who is the chief suspect because he and McPherson seemed to be at odds. But later they became friends, and he even served as McPherson's go-between with Maud Bellamy. What is this? The fierce villain becomes a tame poodle? Though his fierceness flares up again when challenged over his visit to the Bellamys (where we have another couple of fierce men, who, however, seem easily put in their place by Maud). Is all this fierceness just a male facade, easily destroyed by a woman or a jellyfish? Even the athletic McPherson is not only killed by a jellyfish, but first weakened by rheumatic fever. Joseph Kestner sees triumphant masculinity in this story, but it seems more like male defeat to me.

And defeat by whom (or what)? Nature, I guess you'd say. The jellyfish, of course, brought in by the gale, the gale that seemed to leave Nature newly washed and fresh, creating beautiful crystal pools. But beware! beware! Nature may seem soothing and lovely, even exquisite, but death lies there, ugly horrible death looking like the results of medieval torture. At least that is the picture of the world conjured up by an aging writer writing of his aging detective.

And what about the dog? Is it the same dog, by the way? Thrown through a plate-glass window, then poisoned by the jellyfish. McPherson's dog (or dogs). Poor dog. What does it mean? Why should the dog suffer so? Is there something about McPherson that attracts calamity and affects even his dog? What? There do seem to be a lot of dogs in the canon. The Hound of the Baskervilles, of course, the wolfhound in "The Creeping Man," and not to forget the dog that did nothing in the night-time. Holmes even wanted to do a monograph on dogs and detection, suggesting that dogs reflect their masters. So what does this dog reflect? Victimhood?

And if the dog and his master are victims, who are the victors? Not Holmes, who berates himself for slowness. Maud? But she has lost her fiancé. Speaking of fiancés, they often get sidelined in the canon, but not as spectacularly as here, and in this case McPherson's status as fiancé is not even revealed till late in the story; that is not his main role. He is here as the victim, and his "murderer" is the jellyfish: is the jellyfish the victor? But it gets smashed to pieces. Is it Nature more generally, triumphing over us poor mortals? Or is it Stackhurst and Murdoch, reconciled at last, strolling off arm in arm at the end? If you have a friend, you're all right? But then poor Holmes is even worse off, without his Watson.

Secrets: Maud keeps the engagement secret because an uncle of McPherson's would have disapproved and because her father and brother were unsympathetic. The father is concerned that McPherson hasn't made an offer of marriage, so shouldn't Maud have told him about the engagement? That's puzzling. I'm also puzzled by his comment about Maud taking up with a man "outside her own station." Does he mean McPherson was too high or too low? The Bellamys have grown prosperous and own boats and bathing machines, but the father started as a mere fisherman. McPherson is a science master at a prep school. Who is higher than whom? Is there actual confusion here, the confusion of the postwar, or would it have been clear at the time that, say, the science master came from a higher class than a man of commerce?

Secrets (continued): Maud also won't say how she got the notes from McPherson. It turns out Murdoch brought them, but the point of the secret was to make sure Stackhurst, McPherson's boss, didn't find out and object. But why would he object, unless this is all part of some contest for attention and friendship: was Maud disrupting a potential friendship between Murdoch and Stackhurst? Did she disrupt the friendship between Murdoch and McPherson? But they seemed on perfectly good terms at the end. Is there some opposition here between male friendships and male-female relationships? It is so confusing. Does Maud have to be excluded, as Kestner puts it, to allow Murdoch and Stackhurst to proceed? Is that the happy ending? But the very end is actually Holmes stuck with the bovine Inspector and his unwarranted praise. It seems more a failure than a triumph.

The Veiled Lodger

Lion's Mane, Lion's Paw: Not a make-believe lion this time, no jellyfish masquerading as King of the Jungle. It's the real thing this time, Sahara King, the ferocious lion from North Africa, where lions used to roam (though no more). It is perhaps appropriate that he ends up in a place called Abbas Parva, because Abbas is the Arabic word for lion – though Abbas is also old Latin for "abbot" or "father," and here we have a story in which Sherlock Holmes acts as a father confessor. Abbas is part of a few English place names (such as Cerne Abbas in Dorset), and so is Parva (meaning "small" in Latin), though it is also a word from Sanskrit, meaning one of the eighteen books of a great Sanskrit epic of war and conflict, the *Mahabharata*, which also includes a discussion of the four major goals of life: *dharma* (virtue), *artha* (wealth), *kama* (pleasure), and *moksha* (spiritual liberation).

Wait, wait, wait: This is just a story about murder in an English circus; what is all this Eastern philosophy? But consider: in what other story is Holmes described as a "strange Buddha"? And isn't the story about virtue, wealth, pleasure, and spiritual liberation? There's the landlady, interested in wealth. There's the two lovers, interested in, well, you know. There is the virtue of patience that Sherlock Holmes preaches that presumably will lead to spiritual liberation. And there is the world beyond, smuggled in again, when he says that there must be some "compensation hereafter" or else the world is just a "cruel jest."

But back to lions and conflict: There's certainly plenty of conflict in the story: the abuse of poor Eugenia Ronder by her pig-like husband, Eugenia and Leonardo's plot to kill the husband, the mauling of Eugenia by the lion … And lions, or one lion, and a phony lion's paw. Makes me think of a cat's paw, which I looked up, and it's an instrument or tool you use, a person really that you make use of, your dupe or stooge. From an old fable in which a monkey gets a cat to put its paw in the fire to pull out chestnuts.

A monkey? Yes, like in "The Creeping Man," where some see something positive in animal energy. Here there's no monkey, and nothing much positive from the animals. There's the actual lion that mauls Mrs. Ronder, and her husband who's nasty like a wild boar, and the mercenary Mrs. Merrilow, who waddles like a duck. Well, it doesn't say "duck," but Watson insists on the verb waddle.

So sometimes animal energy is positive and sometimes not. Just like foreign things, and though there is nothing overtly foreign in this story, there's Abbas Parva, with its double derivation, both local and exotic, and of course Holmes the Buddha.

But is the lion so bad? The lion's just doing what lions do. In "The Lion's Mane" Holmes calls the lion-like jellyfish a murderer, but here we're told the lion was just reacting to the scent of human blood – and why was there human blood? Not from any real animal, but from the club created by Leonardo, the club meant to frame the poor lion. Sometimes Nature will get you, but sometimes it's your fellow humans you have to look out for.

And sometimes a human taking on animal qualities, like the leaping Professor Presbury in "The Creeping Man," can seem almost inspiring, and sometimes such a person is just bestial, like the horrible husband who abused his wife.

Abused wife or adulterous wife? Well, both I guess. We saw something similar in "The Abbey Grange," but in that case, despite the other man, there was no actual adultery. And the other man in that story killed the husband in self-defence. Here the other man kills the husband from behind (coward!) and then runs away when his woman is attacked by the lion (doubly a coward). And the killing was premeditated this time, and the wife was definitely involved.

Oh, well, she pays for her crime with a life of virtual imprisonment and of course disfigurement. And she wants to kill herself now, but Holmes won't let her: she must stand as a model of patience. Hmm. Isn't she rather a model of villainy for killing her husband? True, he abused her, and one commentator (Joseph Kestner) calls her the most abused wife in the canon, but still …

Perhaps she is a model for patiently bearing one's punishment.

And let's not forget the cormorant: At the beginning Watson warns that he may publish the story of the politician, the lighthouse, and the cormorant if further attempts are made to suppress it. We're in the land of reputation here, something more common in the earlier stories, but conjured up at times in the later tales to explain why some cases can just not be reported, or must be reported discreetly or after everyone involved is dead.

Yes, but what about the cormorant? This seems similar to the cat's paw: a cormorant is a bird that is trained to catch fish and bring the fish back uneaten. So again a tool or instrument, like the fake lion's paw or if we're looking for a human instrument in the story, Leonardo? Was he really the Angel Gabriel, that announcer of the Christian glory, or was he being used by Eugenia to rid herself of a troublesome husband? Well, okay, a violently cruel husband, who whipped her, she says – do we have confirmation? Well, Sherlock Holmes seems to believe her, is sympathetic, and does not turn her in. Like a good confessor, he maintains her privacy.

And the lighthouse: Somehow that "politician, lighthouse, cormorant" trinity reminded me of the old sea shanty, the "Eddystone Light," popularized in the 1950's, but known much before that. "My father was the keeper of the Eddystone Light; he slept with a mermaid one fine night." You know the one. "From that union there came three, a porpoise, a porgy, and the other was me." That would be a scandal to hush up. And it's more animal-human hybrid stuff. Where is Conan Doyle going with all this? He's turning into a veritable Dr. Dolittle. All these animals in the later cases, along with mutilation.

And are we channelling Hamlet? Look on this picture and on this, says Eugenia, showing her husband and Leonardo. A pig-man and an angel. Like Hamlet comparing pictures of his father and uncle: Hyperion and a satyr, he says, his father being the godlike Hyperion and his uncle being the half-man, half-beast satyr. And the violent satyr (his uncle) committed murder so he could marry his brother's wife. Except here it is the Hyperion (or Angel Gabriel) who commits the murder. Something has gone wrong. Maybe there are no more angels and Hyperions, sigh, just beasts. Is there any positive male figure in this story? There's just the abusive circus owner and the predatory Leonardo, smiling over his conquests. Of course, there is also Griggs the clown, but he had not much to be funny about. This is no comedy, I don't think. Not a Garrideb in sight.

The problem is not to find, but to choose: So says Watson, and he has chosen this story for us. Because it is sad? Certainly not to show off the powers of Sherlock Holmes, as he says himself. To show what a sad world it is? A world in which men (and women) can become beasts? Eugenia herself ends like a beast in a cage, suffering retribution at the hands of the lion she would have blamed for her crime. Can she truly be a model for us in any way? She did protect her lover (though not her husband). She renounces suicide and goes along with the patient suffering Holmes urges on her. Is that the best we can do in this fallen world: suffer for our sins? But at least there is the hope of the world to come.

Shoscombe Old Place

Holding off the Jews: That's what Sir Robert Norberton is doing, according to his head trainer, John Mason. What does that mean? Well, it means "the Jews" are here functioning as a sort of figure of speech representing all moneylenders because stereotypically the Jews were moneylenders. (As Les Klinger notes, this is a bit of a slur because in fact not all Jews were moneylenders, and not all moneylenders were Jews. Dickens felt obliged to write a whole novel, *Our Mutual Friend*, to point this out and make amends for creating Fagin. Still, it was a common thing to say someone was "in the hands of the Jews," as both Norberton and Sherlock Holmes do later in the story, and this would simply mean the person was in debt.)

So a little casual anti-Semitism: Yes, and odd in a way to have it expressed by a Mason because after all weren't Masons working together with the Jews in the worldwide conspiracy? (Sorry, a little joke.) But let's look at the underlying issue here: the fact that Sir Robert, acting like a Regency buck out of his time, has been squandering the fortunes of the ancient Falder family, so that all will go bust if his Derby horse doesn't win.

Isn't this a rather shaky basis on which to preserve a family fortune? Well, yes: yes, it is. And it's not even his fortune or his family. Did he have a fortune of his own? How did he get to be a baronet? We don't learn anything about that. He's just leeched onto the Falders by way of his sister who married one. He's something of an outsider or cuckoo – or no, a cuckoo lays eggs, and Sir Robert has produced no children. Neither has his sister, Lady Beatrice Falder, and so the estate will go to her late husband's brother: has he any children? Will there be anyone to hand this estate down to even if the horse does win the Derby? It's all very unclear, but what is clear is that we are once again seeing ...

England in decline: Or the old landed aristocracy, with their heraldic griffins (eagles and lions) in decline, with their crumbling chapel and haunted crypt full of ancient bones of Hugos and Odos from centuries past, not to mention the bones of the unnamed ancestor who Sir Robert arranges to burn to make room for his dead sister in a coffin.

What? Yes, inexcusable, as Sherlock Holmes puts it. And why? Disrespect for the dead? Sir Robert says no, but surely that is there. And not just any dead, but the dead of a respected landed family (both the unknown ancient ancestor and Lady Beatrice). And yet Sir Robert gets away with a mere slap on the wrist, his horse does win, the creditors hold off until it does, they all get paid, and there's enough left for Sir Robert to fade into an honoured old age, free of his earlier "shadows" (his violence, gambling, and womanizing).

But is that a good thing? Holmes, as we've seen, does not think so, but the story lets it happen. Is Doyle shrugging and saying, Well, that's where things are going: respect for the dead, respect for Old England, is gone, and we're in a world where your take at the track is what keeps you afloat. Rickety old England? No more grandeur of the ages, but shady dealings involving, ugh, money. The old baronets had money, of course, but that was from renting out land; that was somehow dignified, but this man who horsewhipped his creditor nearly to death and who has essentially defrauded the betting public, not to mention playing fast and loose with his sister's body and the laws on burials (and of course the crypt of his brother-in-law's ancestors) – this is the man who will succeed into an honoured old age? Is this what England has come to?

But fresh blood: Yes, often in the canon there's been a sense that old families need an infusion from somewhere, but from ill-gotten gambling gains? From Regency bucks? Regency bucks were the dissolute gamblers prominent in the early nineteenth century, before Victoria: should we be going back to that? Or are we stuck going back to that? What is Conan Doyle up to?

Some commentators share Holmes's displeasure over Sir Robert, but after all he's committed no murder, contrary to what Holmes rather rashly suggests early on in the story. All he's done is disturb the dead – and when has Conan Doyle cared about that? His stories are usually about murdering the living. I wonder, though, if Spiritualism requires that the body of the departed remain undisturbed in its grave.

And might it not be good to disturb the dead? Or at least shake up the society of old England, especially its old landowning families?   One does get that sense earlier in the canon, as with the Baskervilles, and yet here it's almost as if this shaking up is a regression to an earlier, dissolute time. Are the 1920's no better than the Regency of 1810? Do we need a return to some Victorian propriety? Or at least a return to eagles from carrion crows? Or perhaps just a return to the "humble abode" of Holmes and Watson? Meaning what? A return to "unpretentious middleclass productivity," as W.W. Robson says in a comment on the story. But what could be a better example of middle-class productivity than money-lending: making money out of nothing. We're not celebrating that, are we?

No, so what do we have? Moneylenders, dissolute Regency bucks, decaying landed families – and of course detectives.

Perhaps we should just celebrate Holmes and Watson (and we do). There's also an actor in the story, but he's no role model: the rat-faced, cowardly Norlett. The loyal retainers of Sir Robert? But Mason is not so loyal: he calls his employer mad, suggests he is having an affair with the maid, and warns against his violence. And the maid, who wants to continue the deception about her mistress? No, who else is there? The innkeeper, I suppose, but if we want the most loyal creature in the story it is of course the spaniel. This story was almost called "The Adventure of the Black Spaniel," and who is more loyal than Lady Beatrice's dog, barking madly at the well-house where her body is first kept and then rushing eagerly to her carriage when he thinks she is in it only to bark angrily when he realizes he's been deceived.

So we need to go to the dogs? We *are* going to the dogs? Lady Beatrice has no children and treats her spaniel like a child. Is that all there is? There are other animals, of course, and not just in this story. There's the racehorse of course and even a Green Dragon. Not to mention metaphorical vultures (the moneylenders) and rabbits (the frightened Mason and Stephens the butler). And in other late stories, lions and jellyfish and monkeys. Also, another loyal dog: McPherson's in "The Lion's Mane," who gets thrown through a plate-glass window in the same way it seems Sir Robert is ready to attack Lady Beatrice's spaniel. Maybe it's the dogs who will inherit (though McPherson's is dead). Ah, well.

The House of Usher: A couple of commentators see parallels with Poe's story about a strange brother-sister relationship and the burial of the sister. It is a strange relationship, isn't it? Holmes at first assumes Lady Beatrice is Sir Richard's wife, and then assumes she lives in his house. No, says Mason, it is her house, the house of the Falders. And she gets buried in the crypt, like Madeline Usher, but at least she doesn't come back from the dead like Madeline, and the house doesn't split in two. Still …

Falder, falter: Is that why the name is Falder? If their house won't split in two, it certainly is in danger of faltering. Maybe all of England is. And that is where Conan Doyle leaves us with his final Sherlock Holmes story. So long, and thanks for all the fish: Holmes and Watson do end up fishing and eating some trout for dinner. And maybe that is a fine way to go.

Or maybe we need something, some glue to hold us together: perhaps that is why the story begins with Holmes looking for glue. Perhaps.

The Retired Colourman

Monkey glands, Watson! Oh, no, not again. Well, actually not. Too bad, really – if only old Josiah Amberley had had some monkey glands like Professor Presbury he too could have been leaping instead of creeping on his damaged legs. Strong above, but damaged below. Made me think of *Lady Chatterley's Lover* – well, not the lover but the husband, paralyzed from the waist down, which drove Lady Chatterley to find a lover – just as Amberley's wife found a … chess player. I wonder if Lawrence read Doyle. *Lady Chatterley's Lover* came out just a year after this story, but …

Chess: Now chess is interesting. The whole story seems like a chess match. Holmes vs. Amberley. The key move is Rook (Knight? whatever Watson is) to Bishop 4. Well, not a Bishop, just a Vicar. But it gets Amberley out of the way so Holmes can burgle his home and find out what's really going on. It's not that Amberley's wife has run off with the chess player, but that Amberley has murdered the two of them.

Yes, the client is the murderer: This gave me pause. Why should the criminal hire Sherlock Holmes to investigate his own crime? Pure swank, says Holmes. Showing off, I think that means. Trying to show that he can best not just the police but the world's greatest consulting detective. Not the only consulting detective, though: we learn in this story that Sherlock Holmes has a rival. Hercule Poirot? Nero Wolfe? No, no, someone named Barker (though perhaps Doyle was thinking of Poirot and others who were beginning to appear in the 1920's).

Time to go? Is it time to take a bow (another bow? like those tenors who keep making farewell concerts?) and leave the stage. Is that what Doyle is suggesting? There's another detective now. Sherlock Holmes can let someone else take over. But does he want to? It seems a bit sad, and the story starts on a sad note. Bleak, one commentator calls it. We strive, we seek, we grasp – it sounds a bit like Tennyson or Browning. A man's reach should exceed his grasp – that sort of thing. But here it's all played in a minor key. All life is pathetic and futile, and what is left in the end? A shadow.

And yet: Perhaps 'tis not too late to seek another world. And after all, for a story that begins with such bleak philosophy and which seems to be almost a handing over of the torch, who triumphs in the end? Oh, he lets Inspector MacKinnon take the credit, but we know who solved the case. There's still a few tricks in the old man yet. Like sending Amberley to Little Purlington and the angry vicar.

An Angry Vicar? That seems wrong somehow. Shouldn't a vicar, the representative of God, the Christian Church, show a little Christian forbearance? But Mr. Elman is furious. His name has been taken in vain. It's a forgery, that telegram. Who really speaks for the Church, for God? Sherlock Holmes? But he angers the gods, or at least the vicar.

But back to Amberley: Why on earth does he invite detection? Pure swank doesn't cut it. An actual criminal would stay away from Sherlock Holmes. Does any other criminal in the canon do such a thing? It makes no sense on a literal level, so I explore the more symbolic regions. Life begins by seeming pathetic and futile; we've reached the end, and there's only shadow. But, but ... No, the story will not accept that. The story will give us Sherlock Holmes's great adversary – Crime with a Capital C – tweaking his nose, as if in mockery of the great detective. But this almost rouses him;

it does rouse him. You will play chess with me? Well, I will show you who's the master.

And so the last story in the last collection ends in Victory against Crime, against the Universe. Maybe it's all shadow, maybe we've reached the end, but we can still rouse ourselves one more time, set off against the billows or the Amberleys and show our mettle.

Messages: And even if we go, there are still messages we can leave behind or communication from beyond the grave. Like the lovers scratching out something in the poisoned vault. "We we –" A cryptic sort of message, which somehow is supposed to mean "We were murdered." You have to be a good medium to derive that message from those feeble table-knockings. Is this a last-minute plea for Spiritualism smuggled into the final story?

Farewell: A long farewell, then, to the Master. But he leaves successors behind. A century's worth of Poirots and Nero Wolfes, not to mention the pastiches. Apocrypha, you might call them. Not really part of the canon. But the canon has survived for a century or more, a pretty good run as canons go, though not of course as long as the one the vicar represents. Still …

And no suicide! For the second time in the last few stories, Holmes prevents a suicide. The Veiled Lodger and now the Retired Colourman have such thoughts, but Holmes will not allow it. See it through to the end. No shortcuts, he tells Amberley. Why? Why should he care? The Veiled Lodger can perhaps provide a model of patience, and the Retired Colourman? Perhaps the futility of trying to best Sherlock Holmes. Everyone should know. This case must become well known, as Watson indeed says it has, becoming "the eager debate of all England."

What is there to debate, I wonder? Whether Sherlock Holmes remains supreme? Whether he will return? He's returned before, of course; there's a whole collection named for his return. And buried in this story is another.

A solitary vigil: That's what Watson must keep, waiting for his friend. Holmes and Barker take Amberley off to the police station, leaving Watson alone in Amberley's house. Why? He keeps vigil there – for what purpose? It is a curious moment. It's an ill-omened house, the scene of a horrifying murder, like something out of Poe, two people walled in and suffocated. Not that we see that happen, as we might in a truly Gothic tale, but will something horrifyingly Gothic happen now? Will someone emerge from the shadows and thrust Watson into the poisoned vault? Will it simply be that Watson must now be alone: is Sherlock Holmes gone forever?

But no, for less than half an hour, actually, less time than Holmes had predicted. He will return, he says, and he does. Have no fear: though he seems to go, he will be back. And I suppose in a way he is. He is always with us, pervading our culture, the world's culture.

Generosity and miserliness: Holmes is the generous one, giving away credit. Amberley is the miser, holding onto his money and also being possessive about his wife, which perhaps is understandable, but the result of that possessiveness is murderously extreme. Maybe it's Amberley who reaches and grasps; he is too grasping by far. What is needed is the generosity of Sherlock Holmes, who lets Inspector MacKinnon take the credit. That is the way, perhaps, to avoid ending with a mere shadow and misery: do not seek and grasp. give away: cast your bread upon the waters and it will come back to you a thousandfold. That perhaps is the very Christian message at the end of the Sherlockian canon.

Foreigners and animals: We can't say goodbye, it seems, without another allusion in this direction. Amberley is a sort of medieval Italian (a poisonous Borgia?) and also a bird of prey, a lion, and a demon. Nothing positive from the animal kingdom this time, nor from foreign lands. Nor even from the progress of British urbanization; much better the oasis of ancient culture and comfort that Watson sees in Amberley's house. "Cut out the poetry," Holmes says, and after all why should we celebrate the murderer's house, especially since he has let it go to seed. But it is The Haven, and maybe we would like to find some ancient oasis to comfort us amidst the jangling of a new era.

Afterword

So there you have it, 56 stories and four novels. The canon as left us by the Master, if Doyle rather than Holmes was the Master. It wasn't Watson, surely, though he is the Teller, the Chronicler, the Boswell.

And forty years of time, with an author aging from late youth to maturity. The early stories are usually seen as the best, but is there something richer in the later ones? More depth, more texture, more tropical tempestuousness and hints of a world to come.

And the themes? These Musings have mostly been about themes, the content of the stories, their message if you will. And what is that? Concern about reputation, certainly. Concern as well about outsiders, foreigners, who play a role especially in the later stories, sometimes for good, sometimes for ill. And also the role of women, especially in the early stories, where they seem threatened by what some might call patriarchal oppression.

There's modernity encroaching in the later stories, and the notion of one great Master Criminal, a notion absent at the beginning, when the game seems to be all about how the Master Detective, in all his eccentricities, can put things right or at least penetrate the eccentricities perpetrated by the respectable and the less than respectable in Victorian England.

Larger forces loom as we enter the Edwardian and post-Edwardian world, and what would Holmes have made of the century after his final disappearance? No one is to know except perhaps the makers of adaptations and pastiches. But if we stick to our canon, we are left with identity and belief and fog and mystery, but fog and mystery always set right. Is there a story in which Holmes remains baffled? Defeated perhaps, but never baffled. There is always an answer for everything, except perhaps the strong forces at the end of *The*

Valley of Fear. But even then, though we are overwhelmed, we are not baffled.

And England may be in decline, but there's always hope for rejuvenation from somewhere: from America or Italy or the lower classes or even monkey glands. Or from dogs or Eastern philosophy. Surely not from opium or cocaine, though, but maybe clouds of tobacco and out-of-body experiences. Or friendship (but not marriage) and arcane bits of knowledge and crawling on the ground with a lens. Or being able to deduce from the barest hints, like a certain doctor in Edinburgh.

And through it all we're really just on one big adventure, aren't we? Like The Hero of a Thousand Faces, journeying into the unknown to bring back some magic elixir or at least some solution to a puzzle. And what jolly fun it is, off with Sherlock chasing down clues, such an escape from humdrum doctoring or whatever else we might have to fill our days with.

Sherlock Holmes has survived in the popular imagination for almost a century and a half now. Why? Who knows? He speaks to something, clearly, that need for adventure or puzzle-solving or companionship. And as we follow him on his adventures we can perhaps explore some of life's meanings as they are revealed to him. And that is what I hope the Musings have helped to do.

Bibliography

Atkinson, Michael. *The Secret Marriage of Sherlock Holmes and Other Eccentric Readings*. Ann Arbor: University of Michigan Press, 1998.

Baring-Gould, William S. *The Annotated Sherlock Holmes*. 2 volumes. New York: Crown, 1967.

Childers, Joseph W. "Foreign Matter: Imperial Filth." In *Filth: Dirt, Disgust, and Modern Life*, ed. William A. Cohen and Ryan Johnson. Minneapolis: University of Minnesota Press, 2004.

Clark, Debbie. "The Copper Beeches." In *About Sixty: Why Every Sherlock Holmes Story Is the Best*, ed. Christopher Redmond. [Rockville MD]: Wildside Press, 2016. pp. 84-88.

Clausson, Nils. *Arthur Conan Doyle's Art of Fiction: A Revaluation*. [Newcastle]: Cambridge Scholars, 2018.

-----. "The Case of the Anomalous Narrative: Gothic 'Surmise' and Trigonometric 'Proof' in Arthur Conan Doyle's 'The Musgrave Ritual'," *Victorian Newsletter* 107 (Spring 2005): 5-10.

Coghill, Bob. "Billy Grows Up," *Canadian Holmes* 40:2 (Spring 2017): 4-12.

Cox, Don Richard. *Arthur Conan Doyle*. New York: Ungar, 1985.

Duffy, Enda, and Maurizia Boscagli, "Selling Jewels: Modernist Commodification and Disappearance as Style," *Modernism/modernity* 14 (2007): 189-207.

Fetherston, Sonia. "A Case of Identity." In *About Sixty: Why Every Sherlock Holmes Story Is the Best*, edited by Christopher Redmond. [Rockville MD]: Wildside Press, 2016. pp. 40-42.

Fowler, Alastair. "Sherlock Holmes and the Adventure of the Dancing Men and Women." In *Sherlock Holmes: The Major Stories with Contemporary Critical Essays*, ed. John A. Hodgson. Boston: Bedford Books, 1994. pp. 353-67.

Green, Richard Lancelyn. Notes to his edition of *The Adventures of Sherlock Holmes*. Oxford: Oxford UP, 1993.

Harris, Susan Cannon. "Pathological Possibilities: Contagion and Empire in Doyle's Sherlock Holmes Stories," *Victorian Literature and Culture* 31 (2003): 447-466.

Hayne, Barrie. "The Comic in the Canon: What's Funny about Sherlock Holmes?" In *Critical Essays on Sir Arthur Conan Doyle*, ed. Harold Orel. New York: G.K. Hall, 1992. pp. 138-59.

Heinz, Sarah. "The Ambivalent Bourgeois: Sherlock Holmes and Late Victorian Subjectivities in Detective Fiction." In *Subject Cultures: The English Novel from the 18th to the 21st Century*, ed. Nora Kuster et al. Tubingen, Germany: Narr Francke Attempto, 2016. pp. 155-191.

Hennessy, Rosemary, and Rajeswari Mohan, " 'The Speckled Band': The Construction of Woman in a Popular Text of Empire." In *Sherlock Holmes: The Major Stories with Contemporary Critical Essays*, ed. John A. Hodgson. Boston: Bedford Books, 1994. pp. 389-401.

Hodgson, John A. "Afterword" to "A Case of Identity." In his *Sherlock Holmes: The Major Stories with Contemporary Critical Essays*. Boston: Bedford Books, 1994. pp. 89-90.

-----. "Confidence and Honor in 'The Second Stain'." In *A Companion to Crime Fiction*, ed. Charles J. Rzepka and Lee Horsley. Chichester: Wiley-Blackwell, 2010. pp. 397-402.

-----. "The Recoil of 'The Speckled Band': Detective Story and Detective Discourse." In his *Sherlock Holmes: The Major Stories with Contemporary Critical Essays*. Boston: Bedford Books, 1994. pp. 335-352.

Jaffe, Jacqueline A. *Arthur Conan Doyle*. Boston: Twayne, 1987.

Jann, Rosemary. *The Adventures of Sherlock Holmes: Detecting Social Order*. New York: Twayne, 1995.

Kestner, Joseph A. *Sherlock's Men: Masculinity, Conan Doyle, and Cultural History*. Aldershot: Ashgate, 1997.

Klinger, Leslie S. *The New Annotated Sherlock Holmes*. 3 volumes. New York: Norton, 2005.

Knight, Stephen. *Form and Ideology in Crime Fiction*. London: Macmillan, 1980.

-----. *Towards Sherlock Holmes: A Thematic History of Crime Fiction in the 19th Century World.* Jefferson NC: McFarland, 2017.

Leitch, Thomas M. "The Other Sherlock Holmes." In *Sherlock Holmes: Victorian Sleuth to Modern Hero,* ed. Charles R. Putney et al. Lanham MD and London: Scarecrow Press, 1996. pp. 102-116.

McLaughlin, Joseph. *Writing the Urban Jungle: Reading Empire in London from Doyle to Eliot.* [Charlottesville VA]: University of Virginia Press, 2000.

Metress, Christopher. "Diplomacy and Detection in Conan Doyle's 'The Second Stain'," *English Literature in Transition (1880-1920),* 37 (1994): 39-51.

Nordon, Pierre. *Conan Doyle.* Translated by Frances Partridge. London: John Murray, 1966.

O'Toole, Michael. "Analytic and Synthetic Approaches to Narrative Structure: Sherlock Holmes and 'The Sussex Vampire'." In *Style and Structure in Literature: Essays in the New Stylistics,* ed. Roger Fowler. Ithaca: Cornell UP, 1975. pp. 143-76.

Pamboukian, Sylvia. "Old Holmes: Sherlock, Testosterone, and 'The Creeping Man'," *Clues: A Journal of Detection* 35:1 (Spring 2017): 31-46.

Priestman, Martin. *Detective Fiction and Literature: The Figure on the Carpet.* London: Macmillan, 1990.

Rassi, Sampo. *Tigers in the Fog: The Foreign in Sherlock Holmes Adventures.* University of Helsinki MA thesis, 2013.

Redmond, Christopher. *In Bed with Sherlock Holmes: Sexual Elements in Arthur Conan Doyle's Stories of The Great Detective.* Toronto: Simon & Pierre, 1984.

Redmond, Donald. *Sherlock Holmes: A Study in Sources.* Kingston: McGill-Queen's University Press, 1982.

Richter, Virginia. "The Civilized Ape." In *Embracing the Other: Addressing Xenophobia in the New Literatures in English*, ed. Dunja M. Mohr. Amsterdam: Rodopi, 2008. pp. 113-24.

Robson, W.W. Notes to his World's Classics edition of *The Case-Book of Sherlock Holmes.* New York: Oxford University Press, 1993.

Rosenberg, Samuel. *Naked Is the Best Disguise: The Death and Resurrection of Sherlock Holmes.* Indianapolis: Bobbs-Merrill, 1974.

The Sherlock Holmes Book, ed. David Stuart Davies et al. New York: Penguin Random House, 2015.

Sherloki1854. "Why The Three Garridebs is known as the gayest ACD Canon story" https://archiveofourown.org/works/4712915 (retrieved January 3, 2019).

Wade, Joshua A. "The Professor Rises: Science, Victorian Viagra, and the Masculine Libido in 'The Creeping

Man'," *Clues: A Journal of Detection* 33:1 (Spring 2015): 82-91.

Wagner, Martin.   "Sherlock Holmes and the Fiction of Agency." In *Sherlock Holmes in Context*, ed. Sam Naidu. London: Palgrave Macmillan, 2017. pp. 133-47.

Wynne, Catherine.   *The Colonial Conan Doyle: British Imperialism, Irish Nationalism, and the Gothic.* Westport CT: Greenwood, 2002.

Also from MX Publishing

MX Publishing is the world's largest specialist Sherlock Holmes publisher, with over a hundred titles and fifty authors creating the latest in Sherlock Holmes fiction and non-fiction.

From traditional short stories and novels to travel guides and quiz books, MX Publishing cater for all Holmes fans.

The collection includes leading titles such as _Benedict Cumberbatch In Transition_ and _The Norwood Author_ which won the 2011 Howlett Award (Sherlock Holmes Book of the Year).

MX Publishing also has one of the largest communities of Holmes fans on Facebook with regular contributions from dozens of authors.

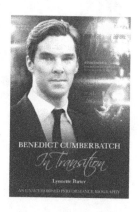

www.mxpublishing.com

CPSIA information can be obtained
at www.ICGtesting.com
Printed in the USA
FSHW011012191119
64253FS